JASON HAWES AND **GRANT WILSON**
WITH **TIM WAGGONER**

GHOST
TRACKERS

Pocket Books
New York   London   Toronto   Sydney   New Delhi

Pocket Books
A Division of Simon & Schuster, Inc.
1230 Avenue of the Americas
New York, NY 10020

This book is a work of fiction. Names, characters, places, and incidents either are products of the authors' imagination or are used fictitiously. Any resemblance to actual events or locales or persons, living or dead, is entirely coincidental.

First Pocket Books paperback edition September 2011

POCKET and colophon are registered trademarks of Simon & Schuster, Inc.

For information about special discounts for bulk purchases, please contact Simon & Schuster Special Sales at 1-866-506-1949 or business@simonandschuster.com.

The Simon & Schuster Speakers Bureau can bring authors to your live event. For more information or to book an event contact the Simon & Schuster Speakers Bureau at 1-866-248-3049 or visit our website at www.simonspeakers.com.

Author photograph © SyFy. Interior designed by Jacquelynne Hudson.

Manufactured in the United States of America

10 9 8 7 6 5 4 3 2 1

ISBN 978-1-4516-1381-0
ISBN 978-1-4516-1383-4 (ebook)

To Jody Hotchkiss, for his unwavering direction.
—Jason

For my father, mother, and all my dearest friends who stood by me and believed in me as I explored the weird and wild depths of the paranormal.
—Grant

For Marty Greenberg, patron saint of the short story and one of the last real gentlemen in publishing. You'll be missed more than even you, with your prodigious imagination could've guessed.
—Tim

GHOST TRACKERS

ONE

Running down a narrow dark corridor, trailing her fingers along the walls to guide her. Heart pounding in her chest, a frightened bird desperate to be free of its cage. Gasping for breath, throat closing up even though she hasn't had an asthma attack in years, rivulets of sweat pouring down her face and neck, trailing along her spine and trickling between her breasts. She's been running for what seems like forever . . . Running and running and running . . . How long *is* this damned hall, anyway?

She's not even sure why she's running. *To* something? *Away* from something? Is there someone pursuing her? She'd stop and turn around to look if she could, if for no other reason than to break the monotony of this endless flight, but she's compelled to keep moving forward, and it seems there's nothing she can do to change that. And so she runs . . .

She doesn't know how much time has passed before she realizes that the distance between the walls is beginning to shrink. What do they say about the span of your outstretched arms—that it's as wide as you are tall? She's a hair over five feet, and for the longest time, she's run with her arms stretched out to the sides, her fingertips brushing across the walls' smooth surfaces. But now her elbows are bent and her palms pressed almost flat against the walls, and they aren't so smooth anymore. They've become rough and craggy, like stone, and they're cold now, ice-cold.

With a stab of fear, she realizes that the walls are closing in on her, and she tells herself it's ridiculous, that no one builds a house with a tapering corridor. Houses don't *do* those kinds of things.

But she knows one house that does, or rather did, and much worse. But that was years ago, and it's long gone. She can't be back there now . . . can she?

A voice echoes in the air, hollow and distant, like a midnight wind blowing through a desolate canyon. A male voice, a familiar one, although she doesn't recognize it.

You're always there, Amber. You never left.

Without warning, the walls rush inward as if propelled by unseen machinery. Amber draws in a breath to scream, but before she can release it, the pain hits, and everything goes black.

Amber Lozier became aware of a sound hovering on the edge of her perception, but it took her several more seconds to put a name to it: *phone*. Eyes still closed, she reached toward her nightstand and fumbled around until her fingers closed around her cell. She brought it to her ear, flipped it open, and answered.

"'Lo," she mumbled.

"Amber? Hi, this is Greg Daniels."

Her stomach dropped at the sound of his voice, and her heart pounded in her ears. She sat up, flung the sweat-sodden sheet off her, and swung her legs over the side of the bed. A wave of dizziness came over her, and for a second, she considered flopping back onto the mattress, but she managed to ride it out and remain upright.

"Greg?" As soon as she said it, she felt like an idiot. After all, he'd just told her who he was. But she couldn't bring herself to believe it. She hadn't seen or heard from Greg Daniels since . . . since . . .

"Don't tell me you've forgotten me." His tone was teasing, but his voice held a bit of an edge, as if he were daring her to pretend she didn't know who he was.

Memories danced at the edge of her consciousness, trying to get her attention. She ignored them, and they remained where they were. Formless shadows, like hazy shapes viewed out of the corner of your eye, indistinct and nonthreatening . . . as long as they behaved and kept their distance. She'd had a lot of practice at keeping her memories at bay over the years, and most of the time, she was successful. As long as she was awake. When she was asleep, well, that was a different story.

"Of course I remember you," she said, well aware of the irony, considering how hard she was fighting *not* to remember. Her mouth and throat were dry, and the words came out soft and raspy. She'd kill for a drink of water, but a glance at the nightstand told her she'd forgotten to pour herself one. Several prescription medicine bottles sat atop the nightstand, and resting next to them was a black sleep mask she wore when it was too bright, even with the heavy curtain drawn across the room's single window. The clock-radio display said it was 4:48, and for a moment, she didn't know if it was morning or evening. Evening, she decided. Greg wouldn't be calling if it was almost five in the morning.

With her free hand, she brushed sweat-matted blond hair off her forehead, the gesture a futile attempt to cudgel her cotton-wrapped brain into working.

"It's been a long time," she said. Banal and predictable, but at least it gave her something to say. She frowned as something occurred to her. "How did you get my number?"

A greasy, burning-food smell filled the air of her small bedroom, the thick odor making her stomach roil with nausea. She lived in a one-bedroom efficiency apartment above the Flaming Wok, a fast-food Chinese restaurant, and her place always stank of fried food and cloying spices. She hated the stink so much that she hadn't eaten Chinese in the two years she'd lived there, and she doubted she'd ever touch the damned stuff again. The apartment wasn't much, and the location sucked, but it was all she could afford on her monthly disability checks. The nausea set off a pounding headache, and she considered asking Greg to hold on so she could take a painkiller, but he was in the middle of saying something, and with an effort, she forced herself to focus on his voice once more.

"—from the alumni organization. They don't normally give out people's numbers, but I told them this was a special case. It didn't hurt that I made a healthy contribution to the alumni fund this year." A small chuckle.

She usually slept in a pair of panties and an oversize T-shirt, and now that the sweat was beginning to cool on her too-thin body, she felt a chill coming on. She drew the damp sheet around her, but it felt cold and clammy and did nothing to prevent her from shivering.

"What do you want?" Then, realizing how that sounded, she added, "Sorry, that was rude."

"No worries. You don't talk to someone for fifteen years, and they suddenly call out of the blue, of course you're curious about why they decided to get in touch again. Do you know what's coming up this weekend?"

"No."

"Our fifteenth reunion."

The news seemed so random that for an instant,

she considered the possibility that, like in a cheesy movie, she only thought she'd woken up and in reality was still dreaming, but she dismissed the notion. The terror quotient was way too low for this to be one of *her* dreams.

"Really?"

"Doesn't seem like it's been that long, does it?"

Her gaze fell on the prescription bottles on her nightstand. "I don't know. Sometimes it seems like it's been a hell of a lot longer."

There was an awkward pause before Greg continued. "Well, like I said, I've been in contact with the alumni organization, and not only did I get your number from them, but they told me you haven't signed up to attend the reunion."

The pounding in her head grew worse, and she reached up with her free hand to massage the back of her neck, not that it did any good. "Yeah, well, what can I say? High school was hard enough the first time."

Greg chuckled again. "I hear you."

Of course you do, she thought. Greg Daniels had been a bona fide geek in high school, the kind of kid everyone else hated and made fun of. He'd been overweight, wore ill-fitting secondhand clothes, and possessed few social skills. But there'd been something else about him, too, a sense of . . . otherness, for lack of a better word. As if no matter what he said or did, no matter how hard he tried, he would never be able to fit in with others, as if he'd been born to be an outsider—something the other kids in school had been only too glad to point out to him. She had felt sorry for him back then, had even befriended him to a certain extent, although now that she tried to remember, she found the details somewhat fuzzy. But that didn't worry her; given the amount of meds she took, she was used to feeling as if her brain were wrapped in layers of wet burlap most of the time.

"So you're calling to, what, exactly?" The words came out harsher than she intended, but her head was really starting to hurt now, and her nausea was getting worse.

If Greg had detected the harshness in her words, he gave no sign. "To try to convince you to come to the reunion. Things have changed for me since high school—a lot." He paused, as if searching for the right words. "I guess you could say that after fifteen years, I finally grew up." He gave a small laugh that held a trace of bitterness. "I've never been to any of the reunions, either, but I'm going to this one. Partly as a 'screw you' to all the people who treated me so badly, to be honest. Show them the ugly duckling has morphed into a swan, that kind of thing. But mostly, I'm going because I hope to get some kind of closure on that part of my life, make peace with my past." Another pause. "I don't know. It sounds stupid, doesn't it?"

It took her a few moments to reply.

"No, it doesn't sound stupid at all."

"I know we weren't close or anything, but I considered you a friend. Probably the only real one I had. It would mean a lot to me if you were there to witness the debut of the new Greg."

She gritted her teeth and forced herself to concentrate past the throbbing in her head and the churning in her gut. What was wrong with her? She hadn't had a reaction to a nightmare this intense in months. And the nightmare she'd had—the walls closing in on her—wasn't all that bad. Not like some of the horror shows that went on inside her skull when her eyes were closed. Why was she reacting so strongly? "That's . . . sweet of you, Greg, but I don't know if I can make it. My . . . health isn't all that great these days."

"I'll understand if you can't make it." Greg sounded sincere enough, but there was an undertone of disappointment in his voice. "But mull it over a little. Who knows? Maybe you'll change your mind. It sure would be great to see you again . . . not to mention Drew and Trevor."

"Amber? Are you all right? Amber!"

A memory slipped past her defenses: Drew shouting, his voice muffled.

He was calling to me, she thought. *From somewhere in the house.* She felt more memories coming then, rising from her subconscious like a vast sea creature leaving the depths of the shadowy ocean where it had lain slumbering in the muddy darkness for far too long. The thought of what those memories might look like once they reached the surface of her mind filled her with a terror she hadn't known since, since . . .

That night.

She spoke then, her voice seeming to operate of its own accord.

"Drew and Trevor are coming?" The words were almost a whisper.

"I hope so," Greg said. His voice was calm, soothing, reassuring, and she grabbed hold of it with the grateful desperation of a drowning woman reaching for a rescuer's outstretched hand. "But that's up to you, Amber. You'll need to convince them. Do you think you can do that for me?"

Blackness nibbled at the edges of her vision as her mind began to shut itself down to protect her from the rush of oncoming memories.

"Yes," she breathed, before giving herself over to darkness and silence.

TWO

Late afternoon at the end of August. Unseasonably cool.

Greg Daniels crossed the street from where he'd parked his Lexus and strode across an open field. He was dressed in a black polo shirt, jeans, and running shoes, so the breeze blowing across the field should have caused him to shiver. At the very least, it should have raised gooseflesh on his arms and the back of his neck, but he didn't notice the wind. It had been fifteen years since he'd been there, and during that time, he'd walked in places far colder.

A lot had changed in the last decade and a half. There was no sign of the house that had once stood there, and the land itself had been reshaped— trees cut down, hilly ground bulldozed and flattened, grass reseeded. It was as if the Ash Creek City Council had done its best to erase every trace of the past, but he knew that was a fool's game, for the past was always part of the present—never gone, merely sleeping, waiting for the right time to come alive again.

A prime example of this was the nearly-completed structure on the property. One story, gray brick, black roof, with high, wide windows and large glass doors. Landscaped with trimmed hedges close to the building and young trees brought in to replace the old ones that had been cut down. A freshly paved parking lot was in front, with painted spaces—white lines, not yellow—and plenty of them, too, seemingly enough for every man, woman, and child in town to have one. The overall effect was modern, friendly, warm, and inviting. But the link to yesterday was plain for all to see, spelled out in shiny new chrome letters above the main entrance: "Lowry Recreation Center."

Greg closed his eyes and stretched out his senses, searching for hints of the power this place had once held. He felt faint echoes but nothing more. To be expected, really, considering what had taken place there fifteen years ago.

Snatches of memory raced through his mind quicksilver-fast: distorted shadows moving with a life of their own, the sound of shoes pounding hard on a wooden floor as someone fled, the shouting of fear-laced voices, and above it all, the terrified screams of a young girl—

The sound of youthful laughter tore him from his memories. He opened his eyes and turned to see a trio of preadolescents—two boys and a girl—riding their bikes down the suburban street toward the rec center. It was still technically a construction site, he supposed, since the center wasn't due to open for another month, as the wooden sign erected near the street proclaimed in large red letters followed by an enthusiastic exclamation point, but as near as he could tell, all of the major structural and exterior cosmetic work had been completed, and only the interior needed to be finished. So there were no "Danger: Construction Zone, Keep Out" signs for the kids to ignore as they hopped their bikes over the curb and pedaled across the field toward the building. Too bad. Ignoring warning signs might have given them a bit of a transgressive thrill; Greg knew it would have for him at that age. Life was all about enjoying the little pleasures, even the dark ones.

He smiled. *Especially* the dark ones.

He expected the children to ignore him. When he'd been their age, he'd rarely noticed adults. They'd been like distant trees or faraway clouds in the sky, something you were dimly aware of off toward the horizon but not on your radar. So he was surprised when the three young bikers rode straight up to him, stopped, and fixed him with bored gazes.

The girl was the tallest of the three and presumably the oldest. She had short, curly black hair and pale skin and wore shorts and a T-shirt displaying the image of some animé character he wasn't familiar with. The girl looked him up and down and pursed her lips, as if she found him more of a disappointment than usual for an adult.

"What are you doing here?" she demanded.

He kept his tone pleasant and allowed his lips to form a suggestion of a smile. "I could ask you the same question, since the rec center's not open yet."

"We *live* on this street," one of the boys said, an edge of whininess in his voice. He was a full head shorter than the girl, stocky, with greasy brown hair and a doughy face that in a couple of years would be covered with pimples. He wore an oversize T-shirt and baggy jeans in an unsuccessful attempt to hide the contours of his body. The boy reminded Greg of himself at that age. He was thin now and looked reasonably attractive, even if he'd never grace the cover of *GQ*, but he still felt a wave of sympathy for the dough-faced boy, mixed with a strong taint of self-loathing. He might no longer resemble this kid outwardly, but on the inside . . .

You've changed, he told himself. *You're nothing like this kid, not anymore.* And mostly, he believed it.

"What are you three?" he asked, still smiling. "The neighborhood watch?"

"Sort of," the second boy said. "Since we live here, we can't be trespassers. Not like you." He was thin, with short brown hair and glasses that lent him a bookish aspect, reinforced by the calm, matter-of-fact way he spoke. His plain red T-shirt and khaki shorts did nothing to dispel his geeky image, especially considering that he wore white socks that rode too high on his calves.

Funny, the little jokes that fate played from

time to time. These three kids were younger than
Amber, Drew, and Trevor had been fifteen years
ago, and they didn't look *exactly* like them, but as
his father had been fond of saying, it was close
enough for government work. It was all too fitting
that these three young doppelgängers should be
the ones to welcome him home.

The girl spoke again, brow still furrowed in sus-
picion. "What are you doing here?"

Greg was old enough to be her father, but that
didn't seem to matter to her. As far as she was concerned, he was an interloper who needed to be
dealt with. He wondered if she'd be so brave if she
didn't have her two friends along to back her up.
Maybe, he decided.

"I grew up in Ash Creek. I'm back visiting and
thought I'd check out the new rec center," he said.
"Looks great, doesn't it?"

"It's all right, I guess," the chubby boy said. "But
you won't catch me going inside when it's done."

Greg tilted his head to the side. "Really? Why
not?" As if he didn't know.

"A long time ago, there used to be a house
here," the boy with glasses said.

"A *haunted* house," the chubby boy added in a
hushed voice.

"It burned down before any of us were born,"
the girl said. "But our parents still talk about the
Lowry House."

"They say the land is cursed," Chubby said.

"Not that we believe any of that stuff," Glasses was quick to add.

"We used to, when I was a kid," Greg said. He kept his tone calm, but inside he felt something cold and dark begin to stir. "Everyone knew the Lowry House was haunted. Kids used to dare each other to go inside."

"Did you?" Chubby asked. "Ever go inside, I mean."

Greg nodded. "Yes, along with three friends of mine."

Despite his earlier profession of skepticism, Glasses sounded eager as he asked, "Did anything happen, anything weird?"

"Many things happened," Greg said. "It was a very eventful night."

Once again, a girl's long-ago screams filled his ears.

"Don't listen to him," the young girl—the girl of today—snapped. "He's trying to scare us. This place isn't haunted, and it never was."

Greg turned to face the girl and gave her a smile that caused her to go pale.

"You're wrong. The Lowry House *was* haunted until that last night, the night it burned down."

Heat washing over him like molten fire, the smell of his own skin burning . . .

He thrust the sensations aside and pinned the girl with his gaze, causing a bit more of the blood to drain out of her face.

"The dark force that inhabited the house left then, and it's been gone for the last fifteen years." He leaned a few inches closer. "But do you want to know a secret?"

All three of the kids were pale now, their gazes fixed on him like those of tiny mammals frozen in the presence of a large predator.

"It's back."

He reached out with his mind, brushed past the children's meager psychic defenses as if they didn't exist, and gave them a glimpse of what dwelled inside him. In response, the wind picked up strength, the sky darkened, and shadows gathered close around the four of them, eager and hungry.

The kids opened their mouths to scream, but nothing came out. Too terrified to produce sound, they stood there, eyes bulging, mouths gawping like fish on dry land. Greg allowed this to continue for another few seconds, reveling in their terrified astonishment, before once more closing his mind off from theirs.

The children found their voices then and shrieked as if they'd been cut to the bone. They whirled their bikes around and began pedaling away from the rec center, still screaming. Greg grinned as he watched them disappear down the street.

Once the kids were gone, the sky cleared, and the shadows that had gathered around him dispersed, but they didn't go too far. They always remained close by, like faithful pets waiting for his next summons.

He headed back to his Lexus. The kids would tell the first trustworthy adult they found about what had happened, and it wouldn't be long before someone—the police, most likely—showed up at the rec center to ask him some pointed questions. He'd prefer not to be there when that happened. Not that he couldn't do the same thing to any adult that he'd done to the children, but as amusing as it had been, he had more important matters to attend to.

He got into his Lexus, put the key into the ignition, and turned the engine over. As he pulled away from the curb, he smiled.

It was good to be home.

THREE

"**. . . and this hallway** is where the maid has been known to appear."

Trevor raised his digital camera, framed the hall in the viewfinder, and took two pictures. He didn't want to take the time to review either shot right now. With any luck, at least one would turn out to be suitably spooky, and if not, well, that's why God invented Photoshop. He would never fake a photo, but he could always darken it a bit and enhance the shadows for effect. After all, this wasn't a scientific expedition, and it wasn't as if he were collecting evidence. Still, the thought of doctoring the photo, even if only a little, made him feel guilty.

He turned to the woman serving as his tour guide that afternoon. She was in her mid-seventies, still very healthy, energetic, and—fortunately— quite talkative. As a writer, Trevor appreciated this last quality. The more information she gave him, the more pages he could fill in the latest book he was working on, a volume going by the working title of *Insidious Inns,* the follow-up to his previous book, *Taverns of Terror.*

"Have you ever seen her yourself?" he asked.

The woman, Anne Waymire by name, owner and operator of the Rise and Shine Bed and Breakfast in scenic Greensburg, Pennsylvania, gave him a look that said she found the question borderline insulting.

"Of course I have!"

He felt a spark of excitement at the woman's words. He loved to listen to people's personal encounters with the paranormal, and they always made great copy. He slipped his camera into the inner pocket of his gray suit jacket and exchanged it for a digital recorder. He'd been recording Mrs. Waymire's accounts of the Rise and Shine's paranormal activity for the last hour, so she was used to speaking into the machine for him, not that she'd been all that nervous to start with. He activated the device and gave Mrs. Waymire a nod to let her know it was working.

She was a tall, slender woman, wearing jeans and a blue button-down shirt with a daisy design stitched below the left shoulder. Since Mrs. Waymire stood a couple of inches taller than he, she bent over to bring her mouth closer to the recorder's microphone. He had assured her at the beginning of his visit that the device's mike was strong enough to pick up her voice without her bending over to talk into it, but she'd leaned over to speak anyway, and she'd continued to do so all afternoon. He was of medium height for a man, but he could be sensitive about his stature at times (almost as much as he was about his thinning hair), and while he was certain that Mrs. Waymire wasn't bending over to point out that she was taller than he, it still made him uncomfortable.

"Now, keep in mind that when I say I've *seen* her, I'm speaking more along the lines of psychic impressions than actual visual contact."

Trevor's excitement gave way to disappointment as Mrs. Waymire went on.

"I can *feel* her presence whenever she's around."

He nodded with a distinct lack of enthusiasm. In his career as an author of books and articles on the paranormal, he'd been down this road too many times before. Just when he hoped he was going to hear something good, something *real,* the person he was interviewing began talking about "impressions," "intuition," and, worst of all, "feelings." Still, he had a book to fill, and he didn't want to hurt the woman, so he tried to keep the disappointment out of his voice as he asked her to continue.

"She feels lost and afraid, like she doesn't know where she is or what's happened to her."

Not bad, he thought. It might make a nice caption to go along with the photo of the hallway. He began to get interested again. "Do you have any sense of what she looked like when she was alive?"

"Petite and pretty. Young. In her early twenties, maybe."

"Has anyone else ever encountered her?"

Mrs. Waymire hesitated. "Well, not encountered per se, but guests often complain about how chilly it gets up here. That's a sign of a ghost, isn't it? Strange cold spots?"

"It's one of the classic signs, yes. So, what's the story behind the maid?"

She frowned. "I'm not sure what you mean."

"Did she work here when she was alive? Under what circumstances did she die? Was there anything about her death that might keep her spirit bound to this place? Some sort of trauma or maybe unfinished business of some kind?"

She gave him a strange look before answering. "I'm sure I don't know."

His disappointment came back full force. "Are you saying you don't know *anything* about the maid?"

"I told you before, I *feel* her. That's how I *know* she's here. But as for being aware of any actual history . . ."

He couldn't help sighing. He should have known better. "So, you have no real evidence that there even was a maid."

Mrs. Waymire pursed her lips and narrowed her eyes, displeased with the implications behind his words. "My feelings *are* my evidence, Mr. Ward."

"Of course they are. I didn't mean to offend you." He switched off the recorder and tucked it back into his suit pocket next to his camera.

"Thank you for your time, Mrs. Waymire. I think I've got all I need."

Her righteous indignation melted away, leaving in its place confused disappointment. "But . . . but I haven't shown you the attic yet! It's the best part!"

He pulled his wallet from the back pocket of his pants, opened it, and removed one of his business cards. White letters on black background, the Os replaced by little white skulls: "Trevor Ward: Author of Paranormal Nonfiction." Below that, his phone number and e-mail address. He handed the card to Mrs. Waymire and tucked his wallet away.

"I'm sorry, but I have to get going. I have another appointment in Pittsburgh at six." Which was a lie. He wasn't scheduled to interview his next B&B owner until eight P.M. But this stop had turned out to be so disappointing that he just wanted to end the interview and get on the road. "You have my card. Why don't you e-mail me the details about the attic, and I'll make sure to include them when I do your entry for the book. All right?"

"Well, OK. If you think that will work . . ."

When he saw the look of disappointment on Mrs. Waymire's face, he couldn't bring himself to go through with his lie. In his line of work, he met a lot of different people. Some were attention seekers who fabricated paranormal experiences, while others were mentally ill, but most were normal, everyday folks who'd seen something strange and didn't know what to make of it. And then there were people like Mrs. Waymire, lonely folks who wanted a bit of human companionship.

"Well, I suppose I could stay a *little* longer," he said.

The woman grinned. "Wonderful! And when we're finished with the attic, maybe you'll have time for a cup of coffee before you leave."

He smiled. "Sounds good."

An hour later, Trevor was on Highway 76, en route to Pittsburgh. The sky was clear and the temperature in the mid-seventies, and he drove with the windows down. He'd visited Pittsburgh before, most recently while working on *Taverns of Terror*. He'd been writing about the strange, weird, and downright bizarre since graduating from Bowling Green University with a bachelor's degree in journalism, almost ten years now. First for magazines barely one step above tabloids, with names like *Unexplained!* and *Spectral Encounters*, and later in books of his own, retellings of regional ghost stories or tour guides of locations with paranormal connections. He'd come across legitimate cases of paranormal activity during his career, but unfortunately, they'd been few and far between. It was often disappointing when he interviewed owners of businesses; they saw the paranormal as another marketing tool, and they weren't above fabricating ghost sightings to bring in trade. Mrs. Waymire had seemed genuine enough to him when he'd first contacted her by phone, and he hadn't changed his opinion after meeting and talking with her. She hadn't tried to con him, and that was refreshing. Besides, she made a damn fine cup of coffee.

His Prius was equipped with satellite radio, and he tuned in a classic jazz channel and cranked up the volume so he could hear the music over the sound of rushing wind. He'd quit smoking six weeks, three days, and . . . around thirteen hours ago, not that he was counting, but he wanted a cigarette then. He'd quit for health reasons—he was carrying about twenty more pounds than his doctor liked, and as high as his cholesterol and triglyceride levels were, if they'd been stocks, he'd be a wealthy man. But why should he bother to try to get healthy? After ten years of writing about the paranormal, it was becoming clear that if he ever wanted to find out what might lie beyond this world, the only way was to kick the proverbial bucket himself. Of course, he wasn't *that* desperate to visit the other side, but he really wanted a smoke right then.

Between the wind gusting through the open windows and the loud jazz music, he didn't hear his cell phone ring, which was too bad, because he'd just downloaded a new ringtone a couple of days ago, "Ghost Riders in the Sky" by Johnny Cash. He loved to hear it play, but he had his phone set to vibrate, so he turned off the radio, removed his cell from his pocket, and answered it.

"Hello?"

Silence at first, stretching on for several seconds, long enough for Trevor to think the call had been dropped. But then he heard a woman's soft voice. "Hi, Trevor."

He could barely hear her over the sound of the wind, but he recognized Amber's voice. "Hold on a sec," he told her. He put the phone in his lap so he could hold on to the steering wheel while he raised the windows, cutting off the wind noise. When the inside of the Prius was silent, he picked up the phone again.

"Sorry about that. I'm driving on the highway, and I had the windows down. It's good to hear from you. How are you doing?"

"All right, I guess. Pretty much the same."

"To what do I owe the honor of this call? Don't tell me you've changed your mind about helping me with a book on the Lowry House." He regretted the words as soon as he spoke them.

"You know how I feel about that."

Amber's voice held a trace of anger, and even though he hadn't wanted to upset her, he was glad to hear some kind of emotion coming from her. "Yeah," he mumbled. "Sorry."

The Lowry House was the reason he'd gotten back in touch with her a year and a half ago. He'd gotten tired of writing articles about ghostly hitchhikers and spectral apparitions who walked up and down stairs in the middle of the night. He'd long understood that his interest in the paranormal stemmed from what had happened during his senior year in high school, when Amber, Drew, and he had entered the Lowry House the night it burned down. That something had happened— something Bad with a capital B—was a given. The problem was that none of them could remember the precise details of what had occurred.

They remembered entering the house, and they remembered fleeing from it as the flames spread, but as for what happened in between, nothing, *nada,* zilch. Which was why he'd decided to contact Amber. Drew, too, for that matter. The three of them had lost touch after graduation, as if they'd decided by some unspoken agreement to go their separate ways so they wouldn't have to be reminded of that night. Or maybe because they didn't want to be reminded of what little they did remember.

Whichever the case, the three of them hadn't talked for more than a decade, until Trevor— who'd tried on numerous occasions to write about the Lowry House without success—had hit on the notion that if the three of them could pool what they did remember, there might be enough for an article, if not a book. And who knew? Once they started talking, more memories might surface. Enough, maybe, so they'd finally understand what had happened to them that night.

But that was what had terrified Amber so much about the idea of talking to him about the Lowry

House, and since Drew hadn't been interested in helping him, either—"Sorry, but I have a lot on my plate right now, Trevor"—the project was dead in the water. Still, he held out hope that one day, he'd remember enough about that night to write about it. Maybe then he'd be able to put it behind him and move on with his life.

Maybe.

"I got a phone call not too long ago," Amber said. "From Greg Daniels, if you can believe it."

For a moment, he didn't have any idea whom she was talking about, but then it hit him. "You mean *our* Greg?"

He remembered that Amber had been kinda-sorta friends with Greg, while he and Drew . . .

Whatever his next thought was, it vanished before it could coalesce in his mind. It was as if he had walked right up to the edge of a memory, and then, *poof*! It was gone. Weird.

He told himself not to worry about the vanishing memory. It had been fifteen years since he'd thought about Greg Daniels, after all. The memory would return to him in time.

Right. Like your memories of what happened that night in the Lowry House.

"What did Greg want?" he asked. "To take a long-distance stroll down memory lane with you?"

"Not exactly." Amber filled Trevor in on her conversation with Greg.

"I can see why he'd want to attend the reunion,"

he said when she was finished. "I mean, it's everyone's fantasy to go to a high-school reunion and rub your former classmates' collective noses in how happy and successful you've become. But—and correct me if I'm wrong—it sounds as if he's got you thinking about going yourself. Not that that's a bad thing," he hastened to add.

"He *did* get me thinking," Amber said. Her tone changed, became kind of dreamy and distant. Trevor had never heard her quite like this before, and he wondered if she was on some new kind of medication. "It would be nice to see you again. And Drew."

"Drew's going?"

"Not yet," she said. "But he might, if *you* talked to him."

"Don't take this the wrong way, Amber, but going to a high-school reunion doesn't"—he searched for the right words—"sound like your kind of thing. When did you become a fan of nostalgia?"

"I told you that I'm not interested in helping you do a book about the Lowry House. But I've been thinking that maybe revisiting the past, at least in some small way, might not be a bad thing. I've tried medicine and therapy to help me deal with the nightmares, and they haven't done much good. The only thing I haven't tried is going home."

When Amber had turned down his first request to work on a Lowry House book, Trevor had decided to pay her a personal visit. It had taken some convincing to get her to agree to see him, but she did, and they met for a coffee at a Starbucks near where she lived. He'd been shocked by her appearance. She'd been so thin, so frail-looking. But what struck him even harder was the way she acted. She'd been full of energy and life in high school, but that day, she was nervous and withdrawn. He had no idea if doing something as simple as going to the reunion would help return Amber to her previous self, but if there was any chance at all that it would . . .

"All right. I'll give Drew a call, see what he says."

"Great!" she said, displaying a hint of enthusiasm for the first time since their conversation began. "Thank you so much, Trevor!"

"No sweat."

They said their good-byes and disconnected. He selected Drew's number from his cell's contacts list but didn't call right away. He'd been glad to hear some life in Amber's voice when they discussed going home, but he doubted that Drew would react quite so positively to the idea. Drew had a sweet gig at a psychiatric hospital outside Chicago, and he'd made it quite clear the last time they'd spoken on the phone that he'd put the past behind him and was determined to keep it that way.

Still, he'd promised Amber.

He was about to call Drew's number when he saw a man standing alongside the highway not too far ahead. At first, he assumed that it was someone whose car had broken down, and he thought about stopping to help. But then he realized that there was no car. The man stood by himself, with no vehicle nearby. He then assumed that the man was a hitchhiker and was less thrilled about the idea of stopping. He'd seen enough suspense movies to know that picking up hitchhikers was never a good move, and while he felt guilty for assuming the worst about a man he'd never met, he didn't lift his foot off the pedal.

As he got closer, Trevor saw that the man was dressed in a black polo shirt and jeans. Hitchhikers should be scruffier than that, he thought. This guy looked as if he worked in an office with a corporate casual dress code—a financial advisor, maybe, or an insurance salesman, who for some strange reason had decided to take a stroll along the highway and had paused to take a rest.

Trevor's mind flashed to a common paranormal experience people had been reporting for decades: the phantom hitchhiker. The stories varied in some details—the hitchhiker might be male or female, for example—but the basic manifestation remained the same. A ghostly apparition appeared on the side of the road, usually at night but sometimes during the day, standing deathly still, not moving, not speaking. If a traveler stopped to offer the person a ride, the ghost would get into the vehicle, saying little until they reached a certain destination, which the driver would later learn was the spot where the spirit had died or perhaps was close to the location where its body was buried. In some variations of the story, the driver would pass by the ghostly hitchhiker and find that the spirit had materialized on the passenger seat, as if determined not to be left behind.

Given what Trevor did for a living, it wasn't uncommon for him to have ghosts on the brain, and as he began to pass the man, he told himself to forget about spectral hitchhikers, and he fixed his gaze straight ahead as he drove by.

Out of the corner of his eye, Trevor saw the man raise a hand as if in greeting, caught a glimpse of a wide grin on his face, teeth a blur of white as his car zoomed past.

He kept on driving, and although he tried to resist glancing at the rearview mirror to check out the man's reflection, in the end, he had to look. He was not surprised to see the image of the road behind him but no sign of the man in the black shirt.

He knew there was probably a mundane explanation for the man's disappearance, such as his having stepped away from the side of the road, but it was damned eerie, coming so close on the heels of his conversation with Amber. Even weirder was the feeling he had that the man had seemed familiar somehow. Something about the way he'd moved, and that smile of his . . .

Trevor realized then that he was still holding his cell phone. Drew's number remained on the display screen, but he hesitated to call it. Despite Amber's decision to return to Ash Creek, maybe she *had* been right when she'd balked at helping him write about that night at the Lowry House. Maybe it wasn't a good idea to go rooting around in the past.

Then again, he was a reporter. That was what he did, wasn't it?

He made the call.

FOUR

"How have you been doing with your hands, Rick?"

Drew Pearson kept his gaze focused on his patient's eyes. The last thing he wanted to do was make Rick feel uncomfortable by training his attention on the man's hands. It was important to make sure patients felt respected and validated while they delivered news, good or ill, about themselves.

The man sitting across from Drew was in his early sixties, bald on top, white hair on the sides of his head trimmed so close to the scalp that pink skin was visible beneath. The lower half of his face was covered with white stubble, and his eyes were tinged an unhealthy yellow. The residents at Oak Grove Wellness Clinic were encouraged to wear regular clothes so they didn't feel like stereotypical mental patients, but Rick Johansen had been institutionalized for a good part of his adult life, and he felt more comfortable wearing clothing that resembled hospital gowns: a loose gray T-shirt, blue sweats, and slippers.

He sat in a chair opposite Drew's, his right leg crossed over his left, foot bouncing nervously. Drew was tempted to make a note of the nervous gesture on the pad resting on his lap, but he didn't want to look away from him to do so.

Rick held up his hands. Each of his ten fingers was wrapped in adhesive strips, and not just on the tips. The entire length of each finger was covered with strips, making Rick's hands look as if they belonged to a mummy swathed in flesh-colored bandages.

"I'm doing OK, I guess. I put these on this morning, and while I've picked at them a little, I haven't torn any of them off."

Drew could tell by the tone of Rick's voice that he was lying, but even if the man hadn't spoken, the adhesive strips would have given him away. They were all fresh—none of them dirty, none of them with edges beginning to peel away from the skin. That meant he'd put them all on just before their session. Maybe he had been picking at the strips throughout the day and scratching at the flesh beneath, prompting him to reapply them before the session. Or it could mean that he hadn't worn any until now and had, as usual, been digging at the skin of his fingers, gouging bloody furrows in them. The only way Drew would know was if blood began to seep through the strips as they talked.

Still, he smiled and nodded. "Looks good." He'd

been working on building trust with Rick, so it was important to take the man at his word—or at least appear to.

Rick smiled, displaying teeth as yellow as his eyes, looking as pleased as a child who had been praised by a beloved adult.

Despite his age, Rick *was* like a child in many ways. He'd been transferred to Oak Grove several months ago, and this was Drew's twelfth session with him. When Rick had first been assigned to his caseload, the man barely uttered a half-dozen words during a session. He'd mostly stared down at his hands, which he kept in his lap, scarred and bleeding fingers scrabbling at each other as if his hands were a pair of crabs determined to kill each other. Over the course of their sessions together, Drew had worked with Rick to gain his trust and get the man to relax in his presence. Slowly, he began speaking more, and his self-mutilating decreased. Drew was encouraged, and he had high hopes for today's session. He thought Rick was on the verge of a breakthrough, and today might well be the day it happened.

To look at Rick now, you'd never suspect he'd killed seven people, but he'd done just that in his twenties. He'd been at a family reunion, sitting at a picnic table in the backyard with various assembled relatives. For no reason that any therapist had ever been able to determine, he had stopped eating his potato salad, stood up, walked to his father's garden shed, picked up a sledgehammer, and caved in the skulls of seven family members. He'd also wounded three others in the process, one of whom had ended up paralyzed for life. Although he fought with an inhuman ferocity, the surviving men in the family eventually managed to restrain him. During his initial psych evaluation, he had claimed he'd heard a voice telling him to kill his family. In fact, he said he'd been hearing such voices all his life. When asked why he'd decided to listen to the voices after so many years, he'd smiled and said, "Because it made them shut up."

His obsessive-compulsive self-mutilating had begun almost immediately afterward, as if he hated the hands that wielded the weapon that had killed his family members.

Unsurprisingly, he had been found unfit to stand trial and was committed to a mental institution. He'd remained institutionalized ever since, transferred from one facility to another as the decades passed. He was what some of the staff referred to as a "lifer," a patient so seriously disturbed—either by his initial problem or by the long years of being confined in an institutional setting—that he'd never be released.

But Drew refused to believe that Rick and others like him were beyond hope. There was *always* hope, even if sometimes it seemed almost impossible to find. He had earned the nickname

"Dr. Die-Hard" because of his stubborn refusal to give up on a patient, no matter how hopeless the case seemed. Some on Oak Grove's staff attributed this to sheer ego on his part. He had graduated from Princeton with his PhD in psychology at age twenty-five, and by his early thirties, he'd become an acknowledged expert in posttraumatic stress disorder. Other staff members believed that he was deeply dedicated to helping people heal.

If he was asked why he worked so hard to reach those patients whom others believed to be helpless cases, he would have smiled and said, "Because it's my job." But the truth was that despite the outward differences between Drew and his patients, inside they were the same, suffering from the aftereffects of encounters with darkness. Deep down, he believed that if he could help his patients, someday he might learn how to help himself.

He was tall and thin, with a narrow, almost aristocratic face whose sharp features were softened by kind brown eyes and a caring smile. His light brown hair was thick and a bit disheveled, as if he'd just woken up from a nap and had neglected to brush it. Doctors at Oak Grove were encouraged to wear suits, but he always dressed casually, and today he had on a dark blue long-sleeved pullover shirt, light blue jeans, and running shoes. As far as he was concerned, doctors who garbed themselves in professional dress were trying to distance themselves from their patients, using their clothing like armor to protect themselves and keep patients from getting too close.

He believed that psychologists should meet their patients on a level playing field, as one person to another, with mutual respect and openness. To this end, not only did he dress more casually than the other doctors on staff, but his office décor was also relaxed. Two comfortable chairs that faced each other, a bookcase filled with novels and nonfiction books about anything *except* psychology. A desk off to the side covered with unsteady mounds of papers and files. White curtains framing a window that looked out on the facility's well-landscaped grounds. And covering the walls, framed photos depicting images from small Midwestern towns like the one he'd grown up in. Hanging on the wall behind the patient's chair so he faced it all the time was a picture of a home that resembled the Lowry House. He kept it there to remind himself of why he did what he did—and to keep him from forgetting any more than he already had about that night so many years ago.

"Tell me how your day's been going, Rick."

Rick's brow furrowed as he thought. He rubbed his bandaged fingers together, but he didn't scratch at them, and Drew took that as a good sign.

"Lunch was good. We had chocolate pudding today. I like chocolate."

Drew smiled. "Me, too. I like a tall glass of cold milk to go along with it."

Rick gave his head a quick shake. "Not me. It takes away from the chocolate taste. Makes it like you never ate it in the first place, you know?"

Drew nodded as if he understood what Rick was talking about. "Anything else?"

Rick's scowl deepened, as if he were having trouble finding the memory. "We made collages during art therapy today. I like cutting pictures out of magazines, but I hate having to use those plastic scissors with the round ends. They don't cut too well."

Which is why residents have to use them, Drew thought. Most of the patients at Oak Grove had a history of violence on some level. The worst ones weren't even allowed to use safety scissors. They had to draw with crayons and eat with plastic spoons under strict supervision. Rick had been nonviolent since the day he'd been committed, but even he wasn't allowed to use real scissors, just in case.

Aloud, Drew said, "What kind of pictures did you use to make your collage?"

Rick shrugged. "Nothing special. Cars. People wearing nice clothes. Disemboweled animals . . ."

His tone didn't change as he said this, but

Drew noted the slight upturn at the corner of his mouth, as if he were enjoying a private smile. Drew wasn't shocked by Rick's words. He'd heard far worse in his career. But Rick had never used any violent imagery in their sessions before. If a patient was delusional, it was sometimes best to let a comment like Rick's pass without comment. But the almost-smile playing about his mouth made Drew suspect that the man was quite aware of what he was saying, so he decided to confront him about it.

"I find it hard to believe Ms. Shewalter would bring any magazines with pictures like that to class."

Rick's smile widened, and his gaze—which was usually a trifle unfocused—sharpened in a way that Drew found disquieting.

"The dog pictures weren't *literally* in the magazines, Drew. I made them out of combinations of other pictures—colors and shapes combined to give the impression of disembodied dogs. Like Rorschach blots."

A mocking edge had come into his voice, one Drew had never heard before, and his speech patterns were different, the phrasing more sophisticated, the rhythms more complex. He remembered how Rick had once claimed to hear voices, and he wondered if the man was hearing one now and if it was telling him what to say or perhaps even speaking through him as if he were a ventriloquist's dummy. Of course, any voice Rick heard would be a manifestation of his own damaged psyche, but the effect was damned eerie.

"What made you decide to make pictures like that, Rick?"

He shrugged again, but the gesture was different this time. Smoother, almost sinuous. It put Drew in mind of the way a reptile might shrug.

"It gave my hands something to do while I imagined burying an ax in Ms. Shewalter's head."

Despite himself, Drew felt a chill at Rick's words. No, he realized. The sensation of cold was more than a simple emotional reaction. The temperature in the office had dropped by several degrees in the last few minutes. He could feel the cold on his face, his hands, the back of his neck, and inside his mouth, throat, and lungs as he breathed. He'd known cold like this before, cold that did more than chill the flesh. Cold that penetrated deep into the core of your being, wrapped its icy fingers around your soul, and began to squeeze.

Drew? Trevor? Why is it so cold?

"You miss them, don't you?" Rick said.

The man's voice yanked Drew out of the memory. "Who?"

He continued as if he hadn't heard Drew's question. "You miss both of them but especially *her*."

He lifted a bandaged hand to his mouth and

began tearing off his adhesive strips with his teeth, spitting them onto the carpeted floor one by one. He continued speaking as he worked, the words muffled at times but clear enough.

"You really haven't had any friends since them, have you? Haven't allowed yourself to get close to anyone. Oh, you have dozens of acquaintances, and you date now and again, but you're going through the motions, aren't you? Pretending to live, when in truth, you're hiding behind walls so thick and high that nothing can get through. Better that way, right? Safer."

Rick finished uncovering the last of his scarred fingertips. He examined his hand for a moment, looking like someone checking out a manicure he'd just received. And then he inserted the tip of his index finger into his mouth.

The room felt as cold as an Arctic plain now, and Drew saw his breath turn to wisps of vapor as it hit the frigid air.

This isn't possible, he told himself. *I'm experiencing some sort of delusion.* But even as he thought these things, he knew he was lying to himself. Whatever the source of the cold, he did his best to ignore it. He had more important things to worry about right then.

"Don't do it. I understand that you're feeling a compulsion to hurt yourself. It's OK to feel that way, but it doesn't mean you have to give in to that compulsion."

Rick's gaze locked onto Drew's, but he didn't remove his finger from his mouth as he talked. "You're going to see them again. Your friends, I mean. Very soon."

Rick bit down on his finger, gently at first, and then with increasing pressure. Drew began shivering from the cold. Whatever was happening here, it wasn't—

Natural.

—helping Rick. He wanted to leap to his feet, rush over to Rick, grab hold of his arm, and yank his hand away from his mouth. But he forced himself to remain seated. He didn't want to sit and watch while Rick mutilated himself, but he knew from both training and experience that it wasn't a good idea to make any sudden moves when a patient began exhibiting violent behavior.

Drew rarely felt threatened when he worked with patients, whatever their pasts, and he'd never felt any threat from Rick during their previous sessions. But he could sense the potential for violence in the air now, like the energy that gathers before a powerful thunderstorm, and for the first time in his career as a psychologist, he was afraid. Afraid for himself and afraid that Rick might hurt himself far worse if he tried to stop him.

And so he watched as the already raw skin on Rick's finger split under the pressure of his jaws, and blood began to flow, running over his lips and onto his chin in a thin trickle. Rick's eyes glimmered with madness, and, still biting down on his index finger, he grinned at Drew.

"I'm starting to get the feeling that our session is about over, but before you send me back to my room wrapped in a straitjacket and carrying a circulatory system full of tranquilizers, allow me to leave you with this. She will call for you again, just as she did before. Only this time, you won't be able to help her."

Drew felt a pit open up in his stomach at Rick's words, but before he could ask the man what he meant, Rick bit down on his finger as hard as he could, and the blood began flowing in earnest. Rick laughed at first, but his laughter quickly faded to silence. His eyes rolled white, his jaw went slack, and his bloody finger slipped out of his mouth as his hand fell to his lap. At first, Drew feared the man had gone catatonic or worse, suffered a stroke, but before he could get up to go check on him, the man's eyes came back into focus, and he blinked in confusion.

"What . . . happened?" His voice was soft, little more than a whisper. "I remember we were talking about something. Pudding, I think, and then . . ." He frowned. "Why does my finger hurt so bad?"

Before Drew could explain, Rick raised his hand and saw his wounded finger.

"Aw, no . . . And I was doing so *good* . . ."

He began to cry, and Drew rose from his chair and—professional distance be damned—walked over to him, leaned down, and put his arms around the sobbing man.

A half-hour later, Drew was back in his office, sitting at his desk, typing up his notes from Rick's disastrous session. A chill still lingered in the air, real or imagined, and he'd turned up the heat.

He had typed several paragraphs so far, but he read over them, scowled, and deleted all but the first couple of lines. He kept *At first, Mr. Johansen appeared to display signs of progress in dealing with his obsessive-compulsive hand mutilation, and our initial conversation proceeded along the usual lines of making small talk about his day.* But he didn't know what to say after that. At first, he'd tried to describe the events as objectively as he could, but when he reached the part about the room temperature dropping, he'd stopped and started hitting the delete key.

Drew was a rational man who used his intelligence and education to help him deal with sometimes very irrational people. In a way, he saw his patients as sailors lost at sea, their ships surrounded by fog and night. Therapy was a lighthouse, a shining beacon of hope that could help them find their way out of the darkness, and he viewed himself as the lighthouse keeper.

He could explain Rick's cryptic pronouncements—*You miss them, don't you? She will call for you again, just as she did before*—as the ramblings of a deeply troubled mind. It had only seemed to have meaning because he himself was tempted to ascribe meaning to it. Basic psychology, the kind of stuff undergrads learned in Intro to Psych. And the temperature drop could be explained as easily. It wasn't uncommon for people to experience sensations of cold during traumatic events. Given his specialty in posttraumatic stress disorder, he knew this better than most. Just because he was a psychologist didn't mean he was immune to experiencing trauma himself. It was always tough to watch a patient have a psychotic break. He'd had an emotional reaction to Rick's meltdown, one that had manifested as a sensation of cold. Simple as that.

But that was his mind talking. His instincts, his *feelings,* told a different story, and over the years, Drew had learned to rely on his feelings as much as his intellect when it came to dealing with patients. And his feelings now told him that whomever he'd been speaking to, it hadn't been Rick, and the temperature drop he'd experienced had been real, not a symptom of intense stress. So that meant . . . what? That Rick had been possessed?

He gave his head a quick shake. No way. It was ridiculous. That was the sort of crazy theory that Trevor might come up with for one of his books. Drew was a man of science. He—

His cell phone sat next to the computer on his desk, within easy reach. It rang, and he picked the phone up and answered it, grateful for the distraction. And while he supposed he should have been surprised to hear Trevor's voice on the other end, he wasn't.

FIVE

Amber knew she shouldn't have a second glass of merlot, not with the meds she was on. She told herself she'd just sip this one slowly and make it last.

The hotel bar was upscale for Ash Creek: chrome, glass, and black-lacquer décor, lighting pitched at just the right level, not so dim as to be depressing but not so bright as to be garish. A banner hung behind the bar, "Welcome Back, Ash Creek Grads!" written in red letters that looked a little too much like blood for her taste. Nineties pop music played in the background, programmed for the reunion crowd by the hotel staff, she guessed. "The Sweetest Taboo" by Sade was on now, the song the aural equivalent of a syringe full of Thorazine, but the effect was lost on her. As nervous as she was, she doubted the real thing could have calmed her down.

She'd chosen a corner table and sat with her back to the wall. She liked having something solid behind her, liked being able to see the entrance. *Less chance of someone sneaking up on you from behind this way, and easier to make a fast escape if you need to,* she thought. She knew it was only partially a joke, and not a very funny one, but she forced a smile and took a sip of her wine.

She managed two more sips before deciding that the alcohol was, if anything, only increasing her anxiety level, and she was about to get up and leave when Drew walked into the bar.

Although she hadn't seen him in fifteen years, she recognized him instantly. He hadn't changed much. A few more pounds, the skin beneath his eyes a bit puffy and discolored, as if he hadn't been getting enough rest. But the changes in Drew's appearance were minor. All in all, he looked as handsome as she remembered. More so, because he carried himself with a casual confidence that she not only found attractive but also envied. It had taken all of the courage she could muster to force herself to leave her room after she'd checked in.

Drew stopped inside the entranceway and looked around. He wore a white polo shirt, dark jeans, and running shoes. He looked more like a grocery-store clerk than a psychologist, but then Drew had never cared what other people thought about him. Another quality he possessed that made her envious.

The bar was about three-quarters full of people drinking, talking, and laughing, and Amber half hoped that Drew wouldn't notice her among the crowd. After all, it *had* been fifteen years, and those years hadn't been kind to her. She was afraid of what Drew would think when he saw her, and she regretted letting Greg talk her into coming here. But then Drew saw her and smiled with such warmth that her regrets melted away. As he approached her table, she rose to meet him.

"Hello, Drew." She held her hand out for him to shake, but she wasn't surprised when he ignored it and gathered her in for a hug. He'd always been a touchy-feely kind of guy but in a genuinely affectionate, noncreepy way. She felt so fragile in his embrace, as if she were made of paper skin and brittle twig bones, but he held her gently, and for the first time in she couldn't remember how long, she felt safe and protected. But then he let go and stepped back, and she was surprised to feel a pang of sadness as the contact ended.

"It's great to see you, Amber." He sounded sincere, but there was a flicker of concern in his gaze, and she guessed that he'd noted her sallow complexion and too-thin body. She'd done her best to disguise her condition with a liberal application of makeup and an oversized black sweater to hide how skinny she was, but it wasn't enough to fool Drew's trained eye. She felt a wave of shame and once again regretted coming here. But then, as if sensing her emotion, he reached out to clasp her hand and said, "*Really* great."

"Same here," she said, and smiled. And then, without thinking, she added, "I was a little afraid that when I saw you, I'd . . ." She'd been about to say, *Have a flashback to that night,* but she didn't want to talk about that, not yet, maybe not ever. So instead, she said, "Make a fool of myself somehow. You know, accidentally spray spit on you when I talked or not realize I had a big piece of spinach stuck in my teeth."

"What are you talking about? Making a fool of myself is *my* specialty!"

Amber and Drew turned as Trevor approached them, a wide grin on his face. He wore a gray suit jacket over a light blue shirt. The extra pounds he carried, along with his thinning hair, made him look as if he were in his early forties instead of his early thirties, but the premature-aging effect was ameliorated by the boyish enthusiasm in his smile and the delight that shone in his eyes upon seeing them. For an instant, she caught a glimpse of the teenager he used to be, and seeing him that way made her feel young again, too, if only for a moment. It was a good feeling.

He gave her a quick but warm hug and then took Drew's hand in both of his and gave it an energetic double pump. When he finished, he stepped back and regarded Amber and Drew.

"Man, it's good to see you two again!" he said.

Drew grinned. "Same here."

Amber smiled and nodded. And then silence descended over the three of them, and they stood there, smiling at one another. She wasn't sure what to do next, and she experienced a small flutter of panic, accompanied by an urge to excuse herself and flee back to her room. Here they were, the three of them, together again for the first time in fifteen years, for the first time since *that night*. She'd been more than a little afraid of what might happen when she saw Drew and Trevor. What she might feel, what she might *remember*. But there had been no flashbacks, no nightmarish images, no disturbing memories of any kind. It was something of a letdown, and she thought she could see the same feeling mirrored in her friends' faces.

It was Trevor who broke the silence. "Is this awkward or what?"

"What," Drew said.

Trevor frowned. "I said, is this awkward or . . ." He trailed off and grinned. And then the three of them were laughing, and Amber could feel the years and the tension melt away.

"What happened to Mrs. Peters?" Trevor asked. "I know she quit teaching art halfway through our senior year, but I can't remember the whole story."

Drew took a sip of his vodka sour—his third—and frowned as he tried to recall the details. "It was a sex scandal of some kind, wasn't it?"

Amber laughed. "Hardly, though it might've seemed that way to people at the time. I was in her class when it happened. She wanted us to do life drawing, you know, like in college when they have models pose nude? But this was high school, so she asked one of the cheerleaders to come in wearing a swimsuit. The girl—I can't remember her name. Bethany? Barbara? Anyway, she wore a bikini that was more than a little on the skimpy side, and that got the kids in class talking, especially the boys. Their parents got wind of what happened, and the next thing you know, there's a concerned group of citizens protesting at a school-board meeting. One thing led to another, and Mrs. Peters decided to take early retirement rather than put up with the bullshit anymore." She took a sip of wine and shook her head. "Small towns, you know?"

"That's right," Trevor said. "I remember now." He finished off his beer, caught their server's eye, and signaled for a refill.

Drew wondered if Trevor really did remember or if he was just saying that. The three of them had spent the last two hours talking about the past, which was to be expected when three old friends got together after fifteen years. The hotel bar was filled with people, many of them fellow classmates back in town for tomorrow night's reunion, and he imagined that a number of similarly nostalgic conversations were taking place at tables around them. The big difference in their case was that they weren't taking a simple stroll down memory lane. They were trying to fill in gaps in their memories, for while none of them had broached the subject of *that night* yet, once they'd begun talking, it had soon become clear that they'd forgotten more than what had happened at the Lowry House.

Huge chunks of their high-school years were missing, the memories not simply dimmed with the passage of time but gone entirely, especially events from their senior year. So, while it had been great seeing Trevor and Amber again, the three of them were doing more than reminiscing; they were playing a very important game of mental fill-in-the-blanks. But just because some missing data were supplied, that didn't automatically translate into an actual memory. Numerous times during their conversation, they had pieced together stories, like the one about Mrs. Peters. And while the facts became clear, Drew at least experienced no real recollection of the events in question.

He *knew* the stories when they were done, but he didn't *remember* them. He felt like someone who was learning phrases in a foreign language by memorizing them phonetically, without any real understanding of the words. It was a strange, frustrating experience, in some ways even worse than not remembering, because it pointed out how much they'd all lost and underscored the reason why.

That night.

Their server brought Trevor his beer, and the three friends fell into a period of silence. It didn't take long to start a new thread of conversation, and

Drew couldn't help smiling as Trevor began talking. He'd never been very comfortable with silence.

"The town's sure changed a lot," he said. "There's a new outlet store off the highway, and did you ever think they'd put a Starbucks in little old Ash Creek, let alone *two*? And then there's the new rec center they're building where the . . ." He paused, and for a moment, Drew thought he wasn't going to continue, but then he went on, his voice subdued. "Where the Lowry House was."

And there it was. It had taken them two hours and more than a few drinks to get around to it, but one of them had finally spoken the words.

"Did you check it out?" Drew asked.

"Eventually." Trevor took a sip of his beer. "I drove around town three times before getting up the courage to go by. You?"

He shook his head. "I thought about it, but I didn't do it. I told myself that I was tired after driving all the way from Chicago and just wanted to check into the hotel, but the truth is that I was too uncomfortable to go there."

Drew and Trevor looked at Amber.

She drained the last of her wine in a single swallow. "Are you kidding me? As often as I visit the damn place in my dreams, I'm in no hurry to see it again for real."

"There's nothing to see," Trevor said. "The only indication that a house was ever there is the sign: 'Lowry Recreation Center.' The place is about finished, and it looks like any other modern building, the kind of anonymous place that might house a dentist's or doctor's office." He looked at Drew and smiled. "Probably like the kind of place where you work." He reached into his jacket pocket and removed a digital camera. "I took some pictures while I was there. If you guys want to see . . ."

"Sure," Drew said, although inside he recoiled at the thought. He glanced at Amber, and she looked even paler than before, and from the panicked look in her eyes, he thought she might bolt from the table any second. But she stood her ground as Trevor turned on his camera, pulled up an image of the Lowry Recreation Center, and held it out for Drew and Amber to see. It was, as he had already told them, almost disappointingly normal, and although Drew felt a slight chill upon reading the word *Lowry,* all in all, the picture did little for him. He looked at Amber and saw the same lack of reaction on her face. He remembered something Rick had said during their last session.

You miss both of them but especially her.

And this was followed by a memory of hearing her speak, the memory so vivid it was almost as if he were hearing her now.

Drew? Trevor? Why is it so cold?

It was so real that he was only able to convince himself that she hadn't spoken because he hadn't seen her mouth move.

When they finished looking at the pictures,

Trevor turned off his camera and put it away. Drew thought then that they might begin talking about that night, now that they'd broken the ice, but they fell into an uneasy silence. Their server came by and asked Amber if she'd like another glass of wine, but she declined. Although he knew it was none of his business, Drew was glad.

He didn't know how many prescriptions Amber was on, but the last thing she needed was to add too much alcohol to her system. Drew understood the urge to self-medicate. It was one reason so many people with psychological problems also had issues with substance abuse. But self-medicating only made things worse.

There are lots of ways to self-medicate, he thought. Some people drank or took drugs. Some people smoked. He glanced at Trevor, who'd told them earlier that he was trying yet again to break his nicotine habit. And some people threw themselves into their work to the exclusion of everything else. He had no illusions; he knew he was guilty of the latter. But at least his self-medicating helped others, right? So it wasn't entirely selfish.

Way to justify an unhealthy lifestyle, he thought, and took a sip of his own drink. He knew he was only exchanging one compensatory habit for another, but right then, he didn't care.

"I think I'm going to call it a night," Amber said. Trevor started to protest, but she held up a hand to cut him off. "I know it's still early, but I think

I've had enough for one evening. It's been great to see you both. It really has. I was worried that being in your presence would make me remember things I didn't want to remember, but it's been nice. I just don't think I can take much more right now. I don't want to talk about the Lowry House, I don't want to look at pictures of it, and I sure don't want to begin comparing scraps of memory with you two in an attempt to piece together what happened that night. I don't *care* what happened. I just want to forget about it and get on with my life, you know?"

"Amber, it's important that we remember," Trevor said. "We experienced something paranormal that night. I'm not talking about a mysterious thump coming from another room or a shadowy figure glimpsed out of the corner of your eye. I'm talking the real shit, and it's important that we try to understand it."

She scowled at him. "Why? So you can write a fucking book about it and get famous?"

At first, he looked hurt by her accusation, but then he got angry. "Back in high school, you were interested in the paranormal as much as Drew and I. It's what brought the three of us together. Or have you forgotten that along with everything else?"

Drew remembered. It was one memory that remained intact. They'd been juniors in high school, enrolled in the same science class. They hadn't known one another at the time, but their teacher assigned them to work together on a group presentation. The topic was up to them, and they'd discovered after a bit of conversation that all three of them were interested in paranormal phenomena, specifically in scientific evidence of life after death. They did their report on that topic, researched it scrupulously, even performed an investigation at Trevor's grandmother's house, which she swore was haunted by the spirit of one of the previous owners.

They'd gotten an A for their presentation, and after that, they'd continued investigating paranormal phenomena, most often reading books and magazines on the subject or watching documentaries on TV, but from time to time, they performed field research, investigating reports of ghostly apparitions that fellow classmates and even teachers would pass along to them. They got a reputation for being a bit weird because of their hobby, but they also gained a certain coolness factor from it, so it all balanced out.

But no matter how many dusty attics, moldy basements, or cold, dark cemeteries they visited, one place stood above them all as the most haunted in town: the Lowry House. Drew, Trevor, and Amber researched everything they could about the house's history, even interviewed some local residents about it, but it took them some time to work up to physically investigating the house.

None of them had ever discussed their reluctance to go there, but it was as if they realized, on an instinctive level if nothing else, that the Lowry House was the real thing, and they wanted to be as prepared as possible before going in.

Whatever had happened the night they'd finally worked up the courage to go in, they hadn't been prepared enough, Drew thought. Not by a long shot.

"I've told you before, and I'll tell you again. I'm not going to help you write about the Lowry House," Amber said to Trevor.

He turned to Drew, a pleading look on his face. "Help me out here."

Drew had to suppress a smile. Even before he'd become a psychologist, his friends had turned to him to mediate any conflict between them. "It's important that we respect Amber's feelings," he began. "If she doesn't want to talk about the Lowry House, that's her choice. But," he hurried to add before Trevor could say anything, "I think you should reconsider, Amber. There's a reason you've come here this weekend, and as much as Trevor and I might like to believe that it was so you could reconnect with a pair of old friends, I suspect it was something more. Have you noticed the people around us? All of them talking and laughing, sharing photos of spouses and children. Catching up on the different paths their lives have taken over the last fifteen years. How much progress have we made in that time? How much have our lives changed since we graduated? Since that night?"

"What are you talking about?" Amber said. "You're a psychologist, and Trevor's a published author. You're both doing pretty well for yourselves, I'd say." She paused and looked down at her empty wineglass, as if regretting not ordering a refill. "Not like me. I can't hold down a job for more than a few months at a time. If it wasn't for disability checks, I'd be homeless."

The pain in Amber's voice prompted Drew to reach across the table and take hold of her hand. "I'm not talking about careers," he said. "I'm talking about how our personal lives have developed. Or, rather, failed to. None of us has been married or had children. For that matter, we haven't been able to hold on to any of the relationships we have managed to form. Do either of you have any lovers, or even close friends?"

Neither Amber nor Trevor said anything.

"It's the same for me," Drew said. "I have my work, and while I get along well enough with my coworkers, it would be a stretch to call them friends."

"And I don't have coworkers," Trevor said. "Unless you count my literary agent, and I've never even met her face-to-face. I travel so much that I'm hardly ever home. I mostly live in cheap hotel rooms and eat too much fast food." He patted his well-padded stomach.

"In a very real sense, the three of us have been frozen in time since that night in the Lowry House," Drew said. He gave Amber's hand a last squeeze before releasing it. "Trevor and I are still looking for answers to what happened, though we've taken very different routes in our search. And you struggle with nightmares. Your subconscious mind is fighting nightly to force you to remember what happened, and your conscious mind fights just as hard to keep those memories suppressed. The conflict wears you down to the point where having a normal life is impossible for you. I think deep down, all three of us are tired of spinning our wheels."

Trevor nodded. "I know I am."

Drew continued. "We want to move on with our lives, and this reunion has provided a handy excuse for us to do something about it. You must recognize that on some level, Amber, or else why would you have come?"

Although she didn't say anything right away, she looked thoughtful, and Drew took the fact that she didn't get up and leave as a good sign.

"So what should we do?" she asked, her voice soft.

Before either Drew or Trevor could respond, a voice cut in. "How about saying hello to an old friend?"

They all turned to face the newcomer, who was standing next to their table, smiling at them. Drew hadn't noticed the man's approach, and he found that puzzling. He was a trained observer, and it wasn't like him to miss an important detail like a man walking up to interrupt their conversation. It was almost as if he had materialized out of thin air, a ridiculous thought, of course, but one that Drew couldn't shake, especially given what the three of them had been talking about when the man arrived.

He was their age, medium height, with a trim physique like that of a runner or a tennis player. His facial features were more distinctive than handsome—he had the kind of face with a lot of character, as Drew's mother might have said—but he wasn't unattractive. He seemed genuine, a regular guy, the kind of man who engendered automatic trust with a ready smile and a warmth-filled gaze. Like a salesman practiced at hiding who and what he really was, Drew thought, surprised a bit at his own cynicism. The man wore a navy-blue suit, black shoes, and a white shirt without a tie. He looked well groomed but relaxed and at ease, as if he owned the place and had come over to see if they were having a good time. But there was something familiar about him, about his voice and lopsided smile, and there was something about his eyes . . . they seemed to sparkle with amusement, as if he were enjoying a private joke.

It was Amber who recognized him first.

"Greg," she said, and that single word triggered Drew's memory.

Drew, Amber, and Trevor might have been the Three Musketeers in high school, but there'd been a d'Artagnan as well, a fourth sometimes-member of their group: Greg Daniels. He hadn't been in the science class where the three of them met, but he got wind of their interest in the paranormal, and that had attracted him to Drew and the others, as he was also interested in strange phenomena. And it hadn't hurt that he'd had a crush on Amber, although it had gone unreciprocated.

Greg had hung around the three friends from time to time and even invited himself along on a few investigations. He'd been something of an outcast in high school—overweight, acne-plagued, socially awkward, and just plain annoying. Plus, he had a bit of a temper and a cruel streak. Drew and Amber had felt sympathy for him, which was why they'd allowed him to tag along sometimes. Trevor hadn't liked him one bit, but he'd put up with him for the sake of his two friends.

There was one thing more, Drew remembered. Greg had been with them the night they'd gone into the Lowry House. He frowned. No, that wasn't quite right. He hadn't gone in with them, had he? The three of them had visited the Lowry House alone that night, he was certain of that. But Greg had been *inside* the Lowry House with them at one point, although the details weren't clear.

Drew was stunned by this sudden inrush of memory. How could he have forgotten Greg? The trauma that Drew, Trevor, and Amber had suffered the night the Lowry House burned down had robbed them of many memories, but they'd never forgotten one another. But he hadn't thought about Greg Daniels once in the last fifteen years. It was as if the man had been erased from existence for the last decade and a half and now, miraculously, had been resurrected.

"What's wrong?" Greg said. "The way you three are looking at me, it's like you don't recognize me." He paused and then let out a small laugh. "I suppose I *do* look a lot different from the last time you saw me."

His smile grew wider, and a dark cast came over his eyes. Looking into those eyes, Drew experienced a moment of vertigo, as if a pit had opened beneath him and he was falling . . . falling . . . His nasal passages were clogged with thick smoke, and he felt intense heat sear his skin. He coughed and fought to keep his eyes open in the superheated air. The sound of crackling flames filled his ears, but the noise was almost drowned out by someone close by screaming in agony. A wall of flames stretched before Drew, and as he watched, Greg staggered through the fire, mouth open wide, and Drew knew then where the screams were coming from.

Greg—the adult version of him—was wreathed in fire. His skin was blistered and blackened, and his hair was ablaze, making him appear to be wearing a halo of flame. His eyes were wild with pain, and Drew wondered how he managed to remain conscious, let alone stay on his feet.

Greg's gaze fixed on him, and he stopped screaming. A terrible calm came over him, even though the fire continued consuming his flesh.

"You did this to me," Greg said, his voice thick, as if his throat were filled with bubbling fat. *"The three of you. It's your fault. All your fault . . ."*

He laughed, flames leaping forth from his mouth as if the fire had eaten its way into his body and was now devouring him from the inside out. He extended his blackened hands toward Drew and stepped forward. Drew recoiled from the flaming apparition, making a small sound in the back of his throat like a tiny animal terrified at a predator's approach. This wasn't real, it *couldn't* be real!

And then, just like that, Drew was sitting in the bar once more, looking at a whole, healthy, unburned adult Greg. He realized that Greg was talking, and while his words were nothing but meaningless noises at first, they eventually became clear.

"—started working out in college and lost a lot of weight. I don't manage to get to the gym as often as I should. Busy-busy, you know? But I still try to take care of myself."

Drew sat and stared at him for a moment, the smell of smoke lingering in his nostrils. He glanced at Amber and Trevor and saw that they looked as shell-shocked as he felt.

Greg continued talking as if he didn't notice anything wrong with them. "I'd love to stay and catch up with you three, but I volunteered to help the alumni committee, and there's lots to do to get ready for tomorrow night. You'll all be at the banquet and the dance afterward, right? I'll make sure to carve out some time for you then. In the meantime, keep having fun." He gave them a last smile and started to go, but he stopped and turned back to look at them once more. "I can't tell you how good it is to see the three of you." His smile widened, and a look came into his eyes that Drew couldn't read. "I've waited a long time for this. A very long time."

Then, with a last wave, Greg departed. Drew watched him as he headed toward the bar's exit, nodding to other reunion attendees at other tables as he passed. When he was gone, Drew turned to Amber and Trevor. He intended to ask them if they'd experienced the same strange vision of Greg being burned in the Lowry House, but then he stopped himself. People didn't share hallucinations. What he'd experienced was some kind of flashback, if a weird one that was a combination of memory and present sensory input. Unsettling, no doubt about it, but nothing supernatural.

Drew glanced at his watch, and even though it was only a little past ten, he said, "It's getting late.

I think I'll turn in. Maybe we can get together for breakfast tomorrow? Say around eight o'clock?"

Trevor and Amber agreed. They exchanged cell numbers and room numbers. They left the bar together, saying little as they headed for the lobby and the main elevators. As they walked, Drew did his best to ignore the smell of burning wood and cooking flesh that seemed to follow them the entire way.

SIX

Amber showered twice before climbing beneath the covers of her bed, but despite her best efforts to rid herself of it, the smell of smoke lingered on her skin—which made sense, since it hadn't been *real* smoke, had it? After drying off, she'd donned a pair of comfortable panties and a cozy oversize T-shirt, but they felt scratchy on her skin, almost as if she were suffering from a sunburn, which was a ridiculous thought. As rarely as she left her apartment, she got about as much sun exposure as one of those blind albino fish that dwelled in caves.

Not a *sun*burn, she realized. A *heat* burn, as if she'd stood too close to a fire for too long.

Despite that, she shivered and burrowed deeper beneath the covers.

At home, she normally lay in bed with all the lights off, but she'd turned them all on the moment she'd gotten back to her hotel room. Even so, it still seemed too dim in there—shadows pooled in the corners, the darkness seeming to watch her as it gathered . . .

Stop it! she told herself. *It's just your imagination.*

And was that her explanation for the vision of Greg burning that she'd experienced at the bar? Imagination? Her throat was still raw from inhaling too much smoke, her skin hot and tight from exposure to the flames' heat. Her body was reacting as if what she'd experienced had been real.

A memory, then . . . a flashback. Though one nightmarishly distorted. In real life, no one could have continued moving and speaking with the kind of burns Greg had sustained. There'd been a fire at the Lowry House the night they'd worked up the nerve to investigate it, that much they knew. Although she had no clear memory of being inside the house when the fire broke out, it's possible that she'd been there. That part could have been a memory. But Greg standing there, covered in flames, laughing, reaching for her with burned and blackened hands . . . no way had that ever happened. Besides, it hadn't been the teenage Greg she'd seen but, rather, an adult version of him.

So, what she'd experienced could have been part memory, part . . . what? Waking dream? Psychotic delusion? She was used to seeing disturbing things in her nightmares, but until this point, such horrifying images had confined themselves to her sleep. They'd never spilled over into her conscious experience before. *Call it what it is,* she decided. *A hallucination.*

"You're losing it, kiddo," she whispered to herself. "Big time."

She'd been afraid that coming here was a mistake, and now she had proof. At first, she'd feared that seeing Drew and Trevor again would dredge up emotions and memories that would be too much for her to handle. But after they'd been talking for a while and everything had been OK—no bad feelings, no bad memories—she'd begun to think that maybe it was a good thing that she'd allowed Greg to talk her into coming to the reunion. That maybe this weekend could be a step forward for her, for all three of them, just as Drew had said it could be. For the first time in a long time, she'd allowed herself to feel hope. Hope that she might be able to begin dealing with the trauma of what happened at the Lowry House and get on with her life.

But the vision-hallucination-whatever-the-hell-it-was of Greg proved that she'd been a fool to allow herself to hope. She was messed up, far beyond the ability of a simple reunion with her two closest friends from high school to fix.

It had been strange seeing Drew and Trevor again. Strange but good. She'd talked to both of them a few times over the years, especially Trevor, who periodically called to nag her to help him write about that night in the Lowry House, and he had visited her once a couple of years back. But this was the first time she'd been in Drew's presence since high school.

They'd never dated; despite the gaps in her memory, she was sure of that. But there had always been an attraction between them, even if they'd never gotten around to acknowledging it. She thought they might have gotten together eventually if that night at the Lowry House hadn't happened. Being around Drew tonight, she'd felt that attraction again, a tightness in her chest, a thrilling fluttery feeling in her stomach, the sensations at once both familiar and brand-new. She wondered if he had experienced similar feelings from being around her, but she dismissed the thought.

Drew was an accomplished professional, and while he claimed also to suffer from the trauma of that night in the Lowry House, he'd handled it a hell of a lot better than she had. There was no way a basket case like her could appeal to a man like him. Still, she thought that maybe she'd sensed something in the way he looked at her, the way he smiled . . .

"Idiot," she muttered. She closed her eyes and concentrated on breathing slowly, as one of the many therapists she'd seen over the years had taught her. She doubted that the technique would relax her enough to help her get to sleep, but she'd be happy if it took the edge off her stress, if only a little. *Breathe in . . . hold . . . breathe out. Breathe in . . .*

Little Eyes woke to darkness and the pressure of a hand clamped over her mouth. She panicked and began to thrash beneath the fur blanket until she heard her father's voice whisper in her ear.

"Be still, my daughter. Visitors have come. White men." He paused. "Not French."

Four Winds was a man of few words, but she could tell from the tone of his voice that he was worried.

Not French? French traders were the only white men her people had ever dealt with. Who were these newcomers, and why would they come in the middle of the night?

"The other men and I will go out to speak to them and see what they want," Four Winds went on. "I want you to stay in here and be quiet. Do not peek outside, no matter how curious you are. I do not wish them to know you are here. Do you understand me?"

She didn't, but she nodded anyway. Besides being her father, Four Winds was leader of their village, and it was her duty to obey.

She heard the smile in his voice as he said, "Good. I shall return soon." He removed his hand from her mouth and kissed her forehead before departing their domed bark house. When he was gone, Little Eyes sat up, wrapped the fur blanket around her buckskin-clad body for additional warmth, and scooted closer to the door. Her father had told her not to peek outside, but he'd said nothing about *listening* to what was happening.

Four Winds was a good father but overprotective. Little Eyes' mother had died of the wasting

sickness two summers ago, and her older sister
had married and gone away to live with her husband in his village the summer after that. She and
her father were alone now, and despite the fact
that she was sixteen, he treated her as if she were
much younger. But she was a woman, old enough
to be married herself, although she had yet to
catch a man's eye. Their village was small, only a
dozen families all told, and right now there weren't
any eligible unattached men of age around. She
thought she might well end up following in her
sister's tracks and marrying someone from another
village. But until that day arrived, she feared that
her father would view her as a little girl, regardless
of her age.

A flap of deer hide hung down over the house's
entrance, and the soft yellow glow of lantern light
was visible through the thin spaces on either side
of it. She knew the lanterns belonged to the visitors, for her people did not use such devices. She
imagined women and children in the other houses,
huddled in fur blankets to ward off the chill of the
autumn night, sitting and listening like her, eager
to know what was happening, hoping everything
would be all right.

She heard her father's voice then. He spoke
French, and while she knew only a few words
in the language, she did not need to be fluent to
guess what he was saying: *Why have you come here,
and why so late?*

A white man answered in a language she had never heard before, but for some strange reason, she understood his words. More, the voice seemed familiar to her, although she was certain that she had never heard the man speak.

"Any of you lot know the King's English?" The man waited. "No?" A sigh. "I suppose bloody French will have to do, then." He switched over to halting broken French, and as before, Little Eyes understood what he was saying. It was as if some sort of wondrous magic had befallen her, but she had no time to marvel at it. She was too busy listening.

"Your village trades with the French," the white man said. "That time is done. Now you will trade with us. With the British."

"We know the French, and we trust them," Four Winds said. "They are our friends. We do not know you and have no reason to trust you—and coming to our village in the middle of the night like this, weapons in hand, is not the best way to introduce yourselves."

Weapons! Little Eyes thought with alarm. That the white men carried guns was no surprise—they needed them for hunting and for protection, of course—but that they should approach the village with their guns out and ready to fire, as Four Winds' words implied, was most disturbing. She wondered how many white men there were, but although she was tempted to push aside the deerhide flap just enough so she could glimpse outside and see for herself, she did not. She had promised her father that she would not peek, and she was beginning to understand the reason for his caution.

The white man laughed. "Well spoken!" he said in that other language. *English,* Little Eyes thought, but she did not know how she knew this. "Maybe you lot aren't quite as savage as you're made out to be, eh?" He switched back to French. "Things are changing. My people are going to drive the French from this land. Our king commands it. He is a mighty monarch, and his army is vast."

At this, a cheer went up from the white man's companions, and while she couldn't judge their numbers from the sound, she knew there were more than a few of them.

The man with the familiar voice continued. "From this day forward, you will trade with us, or you will trade with no one."

"And if we will not?" Four Winds asked.

The white man paused a moment before answering, and when he spoke, she could hear the sly smile in his voice. "Then your memory will be a warning to others not to defy us."

Little Eyes heard a scuffling sound then, as of someone's feet moving across the ground, followed by a muffled grunting noise, as if someone was struggling. Fear gripped her heart, and she could no longer keep her promise to her father. She scooted the rest of the way to the door flap, pushed it aside, and saw two groups of men facing each other in the midst of her people's bark houses. The men from her village stood before a group of white men bearing lanterns and flintlock rifles. Four Winds stood toe-to-toe with one of the white men—the one who had been speaking for the others, she somehow knew. Her father had stepped forward and grabbed hold of the man's rifle and was attempting to wrest it from his grip. Their features were twisted into masks of anger, and the lantern light painted them with an unearthly glow, making the two men seem like a pair of evil spirits battling in the night.

Why weren't any of the other men from her village helping her father? They stood there, watching and doing nothing! But when she looked again at the white men, she understood. While the men of her village outnumbered them, they'd placed their lanterns on the ground near their feet, flintlocks held at the ready. If any of the men from her village made a move, the white men would fire their weapons.

Her father was a tall man, strong and brave, but the white man—while shorter of stature and leaner of limb—was younger, and after several moments of struggling, he broke Four Winds' grip on his rifle, swung the weapon's butt upward in a vicious arc, and struck her father a solid blow on the chin. Four Winds staggered backward, but he did not fall. He remained on his feet and glared at the white man, who grinned, leveled his rifle, aimed, and fired. There was a bright flash accompanied by a crack of thunder, and Four Winds cried out in pain as the gun's round struck him in the chest. The impact spun him around, and Little Eyes saw the agony on her father's face along with the blood spreading on his buckskin shirt as he fell to the ground.

She wailed in anguish, but her voice was drowned out by the crack of gunfire as the rest of the white men began firing. She wanted nothing more than to run outside and go to her father, but instinct prompted her to crawl to the other end of the house and hide beneath the blanket, like a small frightened animal seeking shelter in its burrow. She clapped her hands over her ears, squeezed her eyes shut, and tried not to see her father's face as he fell, tried not to hear once again the sound he made when the rifle ball pierced his flesh.

The first round of gunfire ended, and she wondered how many of the village men survived. Would the survivors, if any, attack the white men now with drawn knives or bare hands, or would they instead take advantage of the time it took the white men to reload their flintlocks to get their wives and children and flee into the woods?

Running. That was a good idea. She should

do that. Now, while she still had the chance. But she was too frightened and in too much shock from witnessing her father's murder to move, and so she remained where she was, hiding beneath the blanket, hands over her ears. It didn't take the white men as long to reload as she thought, and a second round of thunder passed through the village. When it ended, the white men cheered, and she knew that the men of her village had fallen.

The screams of women and children came next, and she knew there would be no more gunfire—not for a while, anyway. The white men had conquered her village and would now take their pleasure, and there would be no more killing until they were finished.

Little Eyes heard the soft rustle of the deerhide flap being pushed aside as someone entered her home. And it was hers now, hers alone, for her father was dead, just like her mother. She knew what the man, or men, had come for, and she knew there was nothing she could do to stop them.

"It's OK, Amber. You don't have to be afraid. I'm not going to hurt you."

It was the man who'd killed her father, but he sounded different now. His accent had changed. He no longer sounded British, he sounded . . . something else. And that name he'd called her. *Amber*. A strange name, but familiar somehow, too. There was kindness in his voice, and despite everything that had happened, she found it reassuring, and it prompted her to take her hands from her ears and draw back the blanket so she could look at him.

The man carried a lantern, and its glow filled the bark house. He was dressed in a well-worn wool coat, breeches, and scuffed boots, and he held a flintlock rifle—the weapon that had killed her father—in his other hand. She could smell the harsh tang of burned gunpowder, and she thought that must be what death smelled like. Now that the man was up close, she could make out his features. His black hair was overlong, tangled, and sweat-matted, and his beard was bushy and in need of trimming. But there was something familiar about his ice-blue eyes, and a name whispered through her mind: *Greg*.

He smiled as he crouched down and placed both the lantern and the flintlock on the ground. He remained in that position, keeping still as if he were a hunter and she were an animal he didn't wish to startle with any sudden movements. He spoke then, taking care to keep his voice gentle, but any reassurance his tone might have given her was spoiled by the cries of fear and sorrow coming from the women in the houses around them.

"This is a dream, Amber. Don't get me wrong. It *did* happen, back during the French and Indian

War in the 1700s. The massacre took place on the site where the Lowry House would one day be built, as a matter of fact. But what you're experiencing now is nothing more than a . . . well, a dramatic re-creation, as they say on reality TV. A band of British traders and hunters took it into their heads to attack Native American villages in the Ohio Valley. They figured the fewer Indians there were to fight alongside the French, the better. This is pretty much the way it happened, though your mind reshaped some of the details." His smile widened. "Just like Hollywood, you couldn't resist making a good story even better. The attack originally took place before dawn, and there was no confrontation between the chief and the leader of the British raiders. The British snuck into the village while everyone was sleeping and started killing. Once the men were dealt with, they *did* take their time with the women, though." His smile took on a darker edge. "And some of the children. You got that part right."

Little Eyes' mind was reeling. On the one hand, this white man—this *killer*—was speaking nonsense. But part of her, a part that thought of itself as Amber and not Little Eyes, seemed to understand his words.

"This place may be a dream memory, but *you're* real. *I'm* real." The man—*Greg*—scooted closer to her. He continued to smile, but a hungry look came into his eyes. That look made her want to flee, but she couldn't move. His gaze fixed her in place, as if he were an approaching predator and she were the prey too terrified to do anything but remain frozen and wait for death.

"I can't tell you how good it is to see you again, Amber. To be close to you. To . . . touch you."

He reached out with his right hand and brushed his fingers along her cheek. His flesh was ice-cold, and his touch burned. She gasped in pain and surprise, and without thinking, she lashed out with her hand and raked her fingernails across his own cheek, tearing bloody furrows in his skin.

If the wound hurt, Greg gave no sign of it. Instead, he laughed as a black tarry substance began to ooze forth from the scratches she'd made. It wasn't blood, it was *darkness,* and as it trickled forth, it formed a mass of tiny tendrils that writhed in the air as if alive. They grew longer and thicker and stretched toward her. She tried to draw back, but the tendrils were fast, and they wrapped around the back of her head and held her fast.

Greg continued to smile, but now his eyes had been replaced by orbs of pure black.

"How about a kiss?" he said.

She felt herself pulled forward as Greg opened his mouth. A mass of ebon tendrils slid over his teeth and between his lips, thicker than the ones protruding from his facial wound, darker, too, and coated with a sheen of viscous slime. The tendrils plunged into her mouth and forced their way down her throat, choking off her screams. She thrashed and struggled as Greg's darkness poured into her, and in her mind, she heard the sound of his laughter.

Amber woke gasping for breath. She threw back the covers, jumped out of bed, and ran to the bathroom. She made it to the toilet just in time, and she spent the next several minutes throwing up. When she finished, she flushed, made her way to the sink, and held on to the counter with a death grip to steady herself. The reflection that looked back at her from the mirror was less than attractive. She was pale and shaking, and her hair was so drenched with sweat it looked as if she'd dunked her head under the shower. And if for a second she thought she saw the face of a young Native American girl looking back at her, she told herself that it was an echo of her nightmare and nothing more.

She washed her face, brushed her teeth, and used a copious amount of mouthwash afterward. She dried her hair with a towel, then brushed it so it didn't look too hideous, and then she left the bathroom. Her clothes were damp with sweat, so she peeled them off and donned a fresh set: jeans and a purple T-shirt with an image of Johnny Depp as the Mad Hatter on it. By the time she'd finished, she wasn't shaking anymore, and she looked at the row of prescription bottles waiting for her on the nightstand. She was used to having bad dreams, but that had been a nasty one, even by her standards. If there was ever a time she could use the aid of pharmaceutical science to get her through the rest of the night, it was now.

She stood there for several minutes, looking at her meds, thinking. Maybe what she needed most right now wasn't pills. Maybe what she needed was a friend.

She turned away from the nightstand, slipped on a pair of flip-flops, grabbed her room key, and headed for the door.

Greg opened his eyes and sat up. He'd been lying on his bed on top of the covers, hands folded over his stomach, while he'd paid his little psychic visit to Amber. Her room was on the same floor as his, as were Drew's and Trevor's, as he'd arranged it. Not that he needed close proximity to initiate mental contact, but it did make things a bit easier.

His room was dark. He didn't need light to see by, hadn't since that night in the Lowry House. He was most at home in the dark, *belonged* there like a fish in water or a bird in the sky. The Darkness was both parent and lover to him. It filled him, sustained him, *completed* him, and he would do its bidding forever and ever, amen. But even the Darkness couldn't be everything to him. He wanted more, *needed* more.

And what he wanted most was Amber.

He'd almost had her, too, but she'd pulled away from him and broken the psychic contact. He could have held on to her mind if he'd wanted, could have forced her to remain linked to him. She was mentally strong, stronger than she knew, but her strength was nothing compared with his. Still, he didn't want to take her by force. He wanted her to come to him willingly, to accept the Darkness, submit to it, give herself over to it body and soul, as he had. And that would take some time. That was OK. He could be patient. He'd waited fifteen years, and he could wait a little longer.

What *wasn't* OK was Amber's reaction to her nightmare. Instead of taking some pills and going back to sleep, she'd decided to go talk to an old friend. She was going to see Drew.

Jealousy surged through him. His hands balled into fists, and he gritted his teeth. Sensing his mood, the shadows in the room thickened and began a slow swirl around the bed, like clouds churning in advance of an approaching storm. Amber had always been attracted to Drew, and he knew that Drew felt the same way about her, although the idiot had never admitted it, not even to himself. *Typical psychologist*, he thought. Good at understanding everyone's feelings except his own. But the last thing Greg wanted to do was drive Amber into Drew's arms and perhaps get them to acknowledge their feelings for each other.

The shadows swirled around him like ebon sharks, and they whispered in voices as cold as the ocean depths. *Then why don't you do something about it? Go to Drew's room and confront them. Batter down their psychic defenses and claim their minds as your own. You have the power. You can do whatever you want,* take *whatever you want* . . .

Yes. He could do that. It would be child's play, and there was nothing Amber or Drew could do to stop him. And when he was finished, he'd go to Trevor and claim him, so he would have the full set. It was tempting, but if he gave in to that temptation, all he'd have in the end would be shells of his friends, their bodies hollowed out and replaced with Darkness. And he didn't want that. He wanted more.

So, as much as he hated it, he'd leave Amber and Drew alone—for now. But that didn't mean he had to stay in his room seething with jealousy. He had two main goals for this weekend, and his friends only factored in one of them. What reasons did anyone have for attending a high-school reunion? To rub your fellow classmates' noses in your success and, if possible, settle old scores. The latter was his other motivation for coming to Ash Creek this weekend. A lot of people had treated him like shit back in high school, and he was here for some long-delayed but well-deserved payback. High time he got to it.

He drew the shadows into him, rose from the bed, and headed toward the door. He grinned so wide his mouth hurt.

This was going to be fun.

SEVEN

Sean Houser lay on his bed, shoeless but still wearing a polo shirt and slacks. He was watching an extreme-sports competition on ESPN2 with the sound off and thinking that this was *way* less fun than he'd thought it was going to be. Not the TV program; he was barely paying attention to that. But the reunion. Sure, technically, it was tomorrow night and hadn't really started yet, but he'd come in tonight expecting *something* to be happening. Maybe some people dancing in the bar or at least a few room parties going on. But no one was doing anything in the bar except talking.

He'd seen a few people he recognized, including those three weirdos who chased ghosts back in high school and that feeb who hung around them sometimes. But he hadn't seen anyone cool, so he'd left and gone in search of room parties, going so far as to wander up and down the hallways on various floors, hoping to hear the sound of music playing too loud and people talking and laughing. But all he'd heard were a few TVs playing and a baby or two crying. So he'd retreated to his own room, flipped on the TV, muted the sound, stretched out on the bed, and moped.

He'd been looking forward to this weekend for months, had gotten good and jazzed about it the last couple of weeks. He'd been hoping to reconnect with some friends he hadn't seen for years, relive some of the glory days, get a little wild and crazy. He hadn't gone to college, opting instead to enter the workforce after graduation, and he'd worked in construction ever since. He was employed by a plastering and drywall company, and he had a wife and two kids, with one more on the way, and while he didn't hate his life, he didn't love it, either. He sometimes felt as if he didn't live so much as exist, but that was the way it went, right? Most people were in the same boat as him. Just going through the motions one day after another, taking care of business, paying their bills, marking the days off the calendar one by one. So, this weekend wasn't only a chance to escape his family for a while but also an opportunity to escape himself. The self he'd become over the last fifteen years, anyway. For a couple of days, he'd be able to go back in time and become teenage Sean again, without any worries or responsibilities.

But now that he was here, he was feeling let down. When he'd been growing up, his dad had told him to enjoy his high-school years. "They're the best days of your life, kid," his old man had said. "The last time you really get to live it up. So make sure you do it right." Whenever his dad talked about high school like that, which was often, he'd get a wistful tone in his voice and a faraway look in his eyes. Not sad, exactly. He'd seemed more tired than anything, like a man who knew that his best days were long gone and never coming back. When his dad got like that, it scared Sean, and he'd vowed that whatever else he did with his life, he wasn't going to grow up and look back on his high-school years and wish he'd done more. *Lived* more. He was going to take his dad's advice and Do It Right.

And he had. He hadn't been big man on campus or anything like that. Hadn't gone out for any sports or wanted anything to do with creative activities like band or drama. He hadn't belonged to any clubs and certainly hadn't belonged to the honor society. He'd barely paid attention in class, doing the minimum amount of work necessary to get by. As far as Sean was concerned, high school had one purpose only: to give him opportunities to party. He'd spent those four years drunk or high more often than not, and while he hadn't gotten laid as often as he bragged about to his friends, he'd done OK with the girls. But if there was one thing he liked more than partying—or at least as much—it was playing practical jokes.

He'd started his career as a jokester in middle

school with the usual. Taping "I suck" signs on the backs of unsuspecting victims, leaving dead mice in teachers' desk drawers, dropping M-80s into trash cans, that sort of thing. He stepped it up a notch when he got to high school, taking the tires off teachers' cars in the parking lot and putting them up on blocks, running an inflatable sex doll up the flagpole in front of the school, and replacing the soda in the vending machine in the teachers' lounge with cans of beer. He was slick about it, too, and while the school administration suspected him, he was never caught. He'd come close, though—just once.

He'd taken biology during his junior year, and the teacher, Mr. Bryant, had been a real hard-ass. No matter how hard Sean worked—admittedly not very—he couldn't seem to pull a passing grade on assignments. When it came time to do a term paper for the course, Mr. Bryant, expecting another lackluster performance on Sean's part, assigned him a tutor: Greg Daniels, the feeb he'd seen down in the bar earlier. Greg might have looked like a potato that some mad scientist had evolved into human form, but he was no dummy, and Sean scored a B-minus on his report. Still, he was pissed off at Mr. Bryant on general principles and decided to indulge in a little revenge.

He photocopied a picture of Bryant, made a couple of dozen copies, and cut out the image of his head. He then snuck into the bio lab after school, removed all of the frogs from the storage cabinet, placed them on the dissecting tables, opened them up and spread out their organs, and—for the pièce de résistance—glued the pictures of Mr. Bryant's face onto the frogs' heads. Then, for no other reason than because Bryant had assigned Greg as his tutor, Sean put the leftover photocopied images of a headless Mr. Bryant into the lab drawer Greg had been assigned.

He then went home and looked forward to the next day.

He had biology second period, so the frogs were gone when he got to class, but Mr. Bryant was livid, and the story had already spread throughout the school. Bryant had searched the lab, just as Sean figured he would, to check if anything else had been vandalized, and in Greg's drawer he'd discovered the photocopied pages from which the images of his head had been cut.

He confronted Greg in front of the rest of the class, and of course, he denied committing the prank. Bryant didn't believe him and got more and more agitated as he questioned Greg, his face turning beet-red, spraying spittle from his mouth as he shouted, until Sean thought the son of a bitch would blow a gasket and drop dead right there. Finally, Bryant told the rest of the class to open their books and review chapter eighteen, and he hauled Greg's ass down to the office. Sean felt a little sorry for Greg but only a little.

Watching Bryant lose it like that had been way too entertaining.

But his amusement faded when Bryant returned a few minutes later and told him the principal had requested the honor of his presence as well. It turned out that Greg had told the principal that he suspected Sean of playing the prank, so he had to submit to an interrogation for the better part of an hour. He kept his cool, though, knowing there was no evidence to prove he'd done it, and the principal let him go, but not before giving a month's detention to everyone in Mr. Bryant's biology classes, no matter what period they attended. Parents raised holy hell about that at the next school-board meeting, and the detention ended after a week and a half. It was a great joke, one of Sean's best, but he knew he'd gotten a little too close to being burned, and so he laid off on the pranks for a couple months after that and was careful not to target specific teachers anymore.

Greg didn't say anything to him about the joke, and the two of them never spoke again. Now, fifteen years later, Sean found himself feeling sorry about what he'd done to Greg. The guy *had* helped him pass that report, after all, and he'd already had enough trouble, being such a loser and all. Of course, it didn't look as if he was a loser any longer. When Sean had seen him in the bar, he hadn't recognized him at first. He was fit, dressed well, and carried himself with confidence. He looked better than Sean did these days. Sean had been a beanpole in high school, but years of too much fast food and too much beer had filled him out and given him a significant gut.

It occurred to him then that he'd become his father, a man on the slow, downward slide to the grave, looking back at his youth and wondering where the hell it had gone.

Greg looked like the opposite kind of man, someone whose present was better than his past, someone who'd found the secret to living well. Maybe he should head on back to the bar, see if Greg was still there, maybe ask if he'd like to sit down for a drink. It wasn't as if he had anything better to do. Who knew? Maybe he'd even apologize to the guy for trying to frame him for the frog prank.

Sean turned off the TV and slipped on his shoes. He grabbed his wallet from the dresser, tucked it into the back pocket of his slacks, and walked to the door. He gripped the handle, opened it—

—and stepped into the biology lab.

For a moment, he stood there, staring as he inhaled the sour-sharp odor of formaldehyde. Everything was as he remembered it. Fluorescent lights, tiled floor, long black tables set up in rows, high wooden stools for students to sit on. The teacher's desk was up front, behind it the chalkboard, and on the other side of the room a series of windows, blinds up to show the grassy field outside, the sun shining down on it.

Sun? But it was well after eleven P.M. For some reason, this shift from night to day disturbed Sean even more than finding himself standing in the high-school biology lab. After all, a room could be faked. As difficult as it would be to accomplish, it could be done. All it took was some furniture, false walls, lights . . . like a set constructed for a play. *How* someone could put it up in a hotel hallway—and in the short time since he'd entered his room and zoned out in front of the TV—and *why* were different questions, but the fact of the matter was that it *could* be done. But the world outside those windows—the sunlight, the grass, the breeze blowing through the trees in the yard, the clouds in the powder-blue sky—he didn't see how those things could be faked. They seemed too real. *Felt* too real.

Sean's initial reaction was that this was some kind of joke. Yeah, that was it. Had to be. The reunion organizers were pranking attendees by re-creating settings from their high-school years. It was a wild idea, genius, really, and Sean admired the hell out of whoever had come up with it. How could the reunion committee afford to build something so elaborate? How did they get hold of that kind of money?

But even as he thought these things, part of

him knew they were desperate attempts at ratio-
nalization. There was no way this was some sort
of prank. It was impossible to re-create the bio
lab in such detail, and in a hotel hallway yet. The
damn thing couldn't even *fit* in the hall. And there
were those windows and the sunlit world that lay
beyond them . . .

He wanted to believe it was a joke, but he knew
it wasn't, and that knowledge chilled him to the
core of his being. Because if it wasn't a joke, then
either this was real or he'd gone crazy. Neither
prospect held much appeal.

No, he thought. *You're asleep. You conked out
watching TV, and you only dreamed you got off the
bed and left the room. You were thinking about Greg
Daniels and the prank in the bio lab right before
you drifted off, and that's why you're dreaming about
them now.*

The thought was a reassuring one, until he realized that he'd never in his life been aware that he
was dreaming while in the middle of a dream. He
supposed there was a first time for everything,
but somehow, despite his hope that this was all a
dream, he couldn't shake the feeling that it was
really happening.

He heard the soft sound of chalk moving
across the chalkboard, and he turned to see letters appearing on the board as if by magic. There
was no chalk visible and no hand to wield it. The
letters appeared one by one of their own accord:

"This isn't a dream, Sean. This is karmic retribution. More simply, paybacks are a bitch. Love and kisses, Greg."

Sean stared at the message for several seconds and finally decided that, dream or not, he'd had enough of this shit. He turned back to the door, gripped the knob, turned it, pushed . . . and found the door locked. He shoved harder, even rammed his shoulder against the door, resulting in a very realistic burst of pain, but it refused to budge. He gave the knob one last shake before giving up and turning away from the door. He looked at the windows on the other side of the room. They'd probably be locked as well. Wasn't that the way it always was in dreams? If one exit was blocked to you, all the others were, too. But the glass could be broken, and then he could crawl through and get outside. Outside to a world of sunlight that shone when it should be dark.

That way of escape might have been open to him, but at that moment, it didn't exactly appeal.

The lab's back wall was lined with a row of metal storage cabinets, and the doors began rattling, as if something inside was trying to get out. Sean heard a soft whimpering sound and wondered where it came from. It wasn't until he heard it a second time that he realized it was coming from his own throat.

The cabinet doors flew open, and misshapen

creatures stepped out, thick-bodied and squat, not quite as tall as an adult man. Their naked bodies were covered with mottled green and white rubbery flesh, and their bulging eyes fixed Sean with cold, inhuman appraisal. The frogs, a half-dozen in all, came toward him, walking with an awkward lopsided gait. They were, after all, not creatures designed to stand upright on two legs. Their skin was coated with a liquid sheen, and the smell of formaldehyde in the air grew stronger, making Sean's stomach turn. He covered his nose and mouth with a hand in an attempt to blunt the awful stench, but the stink was too thick for the gesture to do any good.

The frogs made soft little thrumming sounds in their throats as they approached, and Sean found the noise oddly soothing. In their right hands—if *hands* was the correct word—they held gleaming metal scalpels. In their left hands, they carried paper masks with loops of string attached. The frogs now donned their masks, slipping them over their bulging eyes and protruding mouths as best they could, and Sean saw that the image printed on the paper was the face of Mr. Bryant, the biology teacher. But unlike the picture Sean had photocopied from the yearbook so long ago, the expression on Bryant's face was one of contorted hatred: eyes wild, mouth open, teeth bared.

The frogs continued toward Sean, their tiny

feet making wet slapping sounds on the tile as they came. Sean noticed that the pale flesh of each of their abdomens was bisected with a single vertical line, like old scars that hadn't quite healed all the way. The frogs' pudgy little bellies jiggled with each awkward step they took, and seams opened in their abdominal scars. Grayish-green organs peeked through, just a hint at first, but the seams widened, split open all the way, and frog guts splayed forth to dangle in front of the creatures and be dragged across the floor as they continued toward Sean.

The thrumming sounds they made began to resemble human speech, the words deep and liquidy, spoken in a lilting ribbit-ribbit cadence.

"YOUR-turn, YOUR-turn, YOUR-turn . . ."

Sean backed away, hands raised in a gesture that was half defensive, half pleading. He shook his head no, the frogs nodded yes, and when Sean's back came up against the chalkboard and he had nowhere else to go, they rushed the last few feet to him, raising their scalpels . . . and ready to work.

Drew sat at the desk in his hotel room, laptop open in front of him, looking at a photo displayed on the screen. The picture had been taken with a cheap one-use camera, so the quality of the image wasn't very good, although he'd tried to sharpen the detail and brighten the colors when he'd scanned the photo and converted it to a digital file several years ago.

The picture showed teenage versions of Drew, Trevor, and Amber dressed in jeans and light jackets and standing before an old oak tree. Behind them, off to the left, sat the Lowry House. He thought it remarkable how different those three kids were from the adults they would become. It wasn't that the physical changes were all that pronounced. After all, only a decade and a half had passed since the photo was taken—although when it had been taken and who'd been holding the camera, he couldn't remember. The main difference lay in the attitudes of their teenage selves. All three of them were smiling, their eyes clear and bright. Amber stood in the middle, and they had their arms around one another. They'd been so full of energy and potential back then, untroubled by care or worry. Young in the truest, most wonderful sense of the word.

Looking at the photo caused a great sadness to well up in him, and he grieved for those three children who, in a very real sense, had been lost the night the Lowry House burned down.

Had the picture been taken that very day? It was possible, he decided. The Lowry House had burned down in April, and they were dressed for cool weather. They'd likely been documenting the events of that night. They'd always tried to approach their investigations as scientifically as possible, so they documented everything, taking photos, writing notes, making video and audio recordings. He wondered if they'd recorded any information that night, and if so, what had happened to it. Presumably, it had been left in the house and destroyed in the fire. He didn't remember for certain. All he knew was that he had no information other than the single photo he'd found several years ago when cleaning out an old drawer full of junk.

He leaned forward and examined the photo more closely, paying special attention to Amber. She was as lovely today as she'd been then. As he looked at her face, a whisper of memory returned to him: Amber's voice, sounding scared.

I had a dream last night, Drew. A real bad one. About the Lowry House. I think maybe we shouldn't go there tonight.

He tried to hold on to the memory, tried to drag more of it out of the depths of his subconscious, but the harder he fought to recall it, the faster it slipped away from him. And then the memory was gone.

Drew was a rationalist, and even as a teenager, he hadn't believed that Amber's dreams were anything more than dreams. Amber, however, believed they were prophetic, and Trevor had a tendency to agree with her. Drew believed that so-called precognitive dreams were nothing more than the subconscious mind trying to send a message to the conscious mind, a way for two distinct aspects of the brain to communicate with each other. Nothing psychic about it at all. But now, looking at her smiling teenage face and thinking of how scared she'd sounded in the fragment of memory he recalled, he wondered if, in that instance at least, her dream had been something more than a little nighttime self-therapy.

There was a knock on his door then. Three knocks, to be precise, so soft he wasn't sure he heard them. He rose from the desk and walked over to the door on bare feet; he'd removed his shoes and socks when he'd first gotten back to his room but was otherwise still dressed. He opened the door, half expecting to find no one standing there at all, but he was surprised, and more than a little pleased, to see Amber.

"I couldn't sleep," she said. She opened her mouth again, as if she intended to provide further explanation for her visit, but instead of speaking, she smiled and shrugged.

He wasn't fooled by her smile. He saw the haunted look in her eyes and had a pretty good idea of why she'd been unable to sleep.

He gave her what he hoped was a reassuring smile and gestured for her to enter. She did so, and he closed the door behind her, unable to keep from thinking that this scenario, two friends of the opposite gender seeing each other in a hotel room after fifteen years apart, was the stuff that sexual fantasies were made of. He knew it was important to make sure he didn't give her the wrong impression. He didn't have such a high opinion of himself as to assume that she might be attracted to him, but they *were* old friends, and she was likely feeling vulnerable right now. The three of them being together again had been stressful, rousing long-dormant memories and the difficult emotions that came with them. In a situation like this, it would only be natural for one person to reach out to another in search of comfort and reassurance. He'd have to watch for any overtures on Amber's part and make sure he didn't do anything to encourage them.

And he'd have to watch himself as well. After all, he was only human and prone to the same emotional stresses—and needs—as anyone else.

His room had only a single king-size bed, and Amber stopped at the foot of it, as if trying to decide whether or not to sit down. In the end, she chose to sit in the reading chair tucked into the corner. She passed the desk on the way there, saw his open laptop and the picture displayed on the screen, and paused to look at it.

"I don't remember that being taken," she said. "It's a good picture. We look happy." She leaned forward to examine it. "I wonder who took it. Greg, maybe?"

"I don't know," he said. "I don't even remember how I came by that photo. I just found it one day."

She nodded her understanding and closed the laptop, as if she didn't want the image of their teenage selves to intrude on their conversation.

Those are the real ghosts, he thought. *Specters of What Was and Can Never Be Again.* As frightening as anything that might lurk within the shadowed corridors of a haunted house and in many ways more so.

Amber sat in the reading chair, so he sat on the edge of the bed facing her.

"Bad dreams?" he asked.

She looked at him for a moment and then burst out laughing. "I'm sorry," she said once her laughter subsided. "It's just that this situation—both of us sitting down, you asking if I've been having bad dreams, the attitude of caring attentiveness you're projecting—it all seems like a therapy session. I ought to know; I've been through enough of them." Her merriment died away, and she became serious. "I didn't come here in search of free therapy, Drew. I imagine that happens to psychologists a lot—friends and acquaintances coming to you with their problems, hoping to get some expert advice."

"It *is* an occupational hazard," he admitted.

"Like I said, that's not why I'm here. I just . . . need someone to talk to, you know? Someone who understands."

"I get it. You want me to call Trevor and ask him to join us? He's probably feeling the same way right now."

"No. I mean, Trevor's a good guy, but he's pushy, you know? At least when it comes to the subject of the Lowry House. He's determined to make money off that damned place, and he won't rest until we help him do it."

Drew shook his head. "That's Trevor's way of coping. By treating the Lowry House like just another story, he can keep it at a distance, get a measure of control over it, and make it manageable. In the end, he wants the same thing we do: to learn what happened to him, to the three of us, that night."

"Speak for yourself," she said. "I don't care what really happened. I just want to be free, you know? Free of the fragmented memories and the panic that comes along with them. Free of the crippling depression that keeps me from having a normal life.

"But above all, I want to be free of the nightmares. Most people fantasize about winning the lottery or becoming famous. You know what I fantasize about? Dreamless sleep."

They were both silent for a time after that. Finally, he said, "At the risk of sounding like a psychologist instead of a friend, do you want to tell me about it? The dream, I mean. I assume that's why you had trouble sleeping tonight."

"Yeah, it is. This one was weird, even for me. I suppose it was prompted by this bizarre . . . I don't know what to call it. It wasn't a memory, exactly.

More like a hallucination, I guess, though it didn't last very long. It happened earlier, when we were talking with Greg in the bar."

A chill rippled down the length of Drew's spine. Once more, he saw Greg wreathed in flame, smelled the stench of burning wood and flesh, heard his accusing voice.

You did this to me. The three of you. It's your fault. All your fault . . .

"You saw Greg burning," he said. "And it seemed so real, like you weren't remembering but *seeing* it. As if it was happening right in front of your eyes but just for a moment. Then it was gone."

Amber's mouth fell open in shock. "Yes. But how—"

The rest of her question was cut off by a high-pitched shriek. It was followed by a second and then a third, each one louder and higher than the last. Then silence.

"What the hell was *that?*" she said.

The shrieks sounded as if they'd come from right outside Drew's door. He wasn't a medical doctor, but he was used to dealing with emergencies, given the patient population he worked with. He jumped off the bed and ran to the door, dimly aware that Amber followed. He unlocked the door, flung it open, and saw a man lying on the hallway floor. He rested on his back, legs drawn up so that his knees pointed to the ceiling. His arms were folded so that his hands lay palm-up on his chest, giving the impression that he'd been trying to ward off an attacker, although aside from him, the hallway was deserted. His eyes were wide and staring, and his mouth was open as if he were still shrieking, but no sound emerged. The utter stillness of the body, coupled with those unblinking eyes, told Drew that the man was dead. Still, he had to be sure. He knelt next to the man, checked to see if he was breathing, then pressed two fingers against his neck to feel for a pulse. There was a harsh smell in the air, an acrid chemical tang that made Drew's stomach turn. He breathed through his mouth so he wouldn't have to smell it.

Behind Drew, Amber said, "Is he . . . ?"

"Run back in the room and call the front desk and tell them to get an ambulance here as fast as possible!" He started performing CPR. Even though he hadn't been able to detect either breathing or a pulse, he knew better than to assume that there was no hope of reviving the man.

As Amber rushed back inside, doors to nearby rooms began opening, and people emerged, frightened and curious. Among them was Trevor. He hurried over to Drew and stood next to him, gazing down at the man lying on the floor.

"What happened?" he asked.

Drew continued performing CPR on the man as

he spoke. "I don't know. I heard the man scream, and when I came out to check on him, I found him like this. I think he might have had a heart attack or a stroke. Amber's inside calling the front desk about it."

Trevor gave him a look. "She was in your room when it happened?"

"It's not what you think," Drew said.

Trevor looked as if he wanted to press the issue, but he said no more about it. People were beginning to gather around to check out the body and talk among themselves in hushed voices.

"I recognize him," Trevor said. "He's here for the reunion. I saw him wandering around the bar when we were down there earlier. His name is Sean . . . something. I can't remember his last name."

Amber came back out into the hall and joined them.

"The clerk at the front desk said he'll call nine-one-one. Hopefully the paramedics will be here in a few minutes."

Drew doubted there was anything paramedics could do for Sean at this point, but he continued CPR. Even though he knew his actions were most likely futile, he couldn't give up until medical help arrived to take over.

Amber wrinkled her nose. "What's that smell?"

Trevor crouched down next to Drew, reached out, and touched a finger to one of Sean's palms.

Drew hadn't noticed it before, but the man's hands were coated with a thin sheen of slime. Trevor raised his finger to his nose, sniffed, and made a face.

"This is going to sound weird, but it smells like formaldehyde."

EIGHT

Trevor focused his camera on the chrome letters above the entrance that spelled out "Lowry Recreation Center" and zoomed in for a closer shot. He took a couple of pictures, one with the flash, one without. When he checked them on the camera's display, he wasn't satisfied with either one. They both looked so ordinary. No, worse than that. *Drab* was the word he was looking for. Drab and dull and boring as hell. He imagined a bookstore browser paging through his book on the Lowry House, seeing one of these pictures, thinking, *Seriously? That's not creepy at all,* and putting it back on the shelf. Still, he didn't delete the photos. They were better than nothing.

"Disappointed?" Drew asked.

"A little," Trevor admitted, but he was understating the case. "They cleared away the remains of the Lowry House not long after we graduated from high school, so even if the rec center wasn't here, there'd be nothing to look at but an empty field. But I still expected the place to feel . . . *different,* you know?"

Amber nodded. "Me, too. But it's just a building, isn't it?"

The three friends stood on the lawn in front of the rec center. It was a little before ten A.M., the air was still cool, and the slight breeze blowing made it feel even cooler. Although it was the first week of September, it was still summer, and Trevor figured the day would warm up before long. Still, he wished he'd brought a jacket. Drew had on a blue windbreaker and Amber a cream-colored sweater, but he was wearing a yellow polo shirt, and it wasn't doing a whole lot to cut the breeze.

He smiled, amused at himself. Here he was, a professional paranormal investigator, having returned to the site of the haunting where he and his friends had been traumatized, lost large chunks of their memories, and perhaps nearly died, and what was uppermost in his mind? That he was chilly. A man of real emotional depth, that was him.

"The location has changed so much that there's nothing recognizable to trigger our memories," Drew said.

"Yeah, but I expected to *feel* something," Trevor persisted.

"Like what?" Amber asked. It was a bit cloudy this morning, but she wore sunglasses.

He figured she hadn't been able to sleep and her eyes were red and puffy. After what had happened last night, he'd had a hard time getting to sleep himself, and he'd barely managed to wake up in time to meet.Drew and Amber for breakfast in the hotel restaurant.

They'd talked as they ate, and he'd learned that they'd both had the same weird vision he'd had the night before in the hotel bar, that of Greg burning alive. Drew admitted that it was, to say the least, uncommon for three people to experience a shared hallucination, but despite Trevor's best attempts, he hadn't been able to get his friend to acknowledge that the vision might be of paranormal origin. After they'd finished eating, the three of them had decided to take a trip to visit the site of the Lowry House, and Trevor had driven them in his Prius, excited to return to the place where the most important event in their lives had occurred. But now that they were there, he found himself more than a little disappointed.

"I don't know what," he admitted, and before Drew could say anything, he added, "And I'm not necessarily talking about feeling some kind of psychic residue." In truth, though, he *had* been hoping to experience something exactly like that, a profound sense of unnameable dread emanating from the site where the Lowry House, a Bad Place if ever there was one, had once stood. He turned to look at the rec center. "I guess I hoped that coming here with the two of you would be like having the right key to unlock a door, that once we were here, all our memories would come flooding back, and we'd have all the answers."

Drew stepped closer and laid a hand on his shoulder. "You've seen too many movies and TV shows. Recovery from trauma is a long and difficult road. It's a series of small steps taken over time, not a miraculous epiphany that occurs in an instant."

He sighed. "I know." He turned to Drew and smiled. "But it sure would be convenient if it was."

Drew returned his smile. "True, but if it worked like that, I'd be out of a job."

Amber pointed at an oak tree less than a dozen yards away. "That's the tree from the picture, isn't it? The one you had on your computer, Drew."

"Picture?" Trevor asked. He liked the sound of that. Maybe it was something he'd be able to use for his book—assuming he'd ever get to write the damn thing, that is.

"It's an old photo I found of the three of us standing in front of an oak tree with the Lowry House in the background," Drew explained. He looked at the oak for a moment. "Yeah, I think that's the same one." He started toward the tree, and Amber and Trevor followed.

"You two stand over here," Drew said, and directed Trevor and Amber to stand on the side of the tree facing the street. They did so, and he stepped back to look at them. "It's definitely the same tree," he pronounced. "And if I'm looking at it from the right angle, then the rec center is sitting exactly where the Lowry House used to be."

Trevor racked his brain, searching for a memory of once having stood in this very spot when he was a teenager and having his picture taken. He thought there might be something there, some thin will-o'-the-wisp of recollection, more sensed than recalled, but he wasn't certain. Still, the thought that they were standing in the same place was exciting. Small steps, Drew had said, right? Well, they were definitely taking some steps just by being there.

"Switch places with me, Drew," he said. "I want to get a picture of you and Amber in the same position we stood back then. You know, for comparison's sake."

Drew did as he requested and stood next to Amber, while Trevor stepped back, raised his camera, and lined up the shot.

Drew and Amber stood, their hands at their sides, neither one smiling.

Trevor couldn't help laughing. "C'mon, this isn't a funeral. Smile a little!" As soon as he said the words, he regretted them, especially considering what had happened the night before. Still, Drew and Amber managed a pair of smiles, and

Drew even put his arm around her shoulder. He considered teasing them about that, but after his funeral crack, he decided to keep his mouth shut and take the picture. Again, he tried one with the flash and one without. He had Drew and Amber remain in position as he showed them the photos on his camera display to check if they resembled the original picture. Drew confirmed that they did, and, satisfied, Trevor saved the images to the camera's memory stick.

"Want to see if we can get inside?" he asked.

"I'm sure it's locked," Drew said. "And it's probably not safe to enter, anyway. The outer construction may be finished, but I'm sure they're still working on the inside."

"Maybe," Trevor said, "but aren't you curious?"

"Not really," Amber said, and shivered. He doubted that it was because of the breeze. "Not after last night," she added.

"Are you suggesting that Sean's death is somehow connected to what happened to us in the Lowry House?" Drew asked. "You heard what the paramedics said. He had a fatal heart attack. Sure, he was a bit young to have heart trouble, but it happens. It was just a coincidence. Nothing supernatural about it at all."

"Riiiiight," Trevor said. "And while you're at it, maybe you can explain why he smelled like he'd been skinny-dipping in formaldehyde before his ticker gave out on him."

"Whatever the chemical was on him, I doubt it was formaldehyde," Drew said. "It's impossible to say what it was without doing some tests, but if I had to guess, I'd say it was some kind of astringent, likely used to treat a skin condition of some sort."

Trevor eyed his friend skeptically. "His skin looked fine to me. And did you see his face? And the way he was lying there, with his hands raised, as if he'd been trying to fend off an attacker of some sort? Maybe a heart attack is what the coroner is going to put on his death certificate, but it looked to me as if he'd been scared to death."

"You have an overactive imagination," Drew said, not unkindly. But Trevor thought he detected an edge of uncertainty in his friend's tone.

Amber looked at Drew. "Is it possible for someone literally to die of fright?" she asked.

Drew thought a moment before answering. "The mind's a powerful thing," he said, "and people's mental and emotional states can have very real effects on their physical health. So, yes, it's possible someone could be so terrified that they have a heart attack."

"We heard him screaming right before he died," she said. "He sure sounded terrified to me." She shivered again.

"But what could have frightened him that badly?" Drew said. "There were no signs that he'd been attacked. There were no marks on his body, and there was no one else in the hall when we reached him. The hallway's long enough that if someone *had* attacked Sean and fled, we'd have seen him or her running away. And if whoever it was had ducked into a room, we'd have heard the door close."

"Well, whatever the reason, I'm sorry the guy died," Trevor said. He shook his head. "It's a hell of a way to start off a reunion, isn't it? I mean, people are already melancholy at these things. Thinking about the passage of time, wondering about the choices they made, and even more about the ones they *didn't* make. Having one of their classmates die before the festivities begin makes it that much worse. Nothing like getting smacked upside the head with a cold, harsh dose of mortality. And then there's us. We brought a lot more emotional baggage with us this weekend than anyone else, and for Sean to die outside your room, Drew . . . you have to admit it's more than a little weird."

Before he could respond, Amber said, "I had a very strange dream last night, not long before Sean died." She went on to tell them about dreaming that she was a young Native American girl whose village was slaughtered by British hunters, one of whom had turned out to be Greg. As she spoke, she curled her hands into fists and tucked them beneath her arms, as if hugging herself to ward off a chill brought on by relating the details of her dream.

"It seemed so *real*," she said. "I truly believed I was Little Eyes, and I felt everything that she would've felt. But when Greg appeared, he told me I was dreaming, and then it was like I was two people: Little Eyes *and* Amber. It was very strange, like listening to two different songs playing at the same time. But the worst part was at the end, when Greg . . . changed. Those tentacles . . ." She trailed off and hugged herself tighter.

"It's common for dreams to be made up of unrelated elements," Drew said. "You'd seen Greg in the bar earlier, so he made a guest appearance in your dream. As for the rest, well, you *do* have a history of nightmares, and it's not surprising that you'd have one on the night you returned to Ash Creek."

Trevor had listened intently to Amber's story, his excitement building the entire time. "In the dream, Greg told you that the massacre had really happened, right?" he asked. "Right here, on the site where the Lowry House would one day be built."

She nodded.

"I don't know how much you two remember about the history of the Lowry House," he said. "I know we researched the house's background before we did our original investigation, but I don't recall how much we learned back then. At any rate,

I've researched the house's history in greater detail in the years since, and while there are no official records of British hunters massacring a Native American tribe on this soil, I did find a few brief hints here and there of such an event taking place in the general vicinity. If a tragedy like that *did* occur here, it could explain why this land became, for lack of a better word, tainted. All those powerful negative emotions released in one location— the fear and pain of the villagers, the cruelty of the hunters—left a dark psychic imprint on the area, making it a kind of breeding ground for paranormal phenomena."

Amber looked at him. "Are you saying that what I experienced really happened? That it wasn't a dream, that I made some sort of . . . psychic connection to the past?"

"It's possible," he said.

Drew sighed, and from the expression on his face, it looked as if he was trying very hard to maintain his patience with the two of them. "Trevor, you said we researched the history of the Lowry House when we were kids. It's more likely that we learned about the massacre back then, and Amber unconsciously drew on that memory to create her dream."

He started to argue the point, but instead he shrugged. "That's possible, too," he admitted. He gave Drew an irritated look. "You're a real buzzkill sometimes, pal. You know that?"

Drew smiled. Then, as if to mollify him, he asked, "What else did you dig up about the house's past?"

"During Prohibition, a bootlegger named Russell Stockslager lived here," he said. "He was also a serial killer who murdered seven women—seven that the authorities knew of, anyway—and buried them on his property. One of his intended victims managed to escape and went to the police, and he died in a shoot-out with the cops when they came for him. After that, the house remained empty for a while, and then it went through a number of different owners who reported experiencing various paranormal phenomena. Noises at night, objects that moved on their own, whispering voices, ghostly apparitions"—he glanced at Amber—"intense nightmares. Most families moved out after a few months, and the house would remain unoccupied for long stretches of time. Eventually, John Lowry, an electrician, moved his family into the house, and they managed to stick it out for a couple of years, until one night, Lowry picked up his nine-millimeter and killed his wife and two children before turning the gun on himself."

"I think I remember when that happened," Amber said. "We were in grade school then, weren't we?"

Drew nodded. "The Lowry House had a reputation as being haunted long before that, but it got worse after the murder-suicide. It was one of the reasons we were so excited about investigating it, remember? There were so many stories about kids who snuck into the house, only to flee terrified after only a short time inside. It was almost like the house was daring us to investigate it."

"I *do* remember," Trevor said. And he did. Remembered afternoons spent over at Drew's house, the three of them comparing notes from interviews they'd conducted with kids who'd gone into the Lowry House—or at least claimed to. Afternoons during which they'd discussed how they were going to go inside the house themselves one day.

"Me, too," Amber said, a tone of wonderment in her voice. "At least, I *think* I remember."

Drew smiled again. "Looks like coming back home is starting to do us some good, after all. So . . . what next?"

"I'd like to get a few more pictures of the grounds," Trevor said. "After that . . . well, it's been a while since any of us have been in Ash Creek. Want to do a little sightseeing, check out how the town's changed? Might help us shake loose a few more memories. After that, we could have lunch."

Drew and Amber looked at each other before turning back to him.

"Sounds good," Drew said.

"Why not?" Amber said.

He grinned. If things kept up like this, maybe he'd get to write that book about the Lowry House, after all. More important, maybe the three of them would finally remember the details about that night. He tried to imagine what it would be like not having a huge question mark hovering over him all the time, what it would be like to really *know*. Part of him was eager to find out, but part of him was afraid that maybe there was a damned good reason the three of them had repressed the memory of what had happened. Maybe they'd be better off never knowing the truth.

The breeze seemed to turn colder, and Trevor crossed his arms and shivered. He told himself it wasn't an omen, was nothing more than a hint of autumn's approach, but he couldn't quite bring himself to believe it.

Greg watched the three friends get into Trevor's car and drive off. He'd been standing nearby in plain sight the entire time, but none of them had seen him. Oh, their eyes had passed over him often enough, but their brains had failed to register his image. He'd made certain of that.

He'd enjoyed watching them make their first visit back to this place in fifteen years, and it had been a real treat to see Drew and Amber stand in front of the oak tree as they had that afternoon before they'd entered the Lowry House. Of course, Trevor had posed with them back then, and it had been Greg who'd taken the original photo. When they took the new picture, he'd been tempted to sneak into the camera's frame and let it capture his image even though the others couldn't see him. How much fun would it be when they looked at the photo later and saw their old buddy Greg standing there alongside them, grinning? But he'd resisted. He didn't want to reveal too much, too soon. Still, it had been *so* tempting.

He remembered that afternoon well. Amber, Drew, and Trevor had stopped at the Lowry House after school, and he—after following them at a distance—caught up and, when he saw they were taking photos of the house, offered to take one of the three of them. They hadn't entered the house then, though. They'd returned later that night, after it got dark. They hadn't told him of their plans, but he'd guessed what they were up to and snuck into the house after they were already inside. He'd never been a member of their group, even though they'd allowed him to tag along on a few investigations. But he hadn't taken them as seriously as the others—he was primarily interested in being near Amber—and so the boys hadn't wanted him along. He'd been angry at them, and he'd planned to enter the house without them knowing and give the three of them a good scare.

Funny how things worked out sometimes.

Things had gotten off to a good start, he thought, but there was a lot more still to do before the main event later that evening. Best he get to it. Busy, busy, busy. Good thing he enjoyed his work.

He whistled a jaunty tune as he headed back to his car.

NINE

"I can't believe this place is still here!" Amber said as she lifted another slice of pizza to her mouth. She took a big bite, using her fingers to break through the thick strands of mozzarella that still extended from her mouth to the pizza slice. She laughed as she tucked the broken strands into her mouth. "Pardon my manners!"

As for so many other kids who had grown up in Ash Creek, Flying Pizza had been their hangout when they were young. A hole-in-the-wall pizza joint in a strip mall between a dog groomer and a smoothie café, its plain white walls, simple wooden tables, and permanent odor of burned pizza crusts gave it an endearingly seedy quality. The pizza itself wasn't noteworthy, but it was inexpensive and filling, and best of all, it was served in a place that grown-ups tended to avoid. What more could a teen want from a hangout joint?

Not that there were any teens here today, she noticed. The lunch crowd at Flying Pizza consisted almost entirely of men and women who'd come to town for the reunion, all of them there for the same reason as Drew, Trevor, and herself: a short trip down memory lane with oregano and Parmesan cheese sprinkled on top.

They'd ordered the same pizza they'd always gotten when they were kids: half extra cheese, onions, and mushrooms, half pepperoni and Italian sausage. Amber had ordered a Diet Pepsi to drink, while Drew had bottled water. Instead of getting a Dr Pepper as he had when he was a teenager, Trevor had ordered a bottled beer. Not a very good brand, though, given the way he wrinkled his face every time he took a sip.

"Recognize anyone?" Drew asked. From his tone, Amber could tell that he was doing more than making small talk. He wanted to test their memories, maybe check his against theirs. Last night, the thought of purposely testing her memory would have frightened her, but now she was surprised to find that she was looking forward to it, almost as if it were a game. It seemed that being around Drew and Trevor was having a positive effect on her. Especially Drew.

She turned to Drew and gave him a smile. He'd been so kind and understanding last night. She hadn't gone to his room with any thoughts of romance; she'd simply needed a friend to talk to. But now, sitting here and looking at him, she found herself wishing something *had* happened between them.

Suddenly embarrassed, although there was no way he could know what she was thinking, she looked away from him and glanced around the room. Her gaze came to rest on a tall blond woman sitting with a beefy guy who, even sitting down, looked at least a head shorter than his dining companion.

"That's Patty Miller in the corner," Amber said. "She was . . . in the band, wasn't she? Played flute, I think. I don't recognize who she's sitting with, though."

"She played clarinet," Drew corrected. "And the man she's with is Jerry Cottrill."

As soon as she heard the name, she remembered. "He was a bully who used to corner boys in the restroom and beat them up."

"That's him," Trevor said with undisguised contempt. "Although he didn't really beat up anyone. Mostly he just intimidated you, gave you a punch in the stomach, or got you down on the floor in a headlock. Stuff like that."

Amber looked at Drew. "You stopped Jerry from"—she glanced at Trevor—"*intimidating* Greg once, didn't you?"

His brow furrowed in concentration, as if he were trying to make himself remember. "Yes. Yes, I did. Unfortunately, I didn't get there in time to stop Jerry from giving Greg a swirly, but at least he didn't hit him."

"I remember that, too," Trevor said. "Greg was

so mad. He kept talking about getting back at Jerry, but of course, he never did anything. Who would?" He paused. "Funny, but Jerry doesn't look so tough now, does he?"

"Bullies get their power from instilling fear in others," Drew said. "When you think about it, anyone can hurt anyone else. You don't need much physical strength, just the will to commit an act of violence. But in the case of bullies, the threat of violence alone is usually enough to get them what they want. He doesn't seem intimidating to you anymore, because you've matured past the point of being afraid of him. It's as simple as that."

"I guess that means you're not afraid of him, either," Trevor said. "So, why don't you go on over to his table, say hello, and tell him you don't hold the past against him?"

Drew looked at Trevor for a moment. "You first," he said, and Amber laughed.

The three friends continued identifying their classmates for several minutes until the conversation turned back toward the Lowry House, as she knew it would. She was, however, surprised to find herself bringing up the subject this time.

"I think I'm ready to talk about it." She didn't have to say what. She knew Drew and Trevor would understand what she meant. And without waiting for either of them to respond, she began.

"It was a Saturday in September. Later than

now, closer to the end of the month. I remember taking the picture in front of the Lowry House that afternoon. I didn't before, but I do now. You used a disposable camera that had a couple shots left on it. You took them and dropped the camera off at a drugstore on the way home to get the pictures developed." She thought for a moment. "I remember we didn't say anything to Greg about our plans for later that night because the two of you didn't want him tagging along."

"He always got in the way," Trevor said. "Do you remember that time we spent the night on the covered bridge out by the county line? The one where the phantom horseman had been reported? I had equipment set up to capture both video and audio, and Greg the genius managed to knock the camera into the river. My dad was furious, and I got grounded for two weeks."

She smiled. She did remember, although she knew she hadn't before now. The more time she spent with Drew and Trevor, the more she remembered, and she knew the same thing was happening for them as well.

"Like I said, I understood why you didn't want him to come along that night. To make sure Greg didn't find us, we met at Drew's grandmother's instead of one of our houses. We figured he wouldn't think to look for us there. We planned everything out. We went over the research we'd gathered on the Lowry House one last time, and we designated areas to focus our investigation on based on the information we'd gathered from kids who'd gone into the house before."

Drew was nodding. "They'd claimed to hear noises coming from upstairs, presumably from the bedrooms where Mr. Lowry shot his family, so that's where we planned to set up our audio recorders. We had three of them, one for each bedroom."

"There were stories of ghostly figures passing in front of the dining-room windows," Trevor said, "so that's where we were going to set up our video camera." He looked at Drew. "Your parents' camera this time, since mine wouldn't even let me near the new one they bought."

"And I borrowed a regular camera from my folks," Amber said. "One that would take better pictures than the disposable ones we'd used in the past. I remember you carried it, though, Trevor, since you took better pictures than me. We planned to do a room-by-room sweep of the house, so we brought a thermometer to record any temperature changes. I carried that, and Trevor carried another audio recorder so he could record our impressions of what we saw and felt as we made our way through the house."

"I had a flashlight, and I carried a backpack with supplies," Drew said. "Snacks and drinks, along with plastic bags for collecting any physical evidence we found and a first-aid kit in case we fell through rotten floorboards or something."

"We were scared, but excited, too," Amber said. "You guys told your parents that we were getting together at my house to watch movies, and I told mine that we were going to Drew's. We headed for the Lowry House after sunset. Both of you kept a lookout for Greg, in case he showed up and tried to follow us, but we didn't see any sign of him. We reached the Lowry House, stepped onto the property . . ." She trailed off. "And that's it. Everything after that is still a blank." She paused. "No, that's not quite true. I can recall jumbled images and sounds. Running through a hallway, my heart pounding in terror. I remember hearing voices shouting—yours especially, Drew. I remember you calling my name. But that's about it. The next thing I remember is waking up in the hospital Sunday morning with my mom by my bedside. She looked so tired, like she hadn't slept all night, and I could tell she'd been crying. I smelled smoke, too. I guess the smell clung to the inside of my nasal passages, and my throat was so sore I could barely swallow."

"I remember you calling my name," Drew said. "I was desperate to reach you."

He looked so upset by the memory that Amber reached out, placed her hand over his, and squeezed. She left her hand there for several seconds before removing it. He gave her a grateful smile, and she felt a warm fluttering in her stomach.

Down, girl! she told herself. *You're not here on a date.*

"According to what my parents told me, the firefighters found us sitting on the sidewalk when they arrived, watching the house burn," Drew said. "We were conscious but catatonic, and paramedics took us to the hospital. We all suffered from smoke inhalation and second-degree burns. The police questioned us the next day, remember? They thought we'd done something to start the fire, either on purpose or by accident, but since they weren't able to prove anything, they let us go."

She did remember a police officer questioning her. The man was suspicious and did everything but accuse them of starting the fire. She had felt unfairly accused but unable to defend herself, since she had no clear memory of what had happened. For all she knew, she and her friends *had* started a fire. In some ways, that had been the worst part. She'd feared that they had done something bad, something that had almost gotten the three of them killed, but there was no way to know for sure.

"There's something else," Drew said. "I know that we tried to keep Greg out of the Lowry House investigation, and I know he didn't go inside with us, but I have a memory—no, more like a feeling—that he was inside there with us at one point."

"Well, that would explain why we had that weird vision of him being covered in flames," Amber said. "Not that he literally burned to death, just that we associate him with the fire."

"Who knows?" Trevor said. "Maybe he did burn to death, and the Greg we saw was a ghost. That's how he lost all that weight: he's on the Afterlife Diet program."

Amber and Drew smiled at his joke, but she didn't think it was all that funny. The vision of Greg on fire had been way too creepy for her to laugh about it. The three of them grew quiet for a time after that, and eventually, Drew said, "You two remember anything else?"

She racked her brain, but she couldn't think of anything. "No," she said.

"Me, neither," Trevor echoed, "but let me point out another strange thing in a long list of strange things. Does it strike either of you as odd that our memories of that night all end at the same point, when we approached the Lowry House, and that they start up again the next day in the hospital?" He looked at Drew. "You ever run into anything like that before? Missing memories synced up so precisely?"

"No, I haven't," he admitted. "Different individuals experience trauma in different ways. Three people who lived through the same traumatic event might have suppressed memories of it, but for those memories to end and resume at

the same basic points . . . it's virtually impossible."
He frowned. "I wonder why I never noticed that
before?"

"Well, we've never sat down and compared notes
until now," Amber said. "We didn't talk about what
happened much. We didn't really talk at all after
that night." Instead of drawing them closer, their
shared experience in the Lowry House had driven
them apart, and she regretted that. They'd been
young and afraid, struggling to deal with a bizarre
experience, and since their memories refused to
come back to them, it had been easier to try to
forget the whole thing, and that meant staying
away from one another. Their very presences were
reminders of what they'd been through together.
She understood why they'd done what they'd done,
but she wished things had turned out differently. If
they'd remained together back then and supported
one another . . . well, no matter. They were back
together now, and that was what counted.

"Here's something else I've thought about over
the years," Trevor said. "I've done a lot of research
about trauma, and I think that whatever happened
in the house, it had to have been more than a fire.
Sure, that's a traumatic enough experience, but lots
of people go through the same thing or stuff like
it—fires, car wrecks, tornadoes, earthquakes—and
they don't always lose their memories, and even
when they do, they only lose a few minutes here
and there, during the most traumatic parts of the

event. Especially if they suffer a head injury to boot. But we lost *hours*. We weren't injured that badly, so we must've gotten out before the fire spread too far. And none of us received head injuries. So why did we suppress our memories at all, let alone for such a long span of time?"

"Now, that *did* occur to me," Drew said. "And I think you're right. Whatever happened inside the Lowry House was more than a simple fire. It had to be for us to react the way we did."

Trevor leaned forward, and his lips stretched into a triumphant smile. "Are you ready to admit that something paranormal happened to us inside the Lowry House?"

Drew's smile was more subdued and his tone thoughtful as he answered. "Let's just say that I believe something out of the ordinary happened to us. Whether or not it was paranormal remains to be seen." He paused, as if considering whether to continue. "Although something strange *did* happen to me recently that I haven't been able to explain to my satisfaction." He went on to tell them about an experience he had with a patient named Rick. He had barely begun the story before Trevor pulled a small pad out of his pocket and began taking notes.

Amber listened to the story with rapt interest that became a mixture of revulsion and wonderment. When Drew had finished, she said, "It almost sounds like the poor man was possessed."

Trevor, still writing on his pad, said, "My thoughts exactly."

"Like I said, I can't explain it." Drew's tone told her how frustrated he was that an explanation eluded him. He'd always been the most rational of the three of them. Trevor was more imaginative, while she was more intuitive. She supposed that was one of the reasons they were drawn to one another when they were kids. They complemented one another, each contributing an important quality the other two lacked.

Trevor finished writing and looked up. "OK, here's what's happened to us so far this weekend. We shared a vision of Greg Daniels burning alive, Amber had a dream that might relate to the past history of the land on which the Lowry House was built, we saw a man die in front of us under strange circumstances, we visited the site of the Lowry House, we compared notes about what we remember and don't remember, and we listened to Drew tell us a damn spooky story about a possibly possessed patient who made some cryptic predictions that may or may not relate to this weekend. So . . . what's our next step?"

Amber couldn't help smiling. It was as if they were in their teens again, sitting around and planning an investigation over pizza. It felt good, as if she was finally doing something about the past, taking charge for once instead of letting it control her.

"We should talk with Greg," Drew said. "We

need to find out if he was inside the house with us at some point during that night and, if so, how much he remembers."

"He's helping the alumni committee," Amber said, "so he's probably back at the hotel working to get things ready for tonight. We should be able to track him down without too much trouble."

"The two of you should do that," Trevor said. "Though I bet Greg would rather talk with Amber alone." He looked at her and waggled his eyebrows.

Drew scowled at that, but he didn't say anything. Amber was pleased by Drew's display of jealousy, mild as it was, but she kept her own expression neutral. She didn't want him to know that she was glad he was jealous.

Trevor went on. "I'll drop you guys back at the hotel, then I'll run by the police station, see if I can get anyone to talk to me about Sean and tell me if there's any official word yet about what caused his death. I may not be a newspaper reporter, but you'd be surprised how many people will talk with a writer if you approach them the right way. After that, I'll head over to the Historical Society and see what other information I can dig up on the Lowry House. Some of it will be a memory refresher, I'm sure, but with any luck, I'll stumble across something new. How about we get together at the hotel bar later in the afternoon, around four?"

"Sounds good," Drew said, and Amber agreed. They stood up and started toward the door, Amber feeling much better than she had in a long time.

That's when they heard the scream.

". . . and so that was the end of my second marriage. I mean, there was no way I was going to stay with him after *that*, right?"

Jerry nodded and made a vague noise of agreement. Maybe *uh-huh* or *sure*. He really didn't know. He'd been making such noises for the last half-hour—they were the only contributions Patty had allowed him to make in the conversation—and he'd started to lose track of what he'd said. Not that it seemed to matter to Patty what came out of his mouth, as long as he let her keep talking. So she went on, barely pausing to draw a breath as her monologue continued.

"Luckily, I didn't have any kids with Carl. I mean, I already had two, and the last thing I needed was more to deal with, you know? Being a single mom is no picnic! So, after he moved out, I figured I needed to change how I went about finding men. I needed to find someone who could love *me* for *me*, right? So I signed up with one of those Internet dating services . . ."

Jerry tuned her out, though he continued to nod. Back in high school, he'd had something of a crush on Patty, but he'd never even thought about approaching her. She was a clean-cut band kid, and he was a bully, and while he'd thought that maybe she might go for the bad-boy type, as so many girls did, he'd been afraid she'd reject him. Rather than risk that, he'd stayed away from her and admired her from afar.

She was still as beautiful as she had been back then. Maybe a little too tall and bony for some men's tastes, with an aquiline noise that was a touch too long, but he thought she looked sophisticated and intelligent. When he'd come into Flying Pizza for lunch and had seen her sitting by herself, he'd worked up the nerve to ask if he could join her. He'd expected her to look at him as if he were an especially disgusting species of bug that had crawled out of the woodwork, but she'd acted pleased to see him and invited him to sit down. At first, he'd been thrilled, but as the minutes passed, he became less so, until he wished he'd picked somewhere else to eat that afternoon. Jerry had never gotten to know Patty in high school, hadn't exchanged more than a half-dozen words with her the entire four years they were there. Now, after talking with her—actually, *listening* to her—for the better part of an hour, he realized that the impressions he'd formed of her back then had been based on her looks and his own imagination. As it turned out, she was neither sophisticated nor intelligent. She was shallow and annoying, and he was depressed at having his most cherished high-school illusion shattered. Reality could be a real bitch sometimes.

She finally paused to inhale, and he jumped in. "Would you excuse me a minute? I need to use the restroom."

Without waiting for her to answer, he stood up and headed for the back of the restaurant. If there'd been a back door, he'd have been tempted to skip the restroom and make a break for it, but the short hallway ended in a wall where numerous flyers for local businesses, bands, and special events had been posted. No escape there.

He went into the men's room. Like most kids who'd grown up in Ash Creek, he'd spent lots of time at Flying Pizza, and the sour-stale tang of its bathroom was a familiar smell to him and, in its own disgusting way, nostalgic. The restroom was empty, so he had his pick of two urinals or the stall. He chose a urinal, walked up to it, assumed the position, and took care of business. Graffiti was scribbled on the wall at eye level. Some was straightforward, such as "BJ's Saturday 4–6 p.m." or limericks that began with phrases like "Some people come here to sit and think . . ." Other messages were more enigmatic, such as "Bozwell 79 Sux" or "Campground Ladies Sing No Songs." He wondered if the latter type of messages meant anything or if they were random phrases someone wrote in order to give idiots like him something to ponder while they pissed.

So far, this weekend wasn't turning out as he'd expected, but in his case, that wasn't altogether a bad thing. When he'd first received the notice about the reunion in the mail, he'd tossed it into the trash. Who'd want *him* to show up? He hadn't been the nicest guy in high school, and he doubted anyone would miss him. He hadn't gone to the five-year reunion or the ten-year for that reason, and he wasn't about to change his mind for the fifteen. He'd been babysitting his ten-year-old niece, and she'd fished the reunion notice out of the trash and colored on the back of it. When his sister stopped by his apartment to pick up his niece, she saw the reunion notice and told Jerry he should go.

He told her she was crazy, that no one would want to see him after all these years. She said that was probably true but that he shouldn't go for them; he should go for himself. If nothing else, it would be good therapy.

They'd grown up together in the same abusive household, had endured their father's rages, both verbal and physical, and neither of them had been popular in high school. He had become a bully, passing along the abuse he received at home to kids weaker than him, and his sister had become a party girl, drinking, drugging, and having sex with just about anyone who wanted her. After high school, they continued down their self-destructive paths. He got into bar fights on a regular basis, and his sister went from one abusive relationship to another. Once her daughter was born, his sister decided to turn her life around. She stopped dating assholes, starting getting some therapy, and began urging her brother to get help, too. He'd resisted for a while, but he was getting tired of being an asshole himself. Plus, having a little niece who loved her uncle and looked up to him made Jerry want to be a better person.

He started seeing his sister's therapist, learned some anger-management techniques, and began to get his proverbial shit together. He stopped fighting, got a better job, moved out of the roach hotel of an apartment where he'd been living and into a decent condo, and got himself a bona fide life. He hadn't found Mrs. Right yet, but he dated regularly enough and remained hopeful. And he owed it all to his sis.

So, when she told him that it would be a good idea to attend the reunion, he reconsidered. It could be a chance to make peace with the past, say a final farewell to the screwed-up teenager he'd been, and maybe even make some amends in the process. Closure with a side order of redemption. Knowing that there was a better-than-average chance that he'd end up receiving a lot of hate vibes from his fellow classmates, he had decided to attend.

And all in all, it hadn't been that bad so far. Yeah, seeing Patty had turned into a disappointment, and he'd received more than a few scowls from

people, but so far, no one had said anything negative to him. He'd been reluctant, but he'd forced
himself to initiate conversations with people, and
he'd been surprised by how open they'd been to
talking with him. Maybe they didn't see him as
the big bad bogeyman he imagined they did, or
maybe folks were more willing to forgive than he'd
expected. Or maybe so much time had passed that
they'd forgotten how much of a jackass he'd been.
Whichever the case, people had been treating him
as if he was just one more person attending the
reunion, and he was grateful.

He was living proof that people *could* change
for the better, and for that reason, he was proud
to be there. Maybe it was a little arrogant on his
part, but he hoped he might serve as an inspiration
to his former classmates and that by doing so, he
could make up, at least in some small way, for the
things he'd done back in high school.

Jerry finished, zipped up, and washed his hands.
He looked at his face in the streaked mirror hanging over the sink, and after a moment's inspection
decided that he didn't look too bad. He carried a
few pounds more than he had in high school, but
he wasn't fat, and he wasn't in danger of going bald
anytime soon. But what impressed him most when
he looked at his reflection these days was the
gentleness in his eyes. It was something that had
grown slowly over the last few years, and it was his
hardest-won and therefore most prized possession.

He figured he'd stalled long enough, and it was time to get back to Patty. He decided he'd endure her chatter a few more minutes for the sake of politeness, and then he'd say good-bye and head on out. His parents still lived in town, but his dad was the same abusive bastard he'd always been, and Jerry didn't visit them any more often than he had to. Instead, he figured he'd go back to the hotel and chill until the banquet. Maybe he'd check out the bar, see if there was anyone else around to strike up a conversation with.

"You really know how to live the high life, huh? Big-time partier, that's you."

The voice came from behind Jerry, and he turned around to see a teenage boy standing and looking at him with an expression of utter contempt. The boy wore a Skinny Puppy T-shirt, faded jeans, and an old pair of running shoes with holes in them. Jerry understood at once that he was seeing his younger self right then, the recognition occurring on a deep instinctive level. Part of it was the cruel mocking smile on the younger Jerry's face, part of it was the cold, calculating look in his eyes, but what clinched it was those shoes. Jerry—thirty-three-year-old Jerry—*knew* those shoes. Every hole, every scuff mark, from the feel of the dingy threadbare laces as he'd tied them to the soft flapping sound the loose rubber soles made when he'd walked. Those were *his* shoes, no one else's.

He didn't question how this could be happening. He accepted the presence of his younger self, as if it was nothing more than a dream. It sure felt real, though. Smelled that way, too. Even through the restroom's miasma of sour piss and urinal cakes, he could smell that his younger self was in dire need of a shower. He hadn't been big on hygiene back in those days.

Teenage Jerry stood with his head thrust forward, muscles tense, and hands balled into fists, as if he was ready to rush forward and attack any second. He exuded anger and sullen menace, and he reminded Jerry of a tiger he'd once seen in the zoo, pacing back and forth behind a thick glass partition, its mouth open to display sharp white teeth and a moist pink tongue, eyes gleaming with a mixture of hunger and resentment. *You're lucky this glass is here,* those eyes had seemed to say. *Damned lucky.*

Is that what he'd looked like back then? Is that how the kids he'd tormented had seen him? The thought shamed him, twisted his stomach in a knot of nausea, but most of all, it made him feel angry.

Teenage Jerry's mouth twisted into a cruel smile. "You used to be tough. More important, you used to be *feared*. But look at you now. You were a big dog, but now you're about as scary as a toy poodle."

Jerry's jaw muscles bunched as he gritted his

teeth, and his hands curled into fists so tight that the skin over his knuckles turned white.

Teenage Jerry started walking toward him, cruel smile fixed so firmly in place that it might have been painted on. "I bet your balls are shriveled up like prunes, and your dick's retracted into your body like a little turtle head afraid to peek out of its shell. You're pathetic. A joke. Only you're the worst kind of joke, the kind no one laughs at. They look at you, shake their heads, and think, man, what a total fucking pussy!"

Teenage Jerry continued walking toward him as he spoke, and now he stood a few inches away from him. As he said those last three words, he punctuated them by poking Jerry in the chest with his forefinger, each time harder than the last.

White-hot rage raced through him like electricity, and he felt his muscles tingle. Involuntarily, his body wanted to reach out, grab this little motherfucker by the back of his scrawny neck, and slam his face into the porcelain edge of the sink. The bastard wouldn't be smiling anymore once Jerry had knocked his fucking teeth down his throat.

The fingers of his right hand uncurled and flexed a couple of times, as if in anticipation of sinking them into the flesh of his younger self's neck. He imagined the jolt of impact that would race up along his arm as he smashed the kid's face against the sink, imagined teeth ringing on porcelain, blood splattering everywhere. It would be so easy to make it happen. All he had to do was reach out . . .

It was a near thing, but in the end, he relaxed his hands and allowed them to hang at his sides. That wasn't who he was anymore, and no one, not even himself, was going to make him turn back into the sorry son of a bitch he'd once been.

Teenage Jerry, still grinning that insufferable grin, gave his older self slow, mocking applause. "Way to show self-restraint, Jer. I'm impressed. Of course, all I did was say a few nasty things and poke you in the chest a couple times. I wonder if you'll be able to hold back under more . . . direct provocation."

Without waiting for a response from his older self, teenage Jerry drew back his right hand, made a fist, and slammed it into Jerry's gut. Dull pain flooded his abdomen, his breath gusted out of his lungs in a whoosh, and he doubled over, gasping for air. He'd had the breath knocked out of him before and knew that it would take him a couple of seconds before he'd be able to inflate his lungs again. But teenage Jerry wasn't about to give his older self time to recover.

He was still bent over, and his younger self stepped back, took hold of both sides of his older self's head, and, with a single savage motion, brought his knee up against Jerry's jaw. White light exploded behind his eyes, and when his vision cleared, he found himself looking at those oh-so-familiar running shoes. It was strange, though. They were close to his face, and he was looking at them from a funny sideways angle. It took him a few more seconds to realize that this was because he'd fallen to the restroom floor and was lying on his side. His teeth hurt like hell—he wondered if the impact had knocked any of them out—and his mouth was filled with the thick, coppery taste of blood. His tongue throbbed, and he figured he'd bit it. He tried to spit the blood out, but he was barely conscious, and the best he could manage was to make the blood dribble out of the corner of his swollen mouth.

Teenage Jerry crouched down, hands on his knees, head cocked to the side so he could look his older self in the face.

"Jesus, you *have* let yourself go, haven't you? I barely touched you, and you folded like the proverbial fucking house of cards. Pathetic." He straightened then and gazed down on his older self with sorrowful contempt. "Might as well wrap this up. I've got bigger and better fish to fry."

He gestured, and both the toilet in the stall and the urinal began flushing. But instead of flushing once and then stopping, they continued flushing, over and over. Jerry couldn't see the urinal from where he was lying, but he could see into the stall, and he watched as water began to run over the edge of the bowl and splash onto the floor. He heard water splattering behind him, felt it slide across the tile floor and begin soaking into his clothes. It was cold, damned cold, Arctic Ocean cold, and he began shivering as the water touched his skin and the cold began penetrating his flesh. The toilets continued flushing, and water continued pouring onto the floor and sloshing up against him in tiny waves.

He tried to rise, but he still was having trouble catching his breath. His head was pounding, and he felt dizzy. He wondered if the blow he'd taken to the jaw had given him a concussion, or maybe he'd gotten one when he hit his head as he'd fallen to the floor. Either way, he couldn't make his body listen to him when he told it to get up. All he could do was lie there while the freezing water kept pouring out of the toilets and onto the floor, making him colder and wetter with each passing moment.

Teenage Jerry kept looking down at his older self and grinning. Jerry was surprised to see that the water level had risen an inch over the soles of his younger self's shoes.

"You gave more than your fair share of swirlies in your time, old man," teenage Jerry said. "High time you got one, don't you think? But you deserve more than a run-of-the-mill swirly. You're going to get the greatest swirly ever!"

Teenage Jerry laughed, and water bubbled forth from his throat and dribbled over his chin to soak

the front of his Skinny Puppy T-shirt. He continued laughing, water bubbling out of his mouth
like a fountain, the toilets flushing and disgorg-
ing frigid water, the water level rising. Jerry still
couldn't move, and all he could do was lie there
while the water began to cover his face. Finally,
he was able to draw in a breath and did so, but all
he managed to do was suck in water, and when he
tried to scream, it came out in a gurgling burst of
bubbles.

The water's cold seeped into his brain, render-
ing his thoughts sluggish and dim, and if he had
any final profound insight before the darkness
rushed in to claim him, he wasn't aware of it.

TEN

"Now are you willing to believe that something funky is going on?" Trevor said.

Drew ignored him, mostly because he wasn't sure how to answer.

The three friends stood on the sidewalk outside Flying Pizza. The paramedic vehicle was long gone, taking Jerry's body with it, but a police cruiser still sat parked outside the restaurant. They'd spent the last half-hour being questioned by one of Ash Creek's finest before they'd been given permission to leave. The cop was still inside, interviewing some of the other customers.

"I thought that guy was going to haul us down to the station and book us," Amber said.

For a time, Drew had thought the same thing. But evidently, the officer decided that they'd had nothing to do with Jerry's death and let them go. But not before giving them the traditional "Don't leave town" warning. He wondered if it was something cops were trained to say or something they picked up from bad movies and TV shows.

"You can't blame him for being suspicious," he

said. "Two people in town for the reunion have now died, and in both cases, the three of us found the body and reported it. You don't have to be a master detective to suspect there's something more than coincidence at work there."

"So, you *are* admitting the possibility that there's some paranormal aspect to Sean's and Jerry's deaths," Trevor said.

"I'm not sure that I'm willing to go that far yet," Drew said, "but there *are* some strange similarities. Both men died in proximity to us, both screamed before they died, and both bodies were found covered with fluid. Formaldehyde in Sean's case, water in Jerry's."

"Both of them seemed to scream more in fear than in pain," Trevor added. "And while they were covered with their respective fluids, there was, for the most part, none in their vicinity. Seems like there should've been some puddles or at least a few drops somewhere. But in both instances, the floor around them was dry as a bone." Trevor paused, then frowned. "Sorry. Bad choice of phrase."

"There was a sink near Jerry," Amber pointed out. "That's probably where the water came from."

"Again, there was none on the floor," Trevor insisted. "You can't soak yourself from head to toe in a restaurant bathroom without splashing at least some water, and you'd probably end up splashing a lot of it, and it'd end up all over the place."

As frustrating as it was, Drew couldn't fault

Trevor's logic on that point, but he also didn't see how Jerry could have managed to avoid dousing himself without making a mess. He decided to table that problem for later. The paramedics hadn't been able to give them a specific cause of death for Jerry, but there'd been no outward signs of violence—no bruising or bleeding—just as with Sean. Earlier, Drew had told Trevor that while it was uncommon for a man as young as Sean to drop dead unexpectedly, it wasn't unheard of. But for *two* men in their early thirties to die suddenly within twelve hours of each other? That was definitely in the realm of the weird.

"Maybe their deaths weren't natural," he mused aloud, "but that doesn't mean anything paranormal killed them. Maybe they were poisoned." He hurried on before Trevor could interrupt. "Both of them cried out before they died, and both were covered with some sort of liquid. Maybe they cried out in pain and not fear. If that's the case, then we're dealing with a mundane murderer and not malevolent forces from beyond. I'm sure the police will have the chemical found on Sean tested, and they'll do the same with the liquid on Jerry."

"You better hope that it's not poison," Trevor said. "You gave CPR to both Sean and Jerry, which means if they *were* poisoned, you got plenty of the stuff on you."

His thoughts had been running along similar lines. "I didn't get much on me, and I washed my hands afterward both times. Still, if they *had* been poisoned, you'd think I'd have suffered at least some ill effects from contact with the substance. But I feel fine."

"And what sort of killer covers his victims' bodies with poison?" Amber pointed out. "And who'd stand still long enough for him to do it? It seems like an impractical way to murder someone."

Drew smiled at her. "Well, when you put it that way, my poison theory seems a little unlikely, doesn't it?"

"More than a little," Trevor said. "But maybe you should get checked out by a doctor, just in case."

Drew and Amber looked at him.

"What? Just because I believe something paranormal is going on here doesn't mean I think you should take a foolish risk." He smiled. "The last thing I want is for you to drop dead, too, buddy. Better safe than sorry, right?"

"There's an urgent care on the other side of town," Drew said. "I'll head on over and get looked at, but I'm not worried. Any poison strong enough to kill someone as fast as Sean and Jerry died would've had some effect on me by now."

Amber put her hand on his arm. "Trevor's right. You should go, just to be safe. I'll come along and keep you company, OK?"

He wasn't sure how he felt about her offer. On one level, he was happy to have her go with him, but on another, he was concerned that she'd attached to him too strongly, too quickly. They'd only started to get to know each other again after years apart, but now it seemed that she didn't want to leave his side. She'd spent so many years living alone, dealing with the depression that had resulted from the trauma they'd experienced in the Lowry House, and he feared that she was latching on to him emotionally, not only as someone who might help relieve her loneliness but also as someone who could be a stabilizing influence in her life.

One of the drawbacks to being a psychologist was that some people sought out his company because they hoped, consciously or subconsciously, to derive therapeutic benefit from it. He'd dated more than one woman over the years who'd secretly hoped that he could "fix" them. As much as he cared for Amber and as much as he wanted to rekindle their friendship, and perhaps take it further, as a psychologist it would be unethical of him to allow her to get too close to him while she was in such a fragile emotional state. Hell, given the fact that they'd witnessed two men die since returning to Ash Creek, he wasn't sure he was in all that stable a frame of mind himself. Better to keep things more casual between then, for both their sakes.

"Thanks, but I'll be all right on my own," he said. "The last thing you need to do is sit around in a doctor's office reading old magazines while I wait to be seen."

She looked crestfallen. "But I . . . I don't want to be alone right now, not after everything that's happened."

Trevor gave him a look that he couldn't read before turning to Amber. "Tell you what. We'll modify our plans a bit. We'll drop Drew back off at the hotel so he can get his car and drive over to the urgent care, and you can hang out with me for a while. I was going to head over to the police station to ask them some more questions about Sean, but now that a second guy has died in our presence, that might seem a tad on the suspicious side. I think we'll go straight to the Historical Society and see what else we can dig up on the Lowry House. Sound good?"

She looked disappointed and more than a little hurt by Drew's rejection, but she nodded.

Trevor turned to Drew. "And assuming you get a clean bill of health from the doctor, you can head back to the hotel, track down Greg, and see if he remembers anything about what happened that night at the Lowry House."

"Sounds like a plan," he said.

They started walking toward Trevor's Prius, Amber keeping Trevor between herself and Drew. He regretted hurting her feelings, but he told himself that it was for the best, and as a psychologist, he believed it. So, why did he feel so shitty?

"This may sound kind of morbid," Amber said, "but if Sean and Jerry didn't die of natural causes, then I hope they *were* murdered by some ordinary human killer. Because if there *was* some kind of paranormal cause to their deaths, something connected to the Lowry House and to the three of us returning to Ash Creek after all these years, then that means they died because we stirred up something that we shouldn't have." And then, in a voice so soft Drew almost couldn't hear it, she added, "It means *we* killed them."

For the second time that day, Greg watched his friends get into Trevor's car and drive away. He'd been present the entire time they were at Flying Pizza, sitting alone and unseen at a nearby table. Having the power, as the cliché went, to cloud men's minds not only came in handy but was also really amusing sometimes. He hadn't expected Jerry Cottrill to be there, too, but his presence was serendipitous, and offing the son of a bitch and having Drew, Amber, and Trevor discover his body, especially after killing Sean in front of them the night before, well, life—and death, too, for that matter—didn't get much better than that.

Things were moving along quite nicely, and everything was on track for the big event tonight. But that didn't mean he couldn't have a little more fun in the meantime.

He headed for his own car, humming along with the dark music playing in his head.

The Ash Creek Historical Society was housed in an old building cattycorner from the downtown post office, only a few blocks from where Trevor's parents lived. The main room of the building wasn't much to look at. The plaster on the walls was yellowed and cracked, and the warped wooden floor creaked so loudly he feared the boards would give way beneath their weight as they walked.

Framed black-and-white photos lined the walls, displaying images from the town's past: the first firehouse, several covered bridges, farmers posing next to what at the time was brand-new state-of-the-art farm equipment, the first high school. There were no pictures of the Lowry House, though. It wasn't the kind of place that the civic-minded citizens who served on the Historical Society wanted to commemorate. There were also framed front pages of the town newspaper, the *Hue and Cry*, mostly dealing with national events, such as the bombing of Pearl Harbor, Kennedy's assassination, and the first moon landing. There *were* several local stories represented, but again, nothing about the Lowry House.

Most people who visited the Historical Society—and there were a handful here today, mostly people back in town for the reunion—didn't go past the main room. But as far as Trevor was concerned, the best part of the Historical Society was the smaller room in the back, where the reference library was housed. He'd made a beeline for it the instant he entered the building, and Amber had followed, a little reluctantly, he thought. Maybe she was tempted to linger and check out the pictures. Or maybe she was still bummed about Drew ditching her.

On the drive over, he'd tried to cheer Amber up by telling her about a recent interview he'd done for a paranormal magazine with a woman who claimed not only that she saw ghosts everywhere she went but also that they were always naked. Amber had smiled a couple of times, but he could tell she wasn't paying attention, and he'd fallen quiet and stayed that way the rest of the drive.

Now the two of them sat at a small table in the reference room, Trevor on one side, Amber on the other, three huge bound collections of the *Hue and Cry* between them. The woman who'd retrieved the volumes for them looked as if she was 112 and wore a head bun so severe he wouldn't have been surprised to learn that it had been coated in shellac. She'd wanted to hover while he read, especially once she'd learned that he was a writer there to do research, but he'd told her that he and his "assistant" worked better when they were undisturbed, and she'd gone out into the main room, a disappointed expression on her ancient face.

Amber eyed the large volumes of newsprint with an air of disbelief. "Haven't these people heard of scanning and digitizing text?" she asked. "Or at least microfiche?"

Trevor, glad that she was talking again, smiled as he flipped back the stiff cover of one of the volumes and began turning pages. "They probably don't have the budget for it. Besides, I like the smell of old newsprint. It smells like history, you know?"

"Smells more like mold to me."

"That, too," he admitted. He continued turning pages.

Amber watched him for several moments before selecting one of the volumes for herself. "What are we looking for?" she asked.

"I want to refresh my memory about the incidents with the Lowry House," he said. "There are no detailed records of the Native American massacre you dreamed about, but the paper's been around for more than a hundred years. It should've covered the bootlegger serial killer, the Lowry murder-suicide, and the fire. I'm looking through the volume of issues from the year the serial killings took place." He glanced at the volume she'd selected. "You've got the year of the Lowry killings."

For a moment, it looked as if she was going to put that volume aside rather than dig into it in search of the grisly specifics of how Lowry murdered his family. But then she asked, "Do you remember what month it was?"

"November."

She nodded and began turning pages. Before

long, they'd both found the issues they were searching for and fell quiet as they read, Trevor occasionally writing a note in the small pad he always carried.

After a bit, he looked up from the page he'd been reading. "It's weird. I don't have any specific memories of this place, but it feels familiar, like I *almost* remember it."

"Maybe you do," Amber said, looking up from her volume. "I think the three of us coming home and being together has jolted our memories, kind of given them a jump start, you know?"

He smiled. "Sounds like one of Drew's theories. Has he been giving you private headshrinking lessons?" As soon as he said it, Amber dropped her gaze to the table, and he regretted opening his damn mouth. It wasn't that he was jealous of Drew. He cared about Amber, but as a friend. It was just that, no matter how hard he tried to watch what he said, his internal censor was too often asleep at the wheel.

He wanted to say something to make her feel better, but he had no idea what might work. It might have helped if he had a clear idea why Drew had not so subtly told her to accompany him to the Historical Society. Drew was usually so good with people—that was one of the main requirements of his job, after all—but from the way he'd dealt with Amber outside Flying Pizza, he'd seemed clueless. He probably hadn't been thinking straight,

Trevor decided. Hell, he doubted any of them had. They had just discovered a dead body—the second in two days—and had been questioned by the police about it. Even someone with Drew's training would be shaken up after that. Especially if he thought he might be falling for Amber too fast. *That* was it, he realized. Drew was a good man, and he wouldn't want to take advantage of Amber or make any impulsive moves given their current situation.

Now Trevor knew why his friend had insisted that Amber accompany him to the Historical Society. He started to tell her, but for once he kept his mouth shut. It wasn't as if either Drew or Amber had come out and admitted having feelings for each other. They might not have even admitted it to themselves. If he said anything about it now, he'd only end up embarrassing her. So he decided to broach a different subject.

"You doing OK?"

She looked up, frowning. "What do you mean?"

"It's not every day you find a dead body, let alone two. How are you holding up?"

She looked at him for a long moment before answering. "All right, I guess, all things considered. It's funny the different ways people respond to a tragic event, though. Drew becomes a practical problem solver, while you get excited—not because you're happy those men died," she hurried to add, "but because you view their deaths as possible proof of paranormal activity."

Despite her attempt to soften her words, they still stung.

"You're right. I didn't really know Sean or Jerry, and I *do* believe their deaths were too coincidental and bizarre to explain logically. And yes, I'm thrilled by the prospect of being part of a true paranormal experience. But if what you said earlier was right, and we *have* woken up some force that's responsible for Sean's and Jerry's deaths, then it's our responsibility to learn as much about it as we can. Only then will we have a hope of stopping it and preventing more deaths."

"I'm sorry," she said. "I didn't mean to offend you."

He forced a smile. "I guess what you said cut a little too close to the bone, you know?"

"You're a good guy, Trevor Ward. Don't you ever forget that." She reached across the table and gave his hand a squeeze, and then, without either of them saying anything else, they returned to reading.

Trevor soon found himself getting caught up in the story of Russell Stockslager. In the 1920s, Stockslager, who worked by day as a car mechanic in town, was one of the prime producers of moonshine for those citizens of Ash Creek, and there were many, who viewed Prohibition as an annoying inconvenience. Although there was nothing in the articles he read to suggest it, he wouldn't have been surprised if the town's police had been aware of Stockslager's profitable avocation and turned a blind eye to it. After all, the cops had to get *their* booze somewhere, too, right? But what the police hadn't known was that Stockslager was able to use his 'shine for more than making money. It made effective bait for luring women to his home, which in those days was outside city limits.

The newspaper hinted that he accepted—or, more likely, demanded—sex as payment for booze, and when that thrill no longer satisfied, he'd turned to torturing and murdering his female visitors. He'd slain seven women and buried them in the barn where he kept his still. On January 17, 1923, an eighth woman—a girl, really, as she'd been only seventeen—managed to knock him out while he was raping her and escaped. She informed the police, and they headed out to the property in force. Stockslager tried to fight them off with a shotgun, but there were too many cops, and they were too well armed. And while he managed to hold them off for the better part of an hour, in the end, they stormed the barn where he'd been holed up and shot him dead. Afterward, the police discovered the graves of his victims, and overnight, he stopped being a simple bootlegger and became a town legend.

Seven women died on Stockslager's property in

horrible circumstances, and while there was nothing in the news articles written in the days following his death to indicate precisely where the
murders had been committed, Trevor suspected
that they'd happened inside the house and he'd
taken the bodies outside afterward for disposal.
His closest neighbor lived a quarter of a mile away,
but even so, that was close enough for someone to
hear screams coming from the barn. No, he would
have done his dirty work inside, most likely in the
basement, choosing to bury the dead women in the
barn, not only so the smell of their decaying bodies
wouldn't permeate his house but also because the
odors produced by his still would mask the stink.
And who knows? Maybe he liked having his victims near him while he worked.

Those poor women had experienced unimagi-
nable fear and pain before they died, and all of
that negative psychic energy could have remained
trapped in the house. Trevor knew from previous
research he'd done that the Native American massacre had happened in the general vicinity of the
Lowry House. What if it had happened on the
exact spot?

The negative psychic energy released during the
massacre could have soaked into the land, remain-
ing dormant until someone built a house there.
Maybe Stockslager had been a bad man to begin
with, or at least someone with the potential to be
bad, and he'd awakened the negative energy on

his land and been influenced by it. Transformed from a small-time criminal into someone truly evil. And when his victims died, the negative psychic energy *they'd* left behind could have merged with the energy already there, making what was already a Bad Place even worse.

He tried to imagine what it had been like the night Stockslager's bloody career had ended. It had been January, so it had to have been biting cold, but had there been snow on the ground? Hard to say. Snowfall in southwestern Ohio, like all the weather, was unpredictable. The paper said the police arrived at the house sometime after two A.M. Had it been a clear night, the stars spread across the blue-black sky like glittering chips of ice? Or had it been overcast, the clouds blocking the stars and making a dark night even darker?

"It's a beautiful night. A day after the new moon, but the sky's clear and the stars are out. There's a couple inches of snow on the ground, but it's not all that cold, really. Around thirty degrees, I'd guess, though I haven't checked."

Trevor blinked. A moment ago, he'd been sitting across the table from Amber in the Ash Creek Historical Society's reference room. Now he stood inside a small barn lit by several uncovered light-bulbs hanging down from the ceiling on black wires like glowing spiders dangling from ebon threads. The barn had a dirt floor, and on one side of it sat a still, a simpler-looking device than he expected: a couple of barrels connected by metal tubing to a large metal canister erected above a small fire pit. No fire was burning now, though. The acrid tang of raw alcohol hung heavy in the air, along with another odor, cloying and rank, and in a sickening way almost sweet. The other side of the barn was empty, save for seven raised mounds of earth, marked with simple crosses made of small twigs bound with twine.

"What can I say? I always was a sentimental son of a bitch."

The man sat cross-legged on the floor, facing the closed barn door, which Trevor saw was padlocked from the inside. He was grotesquely obese, so much so that it was difficult for Trevor to guess the man's age by looking at him. He could have been anywhere from twenty to sixty, but thanks to the diligent reporters of the *Hue and Cry,* Trevor knew he was forty-six and that he wouldn't live to see forty-seven. He wore a brown jacket, jeans, and brown boots, and with the exception of the latter, his clothes didn't even come close to fitting. They were so tight on the man's fat form that Trevor thought they might split at the seams any second. The man wore his black hair cut short, not quite a buzz cut but close, and he had a mustache so pencil-thin it looked as if it might have been drawn on with ink. He had a shotgun, but as he didn't have a lap for it to rest across, he held it in his right hand, butt end against the ground, barrel pointed toward the ceiling.

Although the man had spoken to him in a low and resonant voice more appropriate for a radio announcer than a car mechanic/bootlegger/serial killer, he hadn't turned to look at him. Rather, he continued facing the barn door, his gaze fixed on the old gray wood as if he could see through it to what lay outside.

"You know what was stupid? Me coming in here and locking myself in when the cops showed up. Guess I panicked, you know? But there was no reason for me to. Sure, some young cooz ran to the cops and told them I tried to rape her, but that was it. She had no idea about the others, didn't have a fucking clue that there were any bodies buried out here. The cops came to check out her story, but not because they gave a damn about her. They wanted an excuse to shake me down for some money. All I would've had to do was keep calm and pay them off, give them a few bottles of shine for the road, and they'd have gone on their merry fucking way. Instead, I tell them that we should have a little something to drink while we talk, and I come out here to get some of my 'shine, and what do I do? I get scared, shut the door, lock it from the inside, and grab hold of my shotgun. Now they know something else is going on besides a little slap-and-tickle that got out of hand. That means they aren't going to leave without wanting to come in here and have a look around, and once that happens . . ." He trailed off. There was no real need for him to finish.

"You're Russell Stockslager," Trevor said. "And this is 1923. January 17, to be precise."

Stockslager didn't answer, but then, he didn't have to.

Trevor looked around. The level of detail was amazing. Not just sights and sounds but smells, too, and temperature. The inside of the barn was cold, and his breath fogged the air.

"What is this?" he said, feeling equal parts fear and excitement. "A hallucination? A psychic replay of past events? Maybe telepathic contact across time?"

"It's the last night of my life," Stockslager said, still not looking away from the door. "That's all you need to know."

Although he stood a good thirty feet away from Stockslager, he made no move to go closer. He was afraid that whatever this experience was—real, imaginary, or something in between—it was unstable, and like a soap bubble, it would pop out of existence if he disturbed it in the slightest way. And there was the minor fact that he was locked in a barn with a gun-toting serial killer. Stockslager might not be real, at least in a physical sense, but Trevor wasn't about to assume that the man couldn't do him any harm. According to common folk wisdom, if you died in a dream, you died in real life, too. This might not be a dream, but whatever it was, he didn't plan to put that particular bit of folklore to the test.

"This is going to sound a little weird," he began. "OK, more than a little, but this is one of the most exciting things that's ever happened to me. I've spent my entire adult life investigating and writing about other people's paranormal experiences, but this is the first time I've actually had one."

Now Stockslager turned to look at him, and Trevor was taken aback by how dead his eyes were. They were cold, hard, and lifeless, without any hint of human feeling. Doll's eyes.

"The first time you remember," Stockslager said. "You may think this is something special, but it's nothing compared with the little party you and your friends had the last time you were here."

Trevor felt a pressure inside his head, as if Stockslager's radio-announcer voice was calling to his memories, urging them to rise out of the subconscious muck where they'd been buried for so long and come shambling forth. He wanted to know the truth about what had happened that night in the Lowry House, but he sensed that now was not the best time for his memories to surface. He knew somehow that if they did, he would be overwhelmed, his mental defenses shattered, and if that happened, he would be lost. He fought to keep the memories at bay, and although he could feel them crowding the threshold of his awareness and screaming to be let free, they stayed where they were—for the moment, at least.

Stockslager's fat earthworm lips formed a small smile. "You're stronger than I thought you'd be. Good for you."

Trevor's initial excitement upon finding himself experiencing what seemed to be an honest-to-God psychic event was waning fast. Whatever sort of apparition Stockslager was, he felt real, and more, he felt *strong*. Malevolent power rolled off the man in waves, and it seemed to be increasing in strength with every passing second. As a kid, Trevor had ridden his bike past a power substation out in the country, and he'd sensed as much as heard the thrum of electricity surging through the machines, felt the air itself vibrate, making his skin tingle and itch. Being in the barn with Stockslager was like that, only much worse.

"I, uh, I think I'd like this to be over now," he said.

Stockslager chuckled with that smooth, deep voice of his. "You think this is like a dream, where you can will yourself to wake up when things get too scary for you? It doesn't work like that, Trevor. Not even close."

Fire whooshed to life beneath the still, startling him. The flames rose high and hot, curling up the sides of the metal canister, which began to ping and rattle as its contents came to a rapid boil. The interior of the barn, so frigid a second ago, became hot, and he felt beads of sweat begin to form on his skin.

"Alcohol's good for a lot of things," Stockslager said, still sitting, still holding his shotgun butt-first against the ground. "It helps loosen people's tongues. Helps lower their inhibitions so they can find the courage to do things they might not otherwise do. Helps them laugh and cry, helps them relax . . ." His lips stretched into a grin. "Helps them get laid. But you know what the best thing about alcohol is, Trevor?"

He squeezed his eyes shut and concentrated on the Historical Society's reference room, its sights and smells. He thought about Amber sitting across the table from him. Presumably, his body was still there, still seated, his face still pointed at an old yellowed newspaper article detailing Stockslager's death at the hands of the police. Whatever was happening here—wherever *here* was—it wasn't real. At least, not as real as the reference room. If he could concentrate hard enough, shut out what was happening here, maybe he could reconnect to his body and shift his consciousness back to where it belonged.

Stockslager went on. "The best thing about alcohol is that it can be used as a preservative."

He heard a new sound over the crackling of flames, the metallic pinging of the still, and the hiss of escaping steam. A soft rustling, followed by a scratching. Despite his attempt to shut them out, the sounds conjured images in his mind: earth being pushed aside, fingernails clawing on the ground . . . He didn't want to open his eyes, was too afraid to look, but that wasn't the only emotion he felt. He was also curious, and in the end, his curiosity won out. He opened his eyes, but he already knew what sight would greet him when he did.

Seven pairs of women's hands had thrust their way upward from their owners' graves and were scrabbling at the ground, as if trying to find enough purchase to pull the rest of their bodies free of the earth's embrace. Their flesh was a mottled bluish white, and they reeked of the moonshine that Stockslager had used to preserve them.

He was grinning, appropriately enough, like a madman, and he now rose to his feet with a silent grace that Trevor found incongruous for a man of his size. He shouldered his shotgun and aimed the muzzle at Trevor's head. The fat man closed his left eye as he sighted with his right.

"See you later, Trevor."

There was a flash like lightning, a crash like thunder, and darkness rushed in to claim Trevor before he could scream.

"Trevor? Trevor? Are you all right?"

He looked at the pretty woman's face for several

seconds without realizing what he was seeing. She was just a shape at first, color and form without any meaning. But as the seconds passed, he began to understand that he was looking at a woman, a woman named Amber, and then, just like that, everything came rushing back to him, and he drew in a gasping breath of air.

She looked worried, and Trevor wondered how long he'd been sitting there, zoned out, while she tried to rouse him. For her sake, he hoped it hadn't been too long.

He forced a smile. "I'm all right." His voice sounded shaky, and the words came out a bit funny, as if his mouth was having trouble remembering how to shape them. "Guess I got a little too caught up in my research."

He closed the book in front of him too forcefully, and the cover thumped shut with a sound that reminded him too much of a shotgun blast.

She gave him a skeptical look. "Bullshit," she said. "Something's wrong, and you're going to tell me what. Or else."

His smile was a little less forced this time. "Or what?"

"I don't know," she admitted. "But I'll think of something."

He sighed. "All right. But let's talk somewhere else, OK? I've had enough of this place for one day."

They found the old woman in charge of the

reference materials, told her they were finished, and thanked her for her help. As they left, Trevor thought about the last thing Stockslager had said to him.

See you later.

Although the air was cool when they stepped out of the building, he felt hot, as if he stood too close to a blazing fire, and the sharp tang of alcohol clung to the inside of his nose.

ELEVEN

Drew entered the hotel lobby feeling like an idiot, mostly because that was how the doctor at the urgent care had treated him. Then again, he supposed he couldn't blame the woman. After all, how often did she have a patient walk in on a Saturday claiming he might have been exposed to some kind of poison even though he wasn't exhibiting any symptoms? Still, she'd given him a thorough examination, including blood work, but it would be a while before the results came back. As best as she could determine, he was in excellent health, and there appeared to be no signs of poisoning. She told him to call if he began displaying any symptoms and then sent him on his way, but not before asking if he'd ever had any therapy.

Drew had been half amused, half irritated by the doctor's implication that he was experiencing paranoid delusions. He'd been tempted to tell her that he was a psychologist himself and would know if he was suffering from mental illness, but he'd kept his mouth shut. He'd been vague when the doctor asked when and how he thought he'd been exposed to poison, if only because he hadn't wanted to complicate the situation further by telling her that he'd discovered two dead bodies in the last twenty-four hours. He'd feared that would make him seem even crazier to her. And the truth was, he could sympathize with the doctor. If a patient came to him with a similar story, he'd be more than a little skeptical himself.

The hotel had been around as long as Drew could remember, but the lobby was newly refurbished, all chrome and glass and reflective surfaces, with strategically placed green plants hanging from the ceiling, sitting on counters, or standing in large pots in a mostly unsuccessful attempt to soften the cold metallic feeling of the décor. Leather chairs and couches were arranged in the center of the lobby so that guests could socialize, but none was tempted to at the moment—which was fine with him, since he didn't feel like talking with anyone right then. He selected a chair, headed to it, sat down, leaned back, and closed his eyes so he could think.

Part of what made the doctor's reaction to him sting so much was that it brought out something he had been feeling but hadn't wanted to face. Returning to Ash Creek, reuniting with Trevor and Amber, visiting the site of the Lowry House again for the first time in fifteen years, not to mention discovering those two men dead and being questioned by the police, all contributed to a weekend that, to put it mildly, wasn't normal. It was hard to maintain a rational perspective in such circumstances.

He'd started falling for Amber again like a lovesick teenager, *and* he'd become willing to entertain the possibility of a paranormal explanation for the events that had occurred since they'd returned to town. Even when he'd been a teenager and investigated reports of paranormal activity in Ash Creek, he'd managed to maintain a healthy, clear-eyed skepticism. He'd been intrigued by the possibility that there was more to existence than science could explain, but he'd never allowed that to color how he viewed the evidence they collected. And what evidence did they have now? None, really. Amber had experienced a strange dream, the three of them had shared a hallucination of Greg on fire, and they'd discovered the bodies of two men who'd died in strange circumstances. That was it. Everything else was half-recalled memories and suppositions. Nothing more. It was all weird, no doubt about it, but it didn't constitute actual proof.

It was bad enough that he, a trained psychologist, had gotten swept up, but he feared that he was enabling Trevor and especially Amber, helping them to indulge their fantasies and, worse, legitimizing those fantasies by giving them his professional sanction. After all, he was a skeptical psychologist, and if *he* believed something paranormal was going on, then there *had* to be, right?

Maybe he'd made a mistake by letting Trevor talk him into coming here this weekend. Maybe it would be better if he left now before things went any further. Trevor and Amber would be upset with him, but he could attempt to explain his reasons for leaving later. And although he knew it wasn't rational, part of him thought that if Amber was right and the three of them reuniting had somehow awakened some kind of strange force that existed in Ash Creek, perhaps if they were no longer together, the whatever-it-was would become quiet again. If that was true, then by leaving, he might actually save lives.

But what if it didn't go back to sleep? How could he leave his friends to face the force alone?

Listen to yourself, he thought. *You have no evidence that there's some sort of bogeyman running around Ash Creek. Keep up this sort of thinking, and when you get back to Chicago, you'll end up as a patient in your own hospital.*

"What's wrong, buddy? You party a little too much last night?"

Drew opened his eyes to see Greg Daniels standing before him, smiling. He wore a navy-blue mock turtleneck, jeans, and running shoes. Fit and handsome, he looked as if he'd stepped out of a clothing catalogue, the image at odds with the Greg whom Drew remembered from high school.

Drew smiled. "Guess I'm not as young as I used to be. How about you? You seem lively enough, considering that you're helping the alumni committee this weekend. I'd think they'd be running you ragged."

"They are, but you know how it is. Sheer adrenaline keeps me going. Well, that and liberal quantities of extra-strong coffee." He grinned. "Still, I *could* use a breather, and I think the committee can make do without me, for a couple minutes, at least." He slid into the chair next to Drew.

He had planned to track down Greg once he returned to the hotel and ask him what he remembered about that night in the Lowry House. But now that he was considering leaving, there didn't seem to be any point in questioning him. Still, Greg *was* there, and despite everything, he couldn't help being curious about what the man did and didn't remember about that night. Besides, asking questions was what he did, right? But before he could start, Greg began talking.

"It must be strange for you . . . being together with Trevor and Amber again, I mean."

Drew tried not to sound too much like a psychologist as he asked, "What makes you say that?"

"The three of you were inside the Lowry House

when it burned down. And from what I gathered when I spoke to Amber on the phone a while back, you haven't seen one another since. And the three of you don't remember what happened. At least, that's the story that went around town afterward. Is it true? You really don't remember anything that took place inside the house?"

"It's true," Drew said. "We recall scattered fragments, but they don't make much sense. So . . . you weren't with us that night?"

"No. You guys ditched me." He smiled. "I guess you don't remember that part, either. I was pretty mad at the time, but considering what happened, I'm glad you left me out. Otherwise, I might've ended up traumatized, too. Or worse." Something cold and hard came into his gaze then, but it vanished so quickly Drew wasn't certain he'd seen it.

"Did any of us talk to you about it afterward? Did we tell you anything that we might have since forgotten?"

Greg shook his head. "I didn't come visit any of you in the hospital, and I avoided talking to you at school after you were released. Like I said, I was pretty angry."

Drew kept his expression neutral, but a thought occurred to him then. Had Greg been angry enough at them for ditching him that he'd not only followed them to the Lowry House that night but also set the fire that had burned the house down?

Maybe he hadn't intended to hurt them, only scare them, but the fire had gotten out of hand and spread, nearly killing them. He supposed it was possible, and it could explain the hallucination the three of them had experienced of Greg wreathed in flame. It might have been not a literal memory but rather a symbolic image of him being associated with the fire that destroyed the Lowry House.

Except that Drew had a strong feeling that Greg *had* been present in the Lowry House that night. If he concentrated hard enough, he could almost see him there, hear his voice . . . but the memories were slippery, shadowy things at best, and despite Drew's efforts, they refused to be dragged into the light. Frustrated, he decided to change the subject.

"So, what's your story? What happened to you after that night?"

Greg chuckled. "You really don't remember, do you? Once you, Amber, and Trevor got out of the hospital, you stopped hanging around together. It wasn't as if you acted like the others didn't exist. You'd talk, but you weren't best buddies anymore. I got over being angry with the three of you, but by that time, you'd pretty much gone your separate ways, and even though I tried to reconnect with you guys, things weren't the same. And then, when my parents died, I went to go live with my aunt in Rhode Island, and I lost touch with everyone in Ohio. I graduated from high school in

Rhode Island, so I guess I shouldn't be here for Ash Creek's reunion, but I've always felt more of a connection to the old hometown. So, this year, I decided to attend. I'm glad I did. It's been great getting to see old friends and catch up with them."

There was something in Greg's tone as he said these last words—a hint of amused playfulness along the lines of a double entendre, with a glint in his eye and a slight upturn of his mouth—that disturbed Drew, but he wasn't sure why.

"I don't remember your parents dying," he said. "What happened?"

"Car accident," Greg said, his tone casual, as if he were discussing the time or the weather. "And speaking of accidents, what do you think about Sean Houser and Jerry Cottrill both dropping dead like that? Weird, huh? And you finding both of them . . . what are the odds?"

There it was again, that undercurrent of amusement, as if he was enjoying a private joke of some sort.

"It was disturbing, to put it mildly, but you don't seem too upset about their deaths."

Greg shrugged. "It's not as if I was close to either of them. Besides, as disturbing as finding them might have been for you, I don't see you crying about it. But then, I suppose they trained you to keep a tight rein on your emotions in psychology school. The whole detached, clinical distance thing, right?"

Greg's words verged on the combative, though his tone remained casual enough. But there was an old cliché that said that the eyes were the windows to the soul, and while the concept might be phrased poetically, in Drew's experience, it held a great deal of truth. You could tell a lot about someone's emotional state by his gaze, and right now, Greg's was hard and flat. Drew had seen similar looks before in the eyes of sociopaths. Cold, calculating, devoid of both empathy and sympathy. They might appear charming enough on the surface, but that was just a tool they used to manipulate the people around them, protective coloration they employed to keep others from recognizing who and what they really were. In truth, they cared about one thing and one thing only: satisfying their desires, regardless of the cost to others.

The Greg Daniels he remembered from high school might have been annoying and socially maladjusted, but he hadn't been a sociopath. Then again, Drew had been a kid himself at the time, his training in psychology still years ahead of him, and it wasn't as if he'd had any experience in spotting a sociopath back then. But on the other hand, he'd always had good people instincts, which was one of the reasons he'd chosen psychology as a career. He liked to think that if Greg had demonstrated signs of being a sociopath back in high school, he'd have noticed, even if he wouldn't have understood what those signs meant. Maybe Greg had been skilled at hiding his true nature; sociopaths learned to blend in with everyone else from a very young age. Or, he thought, maybe somewhere along the line, something had happened to Greg to change him.

He decided to keep the conversation going and see where else it might lead. "Has there been any talk about canceling the reunion? I'd think two deaths would put a damper on the festivities."

"The alumni committee considered it," Greg admitted. "You might expect something like this to happen if we were old farts attending our sixtieth reunion or something, but our fifteenth? It's shocking for one death to occur, let alone two. But the committee decided to go on. They'll devote some time at the banquet tonight to honor Sean and Jerry, have some people get up and speak, share remembrances, that sort of thing. And they'll dedicate the dance afterward to their memory. I suppose it'll put a damper on the party atmosphere, and some folks will skip the dance and head back to their rooms, but as for the others . . ." Another shrug. "Life goes on, you know?"

Greg *sounded* sympathetic, but the lifeless look in his eyes didn't change. They reminded Drew of shark's eyes: cold, dark, and, above all, hungry.

"So, where are Trevor and Amber?" Greg asked. "The three of you looked pretty cozy in the bar last

night. I figured you'd be inseparable this weekend."

His smile widened a touch as he said the word
cozy, and Drew caught the not-so-subtle sexual
innuendo. He chose to ignore it, though.

"Trevor wanted to stop by the Historical Society, and Amber decided to go with him. I figured
I'd catch up with them later." For some reason, he
was reluctant to tell Greg that they'd gone there to
brush up on the history of the Lowry House. He
didn't want him to know that the three of them
were hoping to unlock their repressed memories
this weekend. With sociopaths, the less information you told them, the better. They'd just use it as
ammunition against you.

This is ridiculous, he told himself. *You're treating
Greg like he's some kind of enemy who's out to get
you. Since when did you decide to buy a ticket for
the paranoia train?*

Maybe he was overreacting, but he'd learned
over the years to trust his instincts, and he wasn't
about to start ignoring them now.

"I suppose Trevor wanted to do research for one
of his books," Greg said. "I've read a couple and
found them amusing enough, I suppose, though
a little hard to take seriously." He smiled. "Dry
retellings of old, tired ghost stories, for the most
part. Stairs that creak in the dead of night, strange
shadows glimpsed through windows, voices whispering words one can't quite make out, an unseen

hand trailing cold fingers along one's flesh . . . kid stuff. Parlor tricks that in the end don't amount to much."

"Oh? You don't think they could be an attempt on the part of the dead to communicate, to bridge the gap between our two worlds?"

Greg let out a derisive sniff. "That's what people would like to think, but the reality is so much more . . ." He trailed off with a look of surprise, as if he'd been about to say more than he'd wanted. He covered his discomfort with another smile, this one feigning warmth. "As much as I'm enjoying talking to you, Drew, I should get going. All the major preparations for tonight have been taken care of, but you know how it is, always a million little last-minute details to attend to." He stood. "Good talking with you. I hope we'll get a chance to do it again before the reunion's over."

Still sporting his fake smile, Greg offered his hand for Drew to shake.

Drew hesitated. The thought of touching Greg made his skin crawl, but he didn't know why. Not wishing to appear rude, he ignored his instincts, reached out, and clasped Greg's hand.

A wave of vertigo engulfed him, his vision grayed and went black, and when the world became clear and steady once more, he found himself standing in someone's living room. His first impression of the place was that it was old: the wooden floorboards were warped, the walls needed painting, and the plaster was cracked and chipped in spots. The furniture wasn't much better. Threadbare couch and easy chair, fabric worn and colors faded. Curtains that might have once been white but were now pus-yellow. The smell of stale cigarette smoke and mold hung thick on the air, adding to the overall atmosphere of despair and slow dissolution.

Sitting on the couch, bathed in the harsh light of an old floor lamp, was a middle-aged man. Thin, almost cadaverously so, with sunken cheeks and dark hollows around his eyes, as if he hadn't gotten a decent night's sleep in weeks, maybe months. The lower half of his care-lined face was covered by an unkempt white beard, and he wore his white hair long and bound in a ponytail. He wore a stained T-shirt that sported a faded Corona logo, black jeans, and brown work boots.

The man sat hunched forward, elbows on knees, head hanging down. He looked tired, as tired as anyone Drew had ever seen. A large hunting knife rested on the couch next to him, and held loosely in his right hand—so loose it looked as if it might slip out of his fingers any second and fall to the floor with a heavy metallic thud—was a pistol. Drew didn't know much about guns, but he still recognized the weapon as a nine-millimeter. He knew this because that was the gun John Lowry had used to kill his family, and that's who the tired,

rail-thin figure sitting on the couch was: the infa-
mous murderer who'd given the Lowry House its
name.

Drew understood that he was experiencing a
hallucination of some kind, but rather than being
disturbed by this fact, he was fascinated. It was
astoundingly realistic, and not just the sights and
sounds. He could *feel* his own body—the solid
heft of it, the way the floorboards gave beneath
his weight—feel the air passing in and out of
his lungs, the increasing tempo of his heart as
adrenaline ramped up his system. Like anyone
else, he'd had dreams that he believed were real
while they were taking place, but no matter how
realistic those dreams might have seemed at the
time, they were nothing compared with this.
Those dreams might have *seemed* real, but this
hallucination was indistinguishable from reality.
That meant one of two things: either he had
gone insane, or what he was experiencing was
the result of some kind of paranormal phenom-
enon. He didn't feel crazy, but then, in his professional experience, the craziest people believed
they were sane.

Best assume for the moment that he was sane
and that what he was experiencing was more than
a complex and realistic delusion. But that assump-
tion was a mixed bag, emotionally. On the one
hand, not being insane would come as a huge
relief. But finding himself trapped in some kind

of psychic time warp and transported back to the night Lowry shot his family to death before planting a bullet in his own brain wasn't exactly a comfort.

Was this what Amber, Trevor, and he had seen on that long-ago night when the Lowry House burned to the ground? A vision of Lowry himself, sitting alone and despondent in his living room, holding on to his gun while who knew what dark thoughts slid black and silent through his diseased mind?

"I don't want to. I won't."

Lowry didn't raise his head as he spoke, and his words came out so soft they were more breathed than spoken.

Without thinking about it, Drew took a step closer so he could hear better. A floorboard creaked beneath his foot, the sound loud in the silence of the room, but Lowry didn't react. He wondered if the man heard the sound or if he was too lost in the twisting corridors of his own mind.

Or maybe I'm not here—not completely, anyway, Drew thought. Maybe he and Lowry were somehow out of phase with each other, and while Drew could see and hear him, he was invisible to Lowry.

He decided to test his theory.

"What don't you want to do?" he asked, speaking loudly enough to be heard but keeping his tone calm and gentle, as he'd done hundreds of times when talking to patients.

Lowry sat there for a time, quiet and still. But then he spoke, his words still below the level of a whisper, and Drew had to strain to hear him. "Hurt them."

A chill fingered down the length of Drew's spine. He didn't have to ask whom Lowry referred to. "You don't have to," Drew said.

He started to take another step forward, but as the floorboard creaked a second time, Lowry's head snapped up, and he glared at him with eyes that blazed with equal parts madness and fury. Lowry raised the gun and aimed it at Drew's chest. Drew felt a cold, sick feeling deep in his gut, as if he'd been punched by a fist of ice.

"What the fuck do you know about it?" Lowry raised the volume now, his whispering giving way to a gravelly roughness.

An instant ago, the man had appeared drained of energy, but now he was alert, muscles wire-taut, and he held the gun in a rock-steady grip.

Drew couldn't tell if the gun's safety was off, but he intended to proceed as if it was. If this was a hallucination, then he wouldn't be hurt if Lowry fired. An imaginary bullet wouldn't cause him any harm. But if this was something other than a hallucination, then maybe a bullet could hurt him. No point in taking any chances.

He raised his hands and showed Lowry his empty palms. "You're right. I don't know anything about it."

"Damn straight," Lowry said, sounding only partially mollified. He kept the gun trained on Drew, but his trigger finger relaxed a little.

Drew waited to see if the man was going to add anything else, but after several moments passed without another word from Lowry, he said, "How long have you been sitting there?"

Lowry opened his mouth to answer, then paused and frowned. "I don't know." No anger in his voice now, only confusion. "A long time, I think. Hours, probably. Not days, though." He frowned once more, as if trying to recall. Then he looked at Drew with an almost pleading expression. "Do *you* know?"

Drew shook his head, making sure to keep his hands raised and motionless. "No. I just got here."

Lowry nodded as if this was the answer he'd expected, but if it disappointed him, he gave no sign. "You're not one of them, are you? The voices, I mean. I've never seen any of them before, only heard them. But you don't sound like them."

"What do the voices sound like?" Drew asked.

Lowry's eyes narrowed. "You pulling my leg? You've got to be able to hear them—they've been talking the whole time you've been here. Hell, they're talking right now. Goddamned things are so loud I can barely hear myself think. Some of them tell me to use the gun, others say I should use the knife. But they all want the same thing in the end. They want me to hurt my family. Hurt them *bad*."

"I believe you . . ." Drew searched his memory for the man's first name. "John. I hope you'll believe me when I say I can't hear them. At least, not clearly enough to make out what they're saying."

Drew rarely lied to patients, but over the years, he'd learned that sometimes you had to play along with their delusions in order to keep them talking. Lowry might not be his patient, but the principle was the same.

Lowry's upper lip curled into a sneer. "Well, then, you must be pretty damned hard of hearing." He paused, and his sneer melted away. "Or maybe I've lived with them for so long now that I can hear what nobody else can." His face brightened then. "But I think I can help you."

The man jumped up from the couch so swiftly that Drew had no time to react, let alone think about defending himself as Lowry rushed toward him. But Lowry didn't fire his gun, and neither did he use it as a bludgeon. Instead, he thrust it into Drew's hand, then stepped back and regarded him, head cocked to the side, as if he were an artist examining his work with a critical eye. He smiled and nodded, pleased.

Drew had never held a gun before, and he was surprised by how heavy it felt. Damned cold, too. Far colder than metal should feel, more like ice.

So cold it burned his hand. He tried to let go of the gun, but his fingers refused to pull away from the metal. They felt stuck, almost fused to it, like sticking your tongue to a metal lamppost in the dead of winter. He gave his hand a shake in an attempt to dislodge the gun, and when that didn't work, he tried prying his fingers loose with his left hand. Despite his best efforts, he couldn't separate his fingers from the metal, and he wondered if he would be forced to sacrifice a layer or two of skin in order to divest himself of the weapon.

He felt panic begin to rise, and he forced himself to remain calm. Not only would losing control of his emotions be counterproductive, but he also suspected that in this place—whatever its precise nature—his fear would be used against him.

He looked at Lowry, surprised to feel an urge to raise the nine-millimeter and aim it at the man. He had never held a weapon before, and he'd never contemplated using one against a fellow human being, had never even fantasized about it. But here he was, fighting the urge to train the gun on Lowry, just as Lowry had held the gun on him only a moment ago. What the hell was wrong with him?

Lowry's smile widened. "See? You can hear them now!"

"What are you talking about? I don't . . ." Drew trailed off. Maybe he *did* hear something. A kind of buzz deep within his ears, almost as if tiny insects had infested his aural canal and were crawling around inside. But whatever the sound was—assuming it was real and not a product of his imagination—there were no words to it, nothing even close to an approximation of sense and order. And yet . . . the more he listened, the more the noise seemed to convey a sort of meaning. Not concepts or images but something far more primal. It was the buzz that had caused him to aim the gun at Lowry, he was certain of it. And it was telling him to do more than just point the weapon at the man. Much more.

"Go ahead," Lowry said. "I want you to. I've listened to the voices for so long, it'll be such a relief when they're gone. You know how some people picture heaven as a place filled with beautiful warm light? Not me. I think of heaven as a place of complete and total silence." He drew in a long breath and let it out. "So, please. Do it."

The buzz in Drew's ears got louder, and he felt his finger tighten on the trigger. "No," he whispered.

"It's OK. I want you to." Lowry stepped toward Drew and stopped when his chest touched the muzzle of the gun.

The buzzing grew even louder and rose in pitch, as if the insects were becoming excited. The pounding of Drew's heart formed a desperate backbeat to the insect voices, and he felt a bead of sweat roll down the back of his neck. He focused his will on making his arm lower the gun, but his body refused to obey him. He tried instead to turn to the side so the gun would no longer be pointing at Lowry, but his body didn't respond to this command, either. It seemed there was nothing he could do but stand there, gun barrel jammed against Lowry's chest, his finger tightening on the trigger.

When the explosion came, the impact jolted up Drew's arm and into his shoulder, but his hand remained steady, held frozen in place by the buzzing in his ears. Blood sprayed out of the exit wound in Lowry's back, and the man flew backward as if punched. His eyes rolled white in their sockets, but a beatific smile was fixed on his face as he fell. He landed in a wet red pool of his own blood with a sickening squelch and lay still.

Drew couldn't move, couldn't breathe. He stared down at Lowry's dead body, unable to believe what he'd done.

Not you—the voices! They did it! They made you hold the gun, made you pull the trigger . . . That's what he told himself, but even if it was true, it didn't do anything to blunt the terrible, crushing guilt he felt at having ended another man's life.

The voices had a different reaction to Lowry's death. The excited buzz quieted, became relaxed, almost drowsy, as if its hunger had been sated and it was content.

The silence in the living room was cut by a frantic voice calling down from upstairs.

"John! Are you all right? What happened?"

It was a woman's voice—Lowry's wife, Drew guessed—and she sounded terrified. He didn't blame her. Hearing an unexpected gunshot in your home in the middle of the night was bound to shatter anyone's composure.

Another voice. "Mommy! What's happening? I'm scared!" A little girl, maybe five or so. It was accompanied by a third voice, this one of an even younger child crying. The sound was high-pitched and loud, and Drew couldn't guess the child's gender, but he remembered that Lowry had two children, a girl and a boy. This, then, was presumably the boy crying.

Drew wanted to call out and reassure them, but what could he say? *It's OK. I shot your husband and your daddy, but he's dead now, and there's nothing more to worry about.*

The buzzing once more increased in volume and intensity, and while it still didn't form any words, he had no trouble understanding what it was trying to communicate.

Nothing to worry about? I wouldn't say that.

His right foot slid forward of its own volition, followed by his left. His right slid forward again, and once more his left followed suit. He tried to reassert control over his legs, but he had no more success than when he'd tried to stop himself from shooting Lowry. His feet continued moving him forward, and with a cold, sinking feeling, he realized where they were taking him.

The stairs.

By killing Lowry, he'd prevented the man from harming his wife and children, but it seemed that the voices were determined to make sure that history repeated itself, one way or another. And since Lowry could no longer carry the gun upstairs, the voices had chosen someone else to do it.

Drew mounted the first step. Then the second. The buzzing was loud again, excited and insistent, urging him onward, urging him to climb faster.

The woman's voice came again, uncertain and afraid. "John? Honey, is that you?"

The third step creaked, and the small boy's cries became more strident, as if he sensed what was coming up the stairs for him. The girl called for her mommy once more.

With his left hand, Drew grabbed hold of the wooden railing and tightened his grip. His foot tried to mount the next step, but his hold on the railing prevented it.

The buzzing became angry then, increasing in volume until it felt as if a pair of razor-sharp daggers had been plunged into his ears. His face scrunched up in pain, but he refused to release his grip on the railing. The buzzing grew even louder, and the pain intensified to the point where it felt as if his skull might burst like a rotten melon.

He gritted his teeth against the pain, and tears streamed down his cheeks. The agony inside his head became his entire world, drove out all other thoughts. He could no longer remember his name, was no longer even aware of himself as an entity separate from the pain. He knew two things: that the pain would go away if he let go of the railing and that he would rather die than allow that to happen.

He sensed the shrug in the voice as it said, *If that's the way you want it* . . .

His hand raised the gun to his face, inserted the muzzle into his mouth, and pulled the trigger.

TWELVE

"I'll see you at the banquet."

Drew looked at Greg, struggling to comprehend what the man had said.

Greg gave his hand a last pump before releasing it and starting to walk away. He got a few feet before he stopped and turned back around to face Drew.

"You know, I used to consider you something of a rival," Greg said. "You weren't as smart as I was, but Trevor and Amber looked up to you and followed your lead." His smile verged on a leer. "Especially Amber. I was jealous. I didn't want to just be a member of your group; I wanted to be its leader. I suppose in a way, I wanted to *be* you." He paused and looked thoughtful. "Seems silly now, doesn't it?"

Without waiting for an answer, he turned and walked away. Drew watched him go, dazed and struggling to reorient himself to his surroundings.

You're in the hotel lobby, he reminded himself. *You were sitting and talking with Greg when . . . when whatever it was happened.*

His shirt was damp under the arms and at his lower back, and he felt drained, as if he'd sprinted a mile without stopping.

"Contemplating the mysteries of the universe?"

He looked up to see Trevor and Amber standing in front of him. Trevor smiled, but it seemed forced, much like his opening comment, and Amber was looking at him with an expression of concern. Drew wondered how bad he appeared. If it was even close to the way he felt, he figured it was pretty damned bad.

"You just missed Greg." Drew was surprised by how steady his voice sounded. "We had a nice little chat. And in the middle of it, I . . . experienced something."

Trevor exchanged looks with Amber. "Yeah, there's a lot of that going around," he said.

Amber and Trevor sat, and the three friends spent the next half-hour catching each other up on what had happened since they left Flying Pizza. They kept their voices low in order to prevent being overheard by anyone passing through the lobby. When they were finished, Trevor said, "Still doubt something paranormal is going on?"

Drew gave him a weak smile. "Let's say that while I retain the right to be skeptical, I've decided to concur with your diagnosis." He hadn't told his friends that he'd been considering leaving before his—for lack of a better word—*vision* of the Lowry House. Whatever was going on here, it had become clear that the three of them were bound not only by what had happened to them fifteen years ago but also by what was happening now. Regardless of the outcome, he would no longer consider abandoning his friends. As he'd so often told his patients, sometimes the only way out of a bad situation was to plow ahead and get through it. And one way or another, the three of them would get through this—together.

Trevor grinned. "This may be the first time you've completely agreed with me. Can I get it in writing? I'll have it framed and hang it in my office."

"Do you think that Greg is involved in all this, too?" Amber said.

"He said he wasn't with us in the Lowry House the night it burned down," Drew said. "And while we have some vague sense that he showed up there at one point, we remember going without him."

"Doesn't mean he didn't show up later," Trevor said. "It wouldn't have been the first time. We'd tried to ditch him before that, and somehow he always managed to find us. I used to say he was like a broken maraca, because we couldn't shake him."

Drew smiled. "I remember." He thought for a moment. "Maybe he was there and was traumatized like the rest of us. His memories might be blocked, too." He frowned then. "But that wouldn't explain why he wasn't found at the Lowry House with the rest of us when the emergency crews arrived."

"Maybe he got out before anyone else arrived," Trevor said. "He still could've been traumatized, just not injured like we were." He sighed. "Or maybe he wasn't there. We don't have any evidence one way or another, so unless our memories return—all of them—we may never know."

"You're both missing another possibility," Amber said. "Maybe he's lying."

Drew and Trevor looked at her.

"When did you become so cynical and distrusting?" Trevor said, sounding as if he was only half joking.

She smiled. "Just trying to cover all the bases. But think about it: Greg is the one who called me about the reunion, and I in turn called you, Trevor, and you called Drew. Basically, we're here because he invited us. It's like he wanted us here."

"He could just have wanted to reconnect with some old friends from high school," Drew said. "Still, you make a good point. He did give off more than a few weird vibes during our conversation, and the entire time, he projected a sense of mocking superiority, as if he had some kind of secret knowledge he enjoyed keeping from me. If he was at the Lowry House that night and did retain his memory, that could account for his strange attitude today. Maybe he *does* know something we don't."

"But if he did remember anything, why would he keep it from us?" Trevor said. He turned to Amber.

"I don't know," she admitted. "Maybe he's not sure what he should do. Maybe whatever's happening to us is happening to him, too. Maybe he's scared."

"I don't know," Drew said. "He didn't seem frightened to me. Come to think of it, he didn't seem stressed at all, despite his talk about how much work helping out with the reunion is. He seems calm and relaxed, like someone who's got it all together, or at least thinks he has."

"So what should we do?" Trevor asked. "Go find him and force him to tell us what he does and doesn't know? I'm afraid I forgot to pack my thumbscrews this weekend."

Drew smiled at the joke. "I don't know if we could force him to admit anything. He seems to keep himself under pretty tight control. But before he left, he told me that he'd see me at the banquet. Maybe if the three of us sat down and talked with him, he'd open up to us."

Drew glanced at Amber, and although he didn't say anything, she said, "You mean open up to me."

"He did admit to me that he was . . ." He didn't want to say *jealous,* because that would be admitting that there was an attraction between himself and Amber, one that had been there since they were kids and was as strong today as it had ever been. "Fond of you in high school," he finished.

Trevor rolled his eyes. "That's one way to put it, I suppose."

Amber ignored him. "The banquet's scheduled for five o'clock, which means we have several hours to kill." She paused, looking uncomfortable. "Sorry. Given the way things have been going this weekend, that's a poor choice of words, isn't it? What should we do until then?"

"Whatever we do, we should stick together," Drew said. "So far, the two people who've died don't appear to have any direct connection to the Lowry House, but that doesn't mean we're safe. If something happens to one of us, the others will be there to call nine-one-one, if nothing else."

"And if any of us has another psychic experience, the others will be there to observe," Trevor said. "Maybe we'll learn something that will prove useful later."

"Useful for what?" Amber said.

"For understanding what's happening," Trevor said, as if it were obvious. "That's the whole reason we started investigating paranormal incidents in high school, wasn't it? To gain a deeper understanding of our world—and what might lie beyond."

She shook her head. "That's not enough, not this time. This has gone beyond mere curiosity about the paranormal and even beyond getting our memories back so we can finally understand what happened to us the night the Lowry House burned down. Two people have died already, and who knows how many more might follow? We don't need just to understand what's happening; we need to stop it."

Trevor looked at her. "Not only did I forget my thumbscrews, I left my proton pack and ghost traps at home, too."

She stuck her tongue out at him, but there was no malice in the gesture. It made Drew smile. It reminded him of how the three of them had teased and bantered with one another back in high school. *The more things change . . .*

"In that case," he said, "we should research methods of nullifying negative psychic energy. It seems the Lowry House is an archetypal Bad Place, a storehouse of . . . the scientist in me is reluctant to use the term *evil*, but I can't think of any word that's more appropriate."

"But the Lowry House was destroyed that night," Amber said, and then she frowned. "Wait a minute. Maybe we really *did* set the fire. Maybe we were trying to . . . I don't know, exorcise the place or something."

"Possibly," Drew said. He searched his feelings to see if he had any reaction to Amber's words, but he couldn't find anything. If they had set the fire on purpose to cast out the evil infesting the Lowry House, his memory of it remained buried.

"Well, if we did burn the house down on purpose, it didn't work," Trevor said. "The evil's stronger than it ever was. Now it can reach out to touch minds and even kill people."

"Amber's vision was of a massacre on the site where the Lowry House would one day be built," Drew said. "Maybe the house itself wasn't the nexus for the negative psychic energy that became stored there over the years. Maybe it was the land it sat on."

"The land's still there," Amber said. "And now there's a rec center on top of it."

"When they open the center and people start going there . . ." Trevor said.

They fell into silence after that. The implications were clear. The negative energy that permeated the land there would have hundreds of new victims to prey upon. They had to do something to prevent that from happening.

"Let's go back to one of our rooms," Drew said. "We'll keep an eye on one another until the banquet, and we can brainstorm ideas for our next move."

"I know some experts I can ask for advice on conducting psychic cleansing," Trevor said. "Don't look at me like that, Drew. They're not kooks. They're serious professionals I rely on to supply information for the books and articles I write. When we get to the room, I'll fire off a few e-mails, leave a few postings on message boards, see if I can't get someone on live chat. Maybe they'll be able to give us some information we can use."

Drew wasn't comfortable with consulting Trevor's "experts," but at this point, he was willing to explore any option. The more knowledge they had to draw on, the better, he supposed. The trick would be separating the wheat from the chaff.

"And at the banquet, we'll talk to Greg and see if we can't get him to tell us what he remembers," Amber said.

Drew nodded. "And afterward, I think a nighttime visit to the rec center might be in order. Since that's where everything started, it makes sense that that's where it has to end."

"I wish you'd phrased that differently," Trevor said. "There are lots of ways things can end, and not all of them are good."

"Always the optimist." But he didn't smile, for he shared his friend's misgivings. What could the three of them hope to do against the force that had killed Sean Houser and Jerry Cottrill? But they had to try. After all, who else was there?

"Keep the flashlight steady."

Amber felt Drew's hand wrap around hers to keep it from shaking. She wasn't scared so much as cold, but the moment his flesh came in contact with hers, a warm flush suffused her body, and she forgot all about the temperature.

She looked at Drew's face, illuminated by the side glow from the flashlight's beam, but he wasn't looking at her. He was looking at the gravestone in front of them: "Lucille Dessick, 1898–1966. Beloved wife, mother, and grandmother. Well may she rest."

"I think this is it," he said.

It was early May, and although it had been warm during the daytime, it had gotten cooler after the sun had gone down. It was closing in on midnight now, and the breeze blowing through the cemetery made her wish she'd brought a heavier jacket. The sky was clear, the moon half full, stars glittering like scattered diamonds. It might have been romantic—if they hadn't been standing in the middle of a graveyard checking out a dead woman's headstone.

She looked at Drew again. She liked the way the stars in the sky framed his head, liked the way the breeze ruffled his hair, liked the intensity in his gaze. And she especially liked the feel of his hand on hers.

She couldn't help smiling to herself. Maybe this *was* kind of romantic, in a weird way.

"I need to take a picture." Drew let go of her hand—which she did *not* like—and removed a camera from the pocket of his jacket. She made sure to hold the flashlight steady as he took a couple of pictures of Lucille Dessick's headstone. When he was finished, he tucked the camera back into his pocket, then turned to her and smiled. "That proves one part of the story, at least. There really was a Lucille Dessick."

For decades, people in Ash Creek had reported sightings of a "White Lady," an example of a supernatural apparition common around the world. A White Lady showed herself to only one person at a time, and her appearance was supposed to herald the death of someone close to those who saw her. White Ladies wore all white, and their hair and even their skin were white, so much so that both were indistinguishable from their clothing. White Ladies tended to manifest in rural areas, and Ash Creek's was no exception. She was always spotted along a stretch of Route Four that bordered the Dessick family farm. According to town legend, the White Lady began appearing only after Lucille Dessick, whose family had lived in Ash Creek since the town's founding, had died under mysterious circumstances; of course, legend was vague about *why* her death had been so mysterious.

Amber, Drew, and Trevor had begun investigating the White Lady after Amber's cousin Josh had seen her late one night while driving home from his job at the cinema over in Zephyr, and . . .

She broke off the thought and frowned. Where *was* Trevor? And for that matter, what were they doing here so late? There was no reason for them to be skulking around like this. All they'd come to do was find Lucille's grave and take a picture. The cemetery was open to the public during daylight hours, so there was no need for them to sneak in. And while there was more than a little theatricality in creeping through a graveyard in the dead of night, Drew was a practical person. He wouldn't have come here this late just for the thrill of it. It didn't make any sense.

She turned to him to voice her concerns, panning the flashlight beam around as she did so, in the process illuminating the figure of an elderly woman standing next to the grave site.

Ice water rushed through Amber's veins at the sight of the woman dressed in white strips of sheer cloth, like a nightgown that had been shredded—or an old-fashioned burial shroud. She was bird-thin, emaciated, her ivory-colored flesh stretched so tight across her bones that the skeleton beneath was visible. Her white hair stood out from her head like a thick growth of dandelion fluff, and it swayed in the breeze like grass that had been bleached of all color. Her lips were thin and bloodless, and while her skin was so taut it was impossible to determine how old she was, she projected a palpable sense of age. Amber's parents had taken her to a museum in

Columbus a couple of years ago to see a traveling exhibit of Egyptian artifacts. Amber had been fascinated by a mummy lying in an open sarcophagus sealed in a glass display case. The mummy itself wasn't much to look at—smaller than she would have guessed, its wrappings a dingy gray—all in all, not that frightening. But what had impressed her the most was the feeling that she was standing in the presence of time itself. The White Lady made her feel like that: young, small, and insignificant.

Worst of all were the woman's eyes. Given her extreme pallor, Amber expected her eyes to be cold, smooth, featureless orbs like a marble statue's. But the White Lady's eyes were nothing like that. Her sockets were filled with a living, roiling darkness from which small tendrils emerged and undulated in the air, as if a pair of strange black sea creatures had taken up residence in the woman's skull and were reaching out to sense the world beyond. For some reason, those tendrils seemed familiar to her, but that was crazy. She'd never seen anything like this before . . . had she?

Amber's breath caught in her throat, and her heart pounded so hard she could feel the veins in her neck throb. She wanted nothing more than to turn and run, but she remained rooted to the spot, unable to make herself move. She could sense Drew still standing beside her, and she wanted to turn her head and glance in his direction, if for no other reason than the reassurance the sight of him would offer, but she could no more turn to look at him than she could pick up her feet to run.

The White Lady raised her right arm in a smooth, graceful motion that was at odds with the aura of age she projected and stretched out her index finger to point at Amber. The finger was long and bony, and the nail was black, hooked, and sharp like a raven's claw. The woman opened her mouth to reveal teeth of polished obsidian, and a thick tongue rolled forth, also black, the tip ending in a cluster of thin, wavering tendrils. A low, keening sound emerged from deep within the White Lady's chest, rising in both volume and pitch as it went on. The sound continued without interruption, as if the woman's lungs contained an inexhaustible supply of air and she had no need to pause for breath.

What *was* this creature? Were they looking at the ghost of Lucille Dessick? But this . . . this *thing* didn't look as if it had ever been human. Amber became aware of another sound then, fainter than the woman's keening, a soft *huh-huh-huh* that sounded almost, but not quite, like sobbing. She wasn't surprised when she realized that the sound was coming from herself.

The ebon tendrils protruding from the woman's eyes and mouth shot forward, extending a trio of writhing, tangled masses toward Amber. The sight shocked her out of her paralysis, and she gave voice to a full-throated scream that split the night like a razor.

She felt Drew's hand grab hold of hers then, felt him pull her away from the White Lady. She spun around, dropping the flashlight as she did, and she and Drew ran like hell, the keening of the White Lady following them as they fled.

She let terror take her then, and she ran without thought or reason, barely aware of the ground she and Drew covered. The cemetery flew by in a jumble of images—the silhouettes of headstones, trees, and mausoleums—and then they were out on the street and still running, past houses, parked cars, and streetlights whose cold illumination provided no comfort. They ran until her lungs burned and her leg muscles felt so weary they might slide off the bone like meat from an overcooked chicken. And then they were on her porch, sitting on the concrete, leaning against each other as they gasped for air, sweat drying in the night breeze.

Amber looked out into the street, half expecting the White Lady to be there, having followed them from the cemetery on foot or, as seemed more likely, simply materializing out of thin air. But the empty street was a most welcome sight.

Amber had no idea how long they sat like that, but the burning in her lungs subsided, and her breathing eased. And then she began to laugh. It started out as a soft chuckle at first, but it grew into full-fledged, hurt-your-belly, unable-to-stop laughter. Drew tried to shush her at first, but his efforts only made her laugh harder, until he gave up and joined her. Though part of her worried that they'd wake her parents—hell, the whole neighborhood—she needed to release the tension that had built up inside her, and she didn't care. But the porch light didn't come on, and the front door didn't open. No neighbors stepped out of their houses to see what all the commotion was about. It was as if she and Drew were the only two people in the world, and it was wonderful.

Eventually, their laughter ended, and she began to shiver, partly from the night chill but more, she suspected, as an aftereffect of all of the intense emotions she had experienced that night. She tried to make herself stop shaking through sheer willpower, but her efforts had the opposite effect: the harder she fought to control her trembling, the worse it became. It became so bad it felt almost as if she were having a seizure.

She tried to say something to Drew, but she was shaking too hard to speak. He seemed to understand anyway. He took her in his arms, held her close and tight, and she gave herself over to the trembling and let it run its course. It seemed to take forever, but he continued holding her, and his reassuring strength and warmth comforted her until the shaking diminished and her body grew still. He didn't let go of her then, and she made no move to draw away from him. Instead, she wrapped her arms around him and held him as tightly as he held her.

After a time, he reached up, took hold of her chin between his thumb and forefinger, and tilted her head up so she was looking at him. He gazed at her a moment, his eyes seeming to glitter with the same cool light as the stars above, and then he leaned down and pressed his lips against hers.

Amber was taken by surprise, and at first she stiffened as Drew kissed her, but she soon relaxed and found herself kissing him back. The two of them had been friends since grade school, and she'd never considered him anything more than that. She'd never imagined that she would be sitting there with him, kissing him after fleeing from some horrible spectral apparition that had manifested in front of them in a graveyard in the middle of the night. No, if she were to be honest with herself, that wasn't true. Well, the part about the ghost was, of course. She hadn't imagined something like *that* factoring into any romantic scenarios she might have conjured between herself and Drew. But from time to time, she had wondered what it might be like if the two of them were more than friends.

And she *had* imagined kissing him, although she hadn't gone so far as to practice on her pillow, as one of the teen magazines she read had advised. She was pleased to discover that the reality was turning out to be much nicer than the fantasy, and she wondered why it had taken the two of them so long to admit their feelings for each other.

I wonder if we'll stay together, she thought, knowing it was premature to go down that road but unable to help herself. *What if we got married and had kids? Wouldn't it be funny to tell them their mom and dad got together because they were scared by a ghost in a graveyard?*

Their kiss continued and deepened, and Amber felt Drew's moist tongue tease against her lips. She hesitated. This wasn't the first time she'd kissed a boy. That was Bobbie Ehrnhardt at summer camp last year. But she hadn't let Bobbie put his tongue in her mouth, for it had seemed less romantic than, well, icky, to be frank. But the thought of doing it with Drew didn't seem so bad. In fact, it felt natural.

Up to this point, she'd been kissing him with her eyes closed, but she opened them now because she wanted to see the expression on his face when she opened her mouth and extended her tongue to meet his. His eyes were already open, and they were gazing at her. Not with love, not with anything even approximating warmth. They were cold, those eyes. Cold and hungry. Cold and hungry and *blue.*

Drew's eyes were brown.

She let go of him, put her hands on his shoulders, and shoved. He released his grip on her, and she scooted away. He didn't seem upset, though. Rather, he appeared amused.

His blue eyes glittered with an internal light, and the voice that came out of his mouth next wasn't Drew's, though the face still was.

"Surprise, surprise," Greg said.

Amber woke with a start, sat up, and looked around. She was in her hotel room, on her bed. Drew and Trevor were over at the desk in the corner, Trevor sitting in front of his open laptop, Drew sitting on the edge of the second bed, close enough to see the screen over Trevor's shoulder. As far as she knew, she hadn't made any sound upon awakening, but both men turned to look at her.

"Are you all right?" Drew asked.

His eyes were brown, just as they should be, but even though Amber knew that what she'd experienced hadn't been real, she couldn't help suppressing a shudder at the sight of him.

She forced a shaky smile. "Guess I dozed off." Spread out on the bed next to her were a half-dozen pamphlets she'd picked up at the Historical Society during her visit there with Trevor. She'd been reading over them while the boys researched cleansing rituals online, more to have something to do than because she thought she'd find any useful information in the pamphlets.

She did her best to keep her tone casual, but Drew must have detected something amiss, because he frowned. "Have a bad dream?"

Trevor was frowning now, too, and both of them wore expressions of concern. She didn't have to be a mind reader to know what they were thinking. They thought she'd had another "vision," and they wanted to know what it was, hoped it might provide a little more insight into the bizarre events that had occurred since they'd returned to Ash Creek. At first, she was going to tell them, but she stopped herself. Did her dream qualify as a vision? Both Drew and Trevor had experienced theirs while wide awake, and theirs had both dealt with the past of the Lowry House. Her first dream, the one in which she'd been Little Eyes, fell into this category, but this latest one hadn't had anything to do with the Lowry House in any way, shape, or form. In fact, it had been only partially based on reality. Back in high school, she and Drew had gone to the cemetery to locate and take a photo of Lucille Dessick's headstone. But Trevor had gone with them, and they'd visited the cemetery during the daytime. There'd been no apparition of the White Lady, and while the three of them had later driven past the Dessick farm in the weird-looking aquamarine Toyota Corolla that Trevor owned, they hadn't witnessed any manifestation of Lucille's spirit there. She and Drew hadn't run all the way from the cemetery to her house in a panic, they hadn't collapsed laughing into each other's arms on the porch, and they hadn't kissed. Hell, the entire time they'd known each other, they hadn't so much as held hands.

Amber had been through enough therapy in her life to have heard that old cliché poking fun at Freudian theory: Sometimes a cigar is just a cigar. Well, sometimes a dream was just a dream. Besides, she wasn't comfortable telling the guys about it. Especially Drew.

She hoped her smile appeared more genuine this time.

"Nope. As a matter of fact, I didn't dream at all."

THIRTEEN

"You know, one of the reasons I became a free-lance writer was so I didn't have to wear a tie."

"Stop tugging at it," Amber said. "You look like a little boy who can't sit still in church."

Trevor, who hadn't realized that he'd been pulling at his tie to loosen it, did as Amber said. To give his hands something else to do, he picked up his knife and fork and cut off another piece of the rubber chicken on his plate, popped it into his mouth, and chewed. And chewed and chewed and chewed. He swallowed, with no little amount of difficulty, and took a large gulp of his iced tea to wash the mouthful down.

"It never fails. Whenever I attend a banquet, no matter what entrée I order, I always end up wishing I'd picked something else."

"It's an inalterable law of the universe that banquet food is always lousy," Drew said. "If it's any consolation, my fish is dry and tasteless."

"My eggplant Parmesan is good," Amber said. As if to illustrate, she put another piece in her mouth and chewed. She then pointed to her dessert with her fork. "But not as tasty as that cheese-cake looks!"

Trevor smiled. "Look at the three of us sitting here like real grown-ups. This is a long way from Flying Pizza, huh?"

Both Trevor and Drew wore suits—charcoal gray and navy blue, respectively—and Amber had on a lovely green dress that left her shoulders bare and had a neckline just low enough to reveal a hint of cleavage. She wore her hair up, and with the addition of earrings, a silver necklace, and understated makeup, she looked quite beautiful. More, she looked like a strong, confident woman, unlike the Amber they'd been reintroduced to yesterday. Despite their current situation and all of its dangers and uncertainties, she seemed to be thriving. Then again, maybe she was thriving *because* of those dangers. Crisis situations could create trauma, but they could also jolt people out of their old patterns of behavior. Somehow, though, Trevor doubted that Drew would recommend an encounter with a murderous otherworldly force as an alternative form of therapy.

Not that Drew's mind was on professional matters at the moment. Despite their earlier decision to stick together, Amber had kicked him and Trevor out of her room when it was time to start getting ready for the banquet. Drew had protested, but Amber insisted that she wasn't about to get dressed with the two of them around, and besides, they needed to return to their own rooms to put on their monkey suits.

Trevor had doubted that she had come over all shy around them—after all, she could have gotten ready in the bathroom and kept the door closed. He figured that Amber hadn't wanted Drew to see her until the banquet started. Trevor was hardly a man of the world, but he knew enough about women to know that they liked to maintain a bit of mystery about them and that they liked to control the first impression they made on a man after they'd spent a significant amount of time making themselves look good.

Her efforts had paid off. Drew had been nervous that something bad might happen to her while the three of them were separated, but when she walked into the banquet hall—arriving later than both Drew and Trevor, naturally—the stunned expression on Drew's face, which he, of course, had attempted to cover, proved that she'd succeeded. He had barely taken his eyes off her the entire meal. And she was doing an excellent job of making him think that she didn't notice. Trevor never failed to find it funny that Drew, a trained observer of human behavior, was so often clueless about Amber's feelings for him.

He wasn't jealous of his two friends. He was a red-blooded, hetero male and recognized how attractive Amber was, and he cared deeply about her but in a brotherly way. Ever since the three of them had met as kids, she and Drew had only had eyes for each other, and that was fine with him. He just wished they would acknowledge their feelings for each other and get on with it. Of course, if they did, that would give him one fewer thing to tease them about. He smiled.

"You find something amusing?" Drew asked.

The two of you, he thought. Aloud, he said, "Just wondering what the kids we used to be would think of the adults we became. That we *all* became." He glanced around. The three of them were the only ones sitting at their table, but most of the rest of the tables in the hall were filled. There'd been a good turnout. Their graduating class had close to two hundred people in it, and at a quick guess, it looked to him that around eighty or so had come this weekend. People were eating and talking, but quietly, their voices hushed and expressions subdued. "Why is everything so down? Do they miss being teenagers *that* much?"

"It's not that," Drew said. "Word about Sean's and Jerry's deaths has gotten around, and it's cast a pall over the proceedings. People are already prone to contemplate the passage of time at events like these, which in turn leads to thoughts of mortality. The deaths only serve to strengthen those feelings and bring them even closer to the surface."

"I wish the alumni committee would've canceled the rest of the weekend," Amber said. "All these people together in one place like this . . ."

"It's like fish in a barrel," Trevor said, "just waiting for someone, or in our case, some*thing,* to come along and start shooting."

"That's what I'm afraid of," Amber said.

Speaking of the alumni committee, they all sat at a table toward the front of the room, near a large drop-down screen that displayed a looped presentation of a collage of yearbook photos. When the banquet began and the presentation started, it was accompanied by the Verve's "Bitter Sweet Symphony," which Trevor found an odd choice, considering that the song had come out a couple of years after they'd graduated. It seemed a little downbeat for a celebration, but then, maybe that was why it had been chosen, for it seemed to fit the melancholy mood of the evening. He was thankful that the song had only played once and didn't continue playing while the presentation proceeded along its endless course.

Greg sat with the members of the alumni committee, all of them—not counting him—former big wheels in high school: captain of the football team, head cheerleader, band field commander, valedictorian and salutatorian . . .

"Never thought I'd see Greg Daniels hobnobbing with the in-crowd," Trevor said.

"Things change," Drew said with a shrug. "People change."

"Maybe so, but that much? Besides, isn't the stereotypical dynamic of events like this that people revert back to type? I mean, look at that table. The cool kids are still sitting with the cool kids, like this was the high-school cafeteria instead of a banquet hall. The only difference is that Greg is sitting with them."

"I told you about our conversation in the lobby," Drew said. "How he struck me as having at least some of the features of a sociopathic personality. Sociopaths are masters of manipulation. They can make you like them and think it was all your idea."

"Well, right now, he's not making me think he likes *us*," Trevor said. "He hasn't so much as stopped by our table to say hi."

Drew smiled. "Feeling neglected?"

"Hardly. But we need to talk to him about the night the Lowry House burned down. And as much as I'm enjoying sitting here with you two and trying not to choke to death on this god-awful excuse for chicken, we can't ask Greg any questions if he's sitting all the way on the other side of the damn room."

"If he doesn't come over before the meal's finished, we'll try to catch him before the dance starts," Drew said.

Amber had been silent for the last several minutes while they'd been talking about Greg, but now she spoke. "Is it really that important that we talk with him?"

Trevor and Drew turned to look at her. Although she'd only gotten three-quarters of the way through her eggplant, she pushed it aside and began working on her cheesecake. She kept her attention focused on the dessert and spoke between bites.

"We've been over this before, but we all remember that he didn't go with us to the Lowry House, and he wasn't there when the emergency crews arrived. I don't see how he could have anything important to tell us."

Trevor detected a studied casualness in her tone, as if she was working hard to make it seem as if what she was saying wasn't that big a deal, when in reality it was. The question was *why* it was a big deal.

She went on after another bite of cheesecake. "And if that's the case, why drag him into this mess if we don't have to? What if by talking to him, we cause the force, entity, whatever it is, to notice him? We might end up putting him at risk. Just because we're desperate for answers doesn't give us the right to place other people in danger."

Drew frowned as he looked at Amber, and Trevor could guess what his friend was thinking. She made a good point, but it was the way she was making it. She didn't look at either of them as she spoke, and she didn't look in Greg's direction.

"I'd say talking to him was a calculated risk," Drew began, "except that we have so little data about what's going on that we can't gauge the danger. We could be putting him at risk by not talking to him."

"And none of us spoke with Sean or Jerry," Trevor pointed out. "But that didn't keep either of them alive."

"Is there some other reason you don't want to talk with Greg?" Drew asked. Now it was his turn to speak in a calm, casual manner, and Trevor wondered how often his patients had heard that same tone of voice.

Evidently, Amber recognized Drew's tone for what it was, for she dropped her fork into her plate with a clatter loud enough to make people at nearby tables look in their direction. Amber turned to glare at him.

"Are you suggesting I'm lying?" she asked.

Drew sidestepped the question. "The dream you had about the massacre, the one in which you were Little Eyes . . . Greg was in it, too, wasn't he? It was a disturbing dream, and it would be natural for you to associate him with it, not just the events of the dream but the emotions it evoked. You could find talking with him uncomfortable for that reason."

Drew sounded both rational and empathetic, but it was clear from the angry expression on Amber's face that instead of reassuring her, his words were only making her angrier. Trevor decided to step in before things got any worse.

"I've been thinking about your dream, Amber. At first, I assumed it was the result of some sort of psychic contact, some connection you made with the past. And then, when Drew and I had similar visions that dealt with the history of the Lowry House, I figured we were following in your metaphysical footsteps."

She still looked angry, but her attention was on Trevor rather than Drew now, and she appeared to be listening.

Trevor continued. "But there are some important differences. The most obvious is that you were asleep during your vision, while Drew and I were awake. And you were a different person in the dream, the Native American girl named Little Eyes. Drew and I appeared as ourselves in our visions. The final difference is that Greg showed up in your dream. He looked like someone from that time and place, a British hunter, but he spoke to you as himself. He even told you it was a dream you were having."

"What are you saying? That my dream was just a dream, after all, and nothing more?"

Drew had been listening as Trevor spoke, and now he looked thoughtful. "We haven't found any evidence that proves that a massacre such as the one you dreamed about occurred on the land where the Lowry House would be built. Whereas the visions Trevor and I had were based on historical fact."

"So, my dreams aren't important?" she said. "Why is that? Because I have a history of depression?" Her voice rose on this last word, once more drawing the attention of people at surrounding tables.

It was clear to Trevor that his attempt to keep the peace between Amber and Drew had backfired. He wanted to say something to calm her down, but he feared that anything he might say would only make things worse. He gave Drew a plaintive look, hoping his buddy would employ his psychological training to pull himself out of the cavernous hole he'd dug for himself. But his gaze remained fixed on Amber, and he looked more thoughtful than worried. Trevor found out why a second later when he spoke.

"You said dreams."

Amber looked startled at first, but she recovered. "No, I didn't. I said dream. Just one."

Trevor knew he should let it go, given how upset she had been a moment ago, but he couldn't. It could be important, and given the seriousness of their situation, they couldn't afford to ignore any bit of information, regardless of how insignificant it might seem at first.

"At the risk of making you even angrier, I have to agree with Drew. I heard you say dreams, plural."

"Did you have another dream?" Drew asked. "Maybe when the three of us were in your room and you dozed off for a bit?"

Amber didn't respond right away. Trevor had the sense that she wanted to deny it but that she also didn't want to lie to them any further. Before she could answer, however, a fourth voice joined the conversation.

"Trouble in paradise?"

Greg stood behind Amber. Trevor hadn't seen the man rise from the cool kids' table and come sauntering over to theirs, and while he knew it was possible that he'd been so caught up in what the three of them had been talking about that he hadn't noticed Greg's approach, there was one thing wrong with that theory. Trevor had trained as a journalist, and his observational skills were a vital part of his professional tool kit. It wasn't like him to miss important details, not to mention the fact that he'd been keeping a close eye on Greg from the moment he'd entered the banquet hall. It was as if he had been sitting at his table one instant and then magically appeared standing behind Amber the next.

Amber's response to Greg's arrival was dramatic. Her expression froze, and her body went rigid. She stared straight ahead, not turning to look over her shoulder at him. It wasn't just that she was startled by his sudden appearance; she seemed afraid of him.

"We were just chatting," Drew said. He glanced at Amber once more before turning to face Greg. "It's a nice banquet. You and the rest of the alumni committee did a good job."

Greg smiled. "It's kind of you to say so, but the food's barely passable, and that slide show is god-awful, isn't it? Amateurish and maudlin. I had nothing to do with it. It was all Sherri's doing."

"I assume you mean Sherri Wackler," Trevor said. He nodded toward the head table, where the woman in question still sat with the rest of the alumni committee. "Never thought I'd see you sitting next to a former head cheerleader. She's as beautiful as she was back in high school."

And it was true. Actually, he thought the added maturity granted by the last fifteen years made her even more beautiful. She was tall, with long blond hair, a model's high cheekbones, a narrow waist, hips that flared out just enough, and a generous bustline.

"I suppose," Greg allowed after a brief glance in her direction. "But beauty isn't everything."

"Maybe not," Trevor said, "but it's nothing to sneeze at, either."

Greg gave him an appraising look, and he felt fixed in place, as if he were a lab specimen sandwiched between two glass slides being examined with microscopic scrutiny.

"You had a crush on her in high school," Greg

said in a pleased tone of voice that reminded Trevor a little too much of a cat's satisfied purr.

"I lusted after her, if that's what you mean," he said. "Most of the guys in school did."

"Not me," Greg said. "She wasn't my type."

Trevor might have asked him what his type was, but from the way he looked at Amber, he already knew the answer to the question. For some reason, seeing Greg look at his friend like that filled him with a mix of revulsion and anger, and from the way Drew seemed to be struggling to maintain his composure, he figured he felt the same way.

Drew spoke then, an unaccustomed edge in his voice. "If you can spare a few minutes, why don't you sit down and talk for a bit? We haven't had a chance to catch up with you yet."

Trevor saw the look of near panic in Amber's eyes, and she gave her head an almost imperceptible shake, as if urging Drew to rescind his invitation. Greg gave no sign that he noticed her.

"I'd love to, but now that everyone's almost finished with dessert, it's time to move on to the formal portion of the banquet. The members of the alumni committee are going to give a few speeches. They'll mention the passing of poor Sean and Jerry, of course, then pass out some gag awards to lighten the mood, that sort of thing. But the three of you are coming to the dance afterward, aren't you? Once that gets going, it'll pretty much run itself, and I'll be able to carve out some time to talk. We'll catch up then, OK?"

He reached out and placed a hand on Amber's bare shoulder. She shivered but didn't turn to look at him.

"And maybe you'll save a dance for an old friend?"

She didn't answer, and he removed his hand, gave them a last smile, and turned to go. But he stopped and turned back around to face Trevor.

"I'll put in a good word with Sherri for you. Who knows? Maybe the two of you can hook up later."

With a last glance at Amber, followed by a smug grin that Trevor thought verged uncomfortably close to a leer, he turned and headed back to the alumni committee table.

When he was out of earshot, Trevor said, "That guy is even creepier than he was back in high school."

In a small voice, Amber said, "You have no idea."

Once the banquet was over, Sherri watched the reunion attendees file out while the hotel staff went to work clearing away the tables and getting the hall ready for the dance. Most people headed to the bar to pass the time while the minimal decorations were hung and the DJ hauled in his equipment, although some returned to their rooms in order to change into clothes that were more comfortable to dance in. Sherri wished she could do the latter. The little black dress she was wearing was stylish and made her look good—no, let's be honest, it made her look hot as hell—but it wasn't designed to be easy to move in. Too tight around the waist and hips and cut too low in front. If she wasn't careful, her boobs would end up popping out when she danced, and wouldn't *that* be the hit of the reunion? She could imagine the headline on the alumni committee's Web site: "Former Head Cheerleader Busts Out on Dance Floor!" Even worse were her shoes. She'd only been wearing her high heels for a couple of hours, but her feet ached as if she'd been walking on them all day. The floor was carpeted, so she'd probably end up kicking the shoes off once the dance got under way, but what she wouldn't give for a good pair of tennies with arch supports in them.

Sherri Wackler opting for comfort over fashion? What's the world coming to? She smiled to herself. She had a reputation to maintain or, more accurately, a role to play, and she might as well accept it. She was more than a person to her former classmates—she was a mythic figure, the Eternal Cheerleader, and they expected her to act the part. More than that, they *needed* her to do it. Just as they needed the other former big men and women on campus to fulfill their old roles, at least for one night. She felt like an aging pop musician who'd had a hit single years ago and was now expected to sing her one song for her fans, over and over. She knew she shouldn't complain. She'd chosen to serve on the alumni committee, after all, and in truth, it was fun to pretend that she was the teenager she used to be. She could endure the Heels of Torquemada for a few more hours. It was a small enough price to pay.

She distracted herself from her aching feet by supervising the placement of handcrafted signs, masterpieces of poster board, marker, and glitter, with such pithy slogans as "Class of 1995 Rox!" and "Dance Till You Drop!" She almost didn't allow this last one to be taped up, considering that both Sean Houser and Jerry Cottrill had dropped dead this weekend. But she kept her mouth shut and pointed to the position on the wall where she wanted the hotel staff member who was assisting her to place the poster. The alumni committee had voted to go ahead with the festivities despite the deaths, and she figured that a few signs weren't going to make people feel any better or worse than they already did. Besides, she didn't believe in minimizing or avoiding unpleasantness. Death sucked, but it was a fact of life, and while she was well aware of the irony implicit in that statement, that didn't make it any less true. And the sooner people started dealing with it, the faster they got over it, or at least as over it as they were ever going to get.

Sherri knew all about learning to deal with

death. During her freshman year in college, her Introduction to Biology class had been taught by a graduate student named Brad Taylor. He was smart, cute, and funny, and she'd had a serious crush on him. But she'd been a good girl and kept things professional between them until the class was over and her final grade submitted. The very next day, she showed up at Brad's office and asked him out. He was ten years older than she was, but she'd always been attracted to older men. She knew she was pretty, so she wasn't worried about being attractive to him on that score, but she feared he'd find her inexperienced, immature, and boring. But he was as attracted to her as she was to him, and he agreed to go out with her.

A year later, they got married. A year after that, while Brad was working on his doctoral dissertation, he found a small lump on the inside of his nose. He didn't give it much thought, figured it was an ingrown hair or something. Sherri urged him to go to the doctor and get it checked, and he promised he would. She didn't want to be a nag, so she didn't keep on him about it. Besides, he was getting his doctorate in biology, for God's sake. She figured he understood enough about basic health to take a lump seriously. But he was so wrapped up in his dissertation that he put it off. One month. Two. Before Sherri knew it, six months had passed, and she decided that regardless of whether she wanted to be a nag or not, she had to get Brad off his ass and to a doctor. But by then, it was too late. The little lump turned out to be melanoma. Stage four, to be precise.

Six months later, despite surgery and chemotherapy, Brad was dead, and Sherri became a widow before her twenty-first birthday.

Losing him was hard in ways she couldn't have imagined, and even with the support of family and friends, she struggled with depression for several years afterward. She'd been fine for the last five years or so, although she hadn't remarried and dated only rarely. She had no trouble meeting guys—not the way she looked—but good guys, quality guys? That was another matter. Still, her life was OK these days, and when she thought about Brad, she focused on the good times, and the memories that came were always happy ones.

Nighttime was a different story.

When Sherri was six, her older sister had babysat her one evening while their parents went out. *Night of the Living Dead* was playing on a cable channel, and although she knew their parents wouldn't approve of her showing Sherri a scary movie, especially one *that* scary, she had anyway. Sherri had been terrified but so compelled by the film that she'd watched all the way through, without once moving or making a sound. Her sister made Sherri promise not to tell their parents, and she agreed, but they found out anyway when later that night she woke screaming at three A.M. Her parents rushed into her room, only to have their tearful daughter tell them that zombies were trying to break into the house.

Her sister, of course, was busted. But that began a lifetime of what Sherri thought of as her "zombie dreams." She didn't have them every night, maybe once every month or two, and they were, with slight variations, always the same. She would be trapped somewhere—in a house, in an alley, inside a department store—alone, with nowhere to run, and groups of shuffling, moaning, unblinking zombies were coming toward her, eager to sink their teeth and nails into her flesh. No matter how hard and fast she ran, the zombies always somehow caught her, and she'd wake screaming just as they were about to devour her.

As she got older, the dreams decreased in frequency and intensity, until she had one every six months, if that, and instead of waking up screaming, she'd sleep through them and remember them only vaguely in the morning. But then Brad died, and her zombie dreams roared back full force. Time, therapy, and antidepressants helped, and now she had the dreams only every couple of months, and while she still woke—covered in sweat, heart pounding, lungs heaving—rarely did she scream.

A therapist had told her the dreams were simple to interpret: the slow-moving but unstoppable zombies represented the inexorable approach of death. Death had taken Brad from her, and one day, it would come to claim her as well. Easy-peasy, that will be a hundred dollars, please.

So, Sherri was no stranger to death. But even so, she still had trouble believing that any of her former classmates had died, let alone two in the same weekend *and* during the reunion to boot. What were the odds? She wasn't a physician, but she'd been interested in anything to do with health and medicine ever since she'd been a child, and Brad's death had reinforced that interest. After getting her bachelor's degree in biology, she'd thought about becoming an oncologist, but Brad's death had been too recent, and she didn't think she could handle working with cancer patients. So, since she also loved animals—her family lived on a farm outside town and had all kinds of livestock and pets—she'd decided to become a vet.

While she wasn't trained to doctor humans, she knew enough basics to know how rare it was for two apparently healthy men in their early thirties to keel over, especially within a few hours of each other. Sean's death was disturbing enough, but after Jerry died, a couple of people on the alumni committee, herself included, had been worried that some kind of disease might be going around, like Legionnaire's, only worse. They'd been in favor of canceling the rest of the reunion, if only as a precaution.

But Greg had spoken up. He'd pointed out that

while there was no denying the oddity of two relatively young men dying suddenly, the police had said nothing to them about the possibility of disease, and they'd be the first to urge the cancellation of the reunion if necessary. The fact that they hadn't, while not proof, was a strong indication that whatever had caused the two men's deaths wasn't related, nor was it contagious. Besides, he'd said, what better way to memorialize their fallen classmates than by continuing with the reunion and dedicating the weekend to their memory?

Sherri had wanted to argue that it took time to perform autopsies and even more time to get test results back. There was no way the police would have any evidence one way or the other regarding the possibility of disease yet. But she hadn't said anything. Greg had seemed so *sure,* and he had a quality about him that was hard to define, a self-assured strength that inspired confidence and trust. So, even though she'd known his argument was specious, she'd gone along with the other committee members when they'd decided to continue. She just hoped they wouldn't end up regretting it.

Once the signs were hung to her satisfaction, she went over to the riser where the DJ was setting up to check on his progress. She double-checked to make sure he'd gotten the playlist she'd e-mailed him—songs that were all hits during their high-school years—and he assured her that he had and was ready to, quote, "Make this party happen!"

Sherri nodded and moved on to check the cash bar, thinking that while it was simpler to have booze ready and available legally at a dance, it took all the fun out of sneaking alcohol into the high-school gym. Everything looked good there, so she walked to the center of the room and stopped to take everything in. Half of the tables had been removed to make room to dance, and the rest had been moved off to the sides, tablecloths replaced with clean ones, and flower centerpieces, which she'd designed herself, placed in the middle, and tiny foil 1995s of various colors had been scattered on the tables. Nothing too fancy, but she figured it would do, considering that all people wanted was to dance, get drunk, hit on old flames, and, if all went well, get laid before the night was over.

She grinned. *My, aren't we getting cynical in our old age?*

Greg walked over to join her.

"Think we're ready?" she asked him.

He had a faraway look in his eyes as he answered, and his voice sounded distracted, almost dreamy. "I've waited fifteen years for this moment, Sherri. I'm more than ready."

Then he turned to her and smiled, and for a second, she saw him as bald, his face a ruined mass of scar tissue, his mouth an open slash bisecting the lower half of his face, gums sore and raw, with only a scattering of jagged, twisted teeth cutting through the flesh. But then she blinked, and he looked normal again, his smile warm and reassuring, and the memory of what she saw—or thought she saw—faded from her mind before she could register it.

"Then let's open the doors," she said, "and get this party started."

Greg's smile widened into a grin, and a dark glint came into his eyes. "I couldn't agree more."

FOURTEEN

Drew, Amber, and Trevor were among the first to enter the banquet-room-turned-dance-hall when the doors reopened. They'd visited the bar for a bit, mostly so Amber could have a glass of wine.

"Just need a little something to take the edge off," she'd said.

Something else was going on with her, beyond a reaction to the general events they'd experienced so far. The way she'd reacted to Greg during the banquet when he'd approached their table . . . Drew wondered if Greg had spoken to her alone and, if so, what he'd said to her that might have upset her so. He wanted to ask her, but he also didn't want to pry too much. The therapist in him told him to wait until she was ready to volunteer the information. But as her friend, he chafed with frustration. He wanted to be able to help her now. And if he were to be honest with himself, he wasn't just frustrated. He was jealous, too. It was obvious that Greg was attracted to her, the slimy bastard, and that his attentions made her uncomfortable. He wanted to confront Greg and tell him to back the hell off and leave her alone. And while he knew he was being an overprotective, possessive male, he couldn't help himself. He'd just have to do the best he could to control his feelings and not let them get the better of him.

But he still intended to keep a close eye on Amber, especially when Greg was around.

So when the three of them entered the dance, the first thing he did was look around for Greg. He stood over by the riser where the DJ had set up, talking with Sherri Wackler. He saw them walk in and nodded in their direction, then went back to his conversation with Sherri. That suited Drew just fine. Intellectually, he wanted to finally talk with Greg and discover what, if anything, he knew about the night the Lowry House burned down, but emotionally, he didn't mind waiting a bit longer.

The lights in the room had been dimmed, and the DJ's equipment was rigged with flashing lights, including a mini disco ball, to help foster a party atmosphere. Drew found the lights annoying and hoped none of his former classmates suffered from epilepsy. If so, they'd probably end up having a seizure after the first five minutes. There were about a dozen people in the room already, the alumni committee and a handful of others, and more continued to filter in as the DJ started his spiel.

"Hey, how's everybody doin' tonight?"

This elicited a few tepid cheers, a couple of woo-hoos, and a smattering of applause.

"Awesome!" the DJ shouted with false enthusiasm. He was a skinny guy in his forties, with wire-framed glasses, a salt-and-pepper beard, and a shaved head. He wore a brown suit jacket over a white T-shirt with jeans in an obvious attempt to look hip. But the jacket was the wrong style, fabric too thick and with pads in the shoulders, making him look like a little kid who'd stolen one of his father's old jackets in a vain attempt to play grown-up. "Everyone ready to have a blast?"

A few more cheers, only a little louder this time. People were starting to get drinks from the cash bar, but the alcohol hadn't had time yet to start hitting their systems and artificially bolster their enthusiasm.

The DJ soldiered on, undeterred. "Well, let's get things hoppin' with a little Dave Matthews!" He flipped a switch on his console and "Ants Marching" began to play. Even though it wasn't the most danceable of tunes, a few adventurous souls headed for the middle of the room—drinks in hand, of course—and did their best to move to the music.

"Now, that's just wrong," Trevor said.

"Oh, I don't know," Drew said. "If ants grew to human size and started dancing, it might look a little like that."

Amber giggled.

They picked out one of the tables close to the door so they'd be as far away from the DJ's speakers as possible and sat down.

"I'm going to get something to drink," Trevor said, raising his voice so he could be heard over the music. "Can I bring back anything for the two of you?"

Drew resisted an urge to glance at Amber. "I think it might be a good idea for us to keep our heads clear tonight."

Trevor did look at her before returning his attention to Drew. "Maybe you don't want a drink, but I quit smoking a couple weeks ago. I still get cravings for cigarettes, and they hit worst right after meals and when I'm sitting at a bar."

"This isn't a bar," he said.

"It's *like* a bar," Trevor said. "It's got bad music, bad dancing, and overpriced booze. So, I'm going to go get a beer and hope it blunts the craving for a smoke. At the very least, it'll give me something to do with my hands instead of imagining I'm holding a cigarette. Do you two want anything? My treat."

"I didn't realize haunted hotel books paid so well," Drew said.

Trevor grinned. "They don't. This is a basic bar survival skill. Buy the first round, and you won't have to buy another the rest of the night."

"I'll take another glass of wine," Amber said.

"I'll take whatever you're having," Drew said to Trevor, who nodded and headed off toward the bar.

When Trevor was gone, Amber turned to Drew. "I know I shouldn't have another, but I'm just so nervous. All of these people, gathered in the same place . . . if anything should happen . . ." She shivered.

"Do you feel that something bad is going to happen?" he asked.

She looked at him as if he'd grown a second head and it had begun singing opera. "Are you asking if I'm having a premonition?"

Drew smiled. "Don't tell Trevor. He'd never let me hear the end of it. I'm not asking if you've had some kind of psychic warning that something bad is going to happen here tonight, but the subconscious mind is often more observant than our conscious minds are. The feelings of foreboding we sometimes experience are often the subconscious's way of trying to get our attention and pass along a warning. So, if you want to call that a premonition, I'm fine with that."

She thought for a moment. "Yeah, I guess I am. I feel like an animal that senses a natural disaster coming, like a tornado or an earthquake, hours before it happens."

He noted the way her gaze fell on Greg. He was still hanging out by the DJ's station, only now he was talking with Sam Knapp, who'd played goalie on the varsity soccer team in high school.

"You think Greg's connected to your premonition somehow." It wasn't a question.

She nodded. "There's something not right with him. All three of us sense it. We're just not sure what to make of it."

He had no reason to agree with what she had said—no rational reason, that is. But he couldn't deny that he sensed the very thing she was talking about. And hadn't he been the one who'd said that the subconscious mind sometimes knew more than the conscious one?

The DJ had switched to "Better Man" by Pearl Jam by the time Trevor returned with their drinks.

"Great song," he said as he set their drinks down on the table, "but it's not any easier to dance to than the last one."

As if to illustrate his words, people cleared the dance floor as swiftly as if someone had lobbed a grenade into their midst. Some went off in search of drinks, some found tables to sit at, while others formed conversation groups and stood around talking, presumably waiting for the DJ to put on a more danceable song. Greg finished gabbing with Sam Knapp, and, although Drew managed to catch his eye, he didn't head over to their table. Instead, he joined a group of four people whom Drew recognized as having been in the Drama Club in high school.

He had the sense that Greg was toying with them, that he knew they were waiting to see him and was delaying doing so just to mess with them. Part of him was getting fed up with Greg's petty games and wanted to go over there, take hold of his arm, and drag him back to the table. But he knew better than to give in to his frustration. It might make him feel good to force Greg to talk to them, but he doubted that it would put him in the most cooperative frame of mind. Better to be patient and wait a little longer. Besides, it wasn't as if they would lose track of him. They were sitting by the door, and Greg couldn't attempt to leave without them seeing him. One way or another, they'd get to talk to him before the night was over.

They sat for a bit, working on their drinks, listening to the music, and watching the people around them. And while part of their scrutiny derived from simple curiosity to see how their former classmates would act as adults, Drew knew that they were, in fact, standing guard, keeping a close eye on the crowd, alert for any sign that something bad—something like what happened to Sean and Jerry—might occur here tonight. His professional radar was operating at full strength, and he picked up on the crowd's mood.

During the banquet, people had seemed subdued, but now, the festive atmosphere—aided by the liberal ingestion of alcohol—appeared to be raising everyone's spirits. People hadn't completely shed their emotional reactions to Sean's and Jerry's deaths, but they were well on their way. Drew recognized that a natural process was taking place, that his former classmates sought to release their negative emotions and were going to use the party atmosphere to purge them. That meant they'd drink too much and get a little rowdy, maybe a lot rowdy—all in the name of catharsis.

Everything seemed normal enough, given the circumstances, but he glanced at Amber and Trevor to see if either of them had picked up on anything he'd missed. He raised his eyebrows and cocked his head, and both shook their heads to indicate that so far, they hadn't detected anything wrong. He nodded, thinking that it was a wonderful thing to have friends so close that even after not having been together for the last fifteen years, they could communicate through simple body language.

He noticed that Trevor was paying close attention to Sherri Wackler, who was over at the cash bar.

Amber noticed, too, for she said, "Thinking about doing a little one-on-one investigating, Trevor?"

At first, he looked embarrassed at having been caught staring at Sherri, but then he grinned. "Why not?" He downed the rest of his beer in a gulp, as if looking for a last boost of courage, and then he got up and headed for the bar.

Drew figured that Trevor needed a little catharsis himself. Considering what the three of them had experienced since returning to town, Drew didn't blame him.

Pearl Jam ended, and the DJ leaned in close to his mic. "All right, looks like we got this party off to a good start, people. So, what say we slow things down a bit and give you a chance to get up close and personal? Any old boyfriends or girlfriends out there you'd like to hook up with again or maybe an old crush you never had the courage to ask out? Now's your chance to get 'em out on the dance floor."

The DJ flipped a switch on his console and the dreamlike tones of "Fade into You" by Mazzy Star started playing.

"I love this song!" Amber said. Before Drew could react, she stood, reached over and grabbed his hand, and pulled him out of his seat. The next thing he knew, they were in the middle of the dance floor, and she had her hands on his shoulders. He hesitated only a moment before placing his hands on her waist. He'd never touched her before, not like this, anyway, and he was surprised by how natural it felt, as if his hands belonged there. They began swaying in time to the music, and when she stepped closer and rested her head on his shoulder, that felt natural, too.

"Look at that."

Trevor inclined his head, and when Sherri turned to glance in the direction he indicated, she saw Drew Pearson and Amber Lozier dancing together. When she turned back to Trevor and gave him a questioning look, he said, "Those two have been in love forever. They've just been too dumb to realize it."

"Good for them," she said. She took a sip of her Kahlúa and cream. She and Trevor stood near the bar, watching people filter back onto the dance floor. Her feet were still killing her, but she hadn't kicked off her high heels yet. So far, no one had asked her to dance, but the night was still young, and the DJ hadn't been playing the most dance-able of tunes. One of the paradoxes of being a beautiful woman was that while some guys hit on her because she was so attractive, a lot of guys—maybe more—were intimidated by her looks, figured she was out of their league, and never approached her. It wasn't uncommon for her to end up alone for long stretches of time at a party or a bar, especially if she was by herself. If she had a girlfriend with her, for some reason, guys seemed to feel more comfortable coming up to talk to her, maybe because they figured that if she shot them down, they could always play it off as if they'd come over because they were more interested in her friend. And tonight she had another factor working against her: as the Eternal Cheerleader, she was viewed as out of reach by her former class-mates, especially those guys who'd gained a few pounds and lost some hair since high school.

So, she was glad when Trevor Ward had come over to chat with her, and she'd been a little surprised. He'd never shown interest in her during high school—at least, no more interest than any of the other boys had, which meant that he'd probably lusted after her from afar—and he definitely fell into the "more weight, less hair" category. But while some people's glory years ended when they graduated from high school, other people blossomed later, and it seemed he fell into the latter camp. Despite her physical appearance and near-mystical status as Eternal Cheerleader, he didn't seem intimidated by her. He came off as calm and confident, and best of all, he talked to her as if she was a person instead of a pair of big boobs that happened to be attached to a woman. So what if he'd been a bit of a geek in high school, running around with his two friends investigating ghost stories as if they were Scooby-Doo and the gang? All she cared about was who he was right now: a nice guy who had the balls to talk to her and the intelligence to see beyond her beauty, which put him way ahead of most guys she met.

She was glad that he hadn't asked her to dance right away. A lot of guys would have used slow dancing as an excuse to touch her before getting a chance to know her. But he seemed content to talk, which was fine by her.

"What do you do these days, Trevor?"

He'd already asked her what sort of work she did, and he hadn't batted an eye when she'd told him she was a vet. Most people, women included, acted amazed and more than a little surprised when they learned about her profession, as if it were some sort of miracle that a beautiful woman could also have a brain.

"I'm a writer," he said. "I do nonfiction books and articles dealing with paranormal events and places associated with supernatural activity."

That caught her off guard, but she recovered. "So, you still deal with ghost stories, only now you tell them instead of investigate them."

He grinned. "Something like that."

He didn't seem at all self-conscious about his work, even though he had to know that a lot of people would have cut the conversation short as soon as he said *paranormal* and *supernatural*. Another point in his favor. She found confidence—true confidence, not arrogance or bravado masquerading as confidence—attractive.

She had no special interest in the paranormal or, for that matter, in anything related to spirituality. Her family hadn't been religious, although her mother read the Bible from time to time, and while some people turned to religion after experiencing a tragedy like the early loss of a spouse, or in some cases turned away from religion, she had done neither. After Brad's death, she'd gone on with her life the best she could. If anything, she found the idea of an unseen world of ghosts and psychic phenomena to be morbid and a bit creepy. Not to mention a little too close to her zombie dreams for comfort.

Still, she wanted to be polite, and if she wasn't interested in Trevor's work itself, she *was* interested in getting to know him better, so she said, "What's the scariest thing you ever experienced?"

He kept smiling, but not quite as widely as he had a moment ago. "You don't want to know." He said it as if it was a joke, but there was an undercurrent of seriousness in his voice, and she feared she'd raised a sore subject without meaning to. She decided to change the topic, but before she could do so, she heard a voice whisper close by.

I know what the scariest thing you've ever experienced is, Sherri. And you keep on experiencing it. That's why you hate closing your eyes and drifting off to sleep each night, isn't it? Because you never know which night will be one of those *nights.*

She recognized the voice as Greg's, but when she turned to look, he wasn't anywhere nearby. He was standing over by the DJ, talking to some other people. And even if he had been standing right next to her, how could she have heard him whisper, as loud as the music was? But then, the whisper hadn't been something she'd heard, exactly, not with her ears, anyway. Greg's words had sounded within her mind, as if they were her own thoughts but "spoken" in his voice. Weird.

She glanced in his direction once more, and this time, he was looking at her and grinning. He seemed amused, as if he was enjoying a private joke. And his eyes . . .

She frowned. His eyes were gone, or rather concealed, covered by dark shadowlike smudges. She told herself it was a trick of the light. It had to be! She continued staring at his shadow eyes, felt them pulling at her. She was aware of Trevor calling her name as a wave of dizziness gripped her. She swayed and feared she might fall, but he grabbed hold of her arm and steadied her. The dizziness passed, and she turned to face him.

"Sorry about that. I think the bartender made my drink stronger than I'm used to. I . . ." She trailed off. Trevor had changed. His skin had become a grayish-green color, and his eyes had sunken into the sockets, the irises and pupils clouded over as if by thick cataracts. His mouth hung open, desiccated lips as dry as two strips of leather, his tongue black and swollen. His hair was shaggy, matted, as coarse as straw, and his suit was ripped in numerous places, the fabric dirty and stained with dark patches that looked like dried blood.

Her voice caught in her throat, and she wanted to scream, but no sound came forth. Her almost empty drink slipped from her fingers, and the glass hit the carpet with a solid thump. She backed away from Trevor, shaking her head, as if trying to deny his existence. But he didn't vanish, didn't reassume his normal appearance. Instead, he raised his hands—fingers twisted claws with prominent joints, nails overlong and jagged—let out a gurgling moan, and slid one shuffling foot forward, then the other.

"Fade into You" ended, and the next song began without any patter from the DJ: 10,000 Maniacs' "These Are Days." Trevor moaned louder, the sound a grotesque accompaniment to Natalie Merchant's strong, smooth voice.

He took another step toward her, his leathery lips moving as if he was trying to talk to her, but no recognizable words came out of his mouth, only that sickening, wet moaning, as if he was choking on his own blood.

Sherri couldn't tear her gaze away from his hideous face, and despite the terror that enclosed her heart in a grip of ice, she couldn't flee. All she could do was continue taking tiny steps backward, barely managing to keep out of his reach.

She told herself that this couldn't be happening, that it had to be some kind of delusion, a waking version of her hated zombie dreams. The stress of helping to organize the reunion must have gotten to her, she reasoned. And coupled with the trauma of Sean's and Jerry's deaths, it had dredged up a lot of negative emotions that she'd been suppressing. Trevor wasn't some undead monster coming to kill her. He just seemed that way to her misfiring brain. If she could manage to focus past her fear and concentrate, she should be able to will the delusion away. Trevor would appear normal again, and she could excuse herself and call a cab to take her to the nearest emergency room. But no matter how hard she concentrated, he remained a walking corpse, moaning and reaching for her, staring ahead with milky-white eyes.

"Are you OK, Sherri?"

She felt a hand come down on her shoulder from behind, and she jumped and let out a piercing shriek. She felt stupid, for she recognized the voice as belonging to Julie Weidner, one of her friends who'd been on the cheerleading squad with her back in high school. That feeling was washed away by relief that someone had come to help her, and she turned to face Julie—

—only to find herself looking into a face even more horrifying than Trevor's. Not only because the severity of Julie's condition was worse than his but also because Julie had been a close friend to her once, and seeing her appearance so distorted came as a true shock. Her skin possessed the same grayish-green hue as Trevor's, and her blue dress was in as bad a condition as his clothing. But while his body was intact, hers had numerous injuries. Her flesh was scored with scratches and bite marks, and in some places, large chunks of meat had been torn or bitten away. Worst of all was her face. The skin beneath her milky left eye and down across her upper lip to beneath her chin had been ripped away, revealing muscle that was as dry as old rawhide. Both her upper and lower teeth were exposed on the left side, giving her a grisly, permanent half-grin.

Her hand still lay on Sherri's bare shoulder, the

skin as cold and dry as a lizard's. As Sherri looked into her friend's dead white eyes, Julie tightened her grip, and Sherri felt cracked and broken fingernails dig into her skin.

She found her full voice then and screamed for all she was worth.

As if the scream broke a dam inside her, she was able to move again, and she tore away from Julie and ducked Trevor's grasping hands as he reached for her. She started to run toward the door but stopped short when she saw the faces of the crowd turned toward her, and while Natalie Merchant sang about days of laughter and shafts of light, she saw that everyone in the room was staring at her with eyes of clouded ivory.

And then they all began shuffling toward her, moaning in hunger, hands raised, eager to get a piece of the Eternal Cheerleader.

Amber felt a bit flushed from the wine she'd had, but that was nothing compared with what she felt being in Drew's arms. She knew she shouldn't make more of it than it was—just two old friends sharing a slow dance—but she'd fantasized about being close to him like this since she'd been a girl, and for it to finally happen, well, it was nice to know that dreams did come true sometimes. She told herself not to ruin the moment with expectations about what might happen afterward but just to enjoy it for what it was.

The dance floor had been filled, but when "Fade into You" ended and "These Are Days" started, couples began drifting back to their tables. She expected Drew to release her, but he didn't, and since she didn't want to let go of him, either, the two of them continued swaying, out of time with the music but in sync with each other.

That's when the screaming started.

Amber and Drew stopped dancing, but they didn't separate yet, and both turned to look in the direction of the sound. Sherri Wackler was standing between Trevor and a woman Amber recognized but whose name she couldn't recall, and Sherri looked terrified out of her mind. She kept whipping her head around as she screamed, wild-eyed and frantic, as if she was searching for a way to escape but couldn't find it. Everyone was looking at her, concerned and confused, and the DJ cut the music and asked if there was a doctor present.

"I think that's your cue," Amber said.

She and Drew stepped away from each other and ran over to Sherri.

"I don't know what's wrong," Trevor said when they got there. "We were talking, and suddenly, well, this happened."

Before the three of them could do anything, the other woman—her name was Julie, Amber now remembered—stepped forward and took hold of Sherri's hands. "It's OK, honey. Everything's all right, you're going to be fine. We're going to help—"

Sherri shrieked and hit Julie with a solid right cross to the jaw. She staggered back and might have fallen if Drew hadn't stepped forward to catch her.

Sherri stopped screaming when Drew caught Julie, and her brow furrowed as if she was confused by what he'd done. Trevor took advantage of her distraction to move forward and grab her from behind. He managed to pin her arms to her sides, and while she thrashed back and forth like a wild woman, she wasn't able to break his grip. She tried slamming the back of her head into Trevor's face, but he was ready for that, and he leaned to one side or the other to avoid her blows. She then stomped down on his foot with one of her high heels. He let out an exclamation of pain, but he didn't release her.

Amber hurried over to Drew and took over steadying Julie so he could deal with Sherri. "What's wrong with her?" she asked.

"I think the same thing that happened to Sean and Jerry is also happening to her. She appears to be experiencing some kind of hallucination, one far worse than anything we saw, and if it keeps up, I'm afraid her heart will give out, just as Sean's and Jerry's did."

The sound of slow clapping came from behind them, and Amber turned to see Greg approaching. Sherri still thrashed in Trevor's arms, but everyone else in the room stood and watched as Greg came over to join them.

"You always were so smart, Drew," he said. "But if you were *really* smart, you'd know how to snap Sherri out of her little trance. But that's not the sort of thing they cover in graduate school, is it?"

Drew's eyes narrowed. "You did this to her, didn't you?"

He executed a mocking bow. "Guilty as charged."

"How?" Drew demanded. "Did you spike her drink with some sort of psychotropic drug?"

He laughed. "Nothing so crude! You don't need to use drugs when you have mojo, and I've got some *serious* mojo, my friend."

Although Sherri was no longer screaming, she continued to struggle. Trevor still fought to hold on to her as he turned his attention to Greg. "Are you saying you did this *psychically*?"

His smile held a cold, cruel edge. "You're the paranormal investigator, Trevor. You tell me."

Julie was steady once more, so Amber let go of her and stepped to Drew's side, keeping her gaze fixed on Greg.

"You were there with us the night the Lowry House burned down," she said. "And something happened to you, something that changed you. Gave you powers. You caused the hallucinations we experienced, and you killed Sean and Jerry." She wasn't sure how she was aware of all this, but she knew it was true.

Drew stepped forward, his hands balled into

fists at his sides. She hoped he wouldn't take a swing at Greg. If he possessed the power to kill with his thoughts, what could fists do against him?

"Whatever you're doing to Sherri, stop it now, before she suffers any permanent damage," Drew said.

Greg's tone was one of amusement, but his gaze was devoid of emotion as he spoke. "Why should I? Because it's *wrong* to hurt people? Or maybe because you're asking me as a favor since we used to be such *good* friends in high school? Let me tell you how this is going to play out. Sherri is going to stay trapped in her private little nightmare until her heart explodes, and you and Trevor are going to watch it happen, knowing that there's nothing you can do to stop it. Unless, of course, you manage to think of something clever in the next few minutes."

Trevor's face clouded over with anger, and Amber knew that if he hadn't been restraining Sherri, he'd probably have attacked Greg. From the way Drew's jaw muscles bunched, she knew he felt the same way but was fighting to maintain control of his emotions. Most likely, he feared that any move he might make against Greg would only provoke him into doing something worse. Then she realized something.

"You didn't say anything about me."

Greg turned to her, still smiling. "That's because you're not going to be staying. It's getting a bit stuffy in here, and I thought you might like to come with me and get a little fresh air."

He gestured, and she found herself walking toward him. She didn't want to, but while she tried to stop herself, her body moved of its own accord until she was standing next to him.

Drew took a step forward, but Greg held up a warning finger and waggled it from side to side.

"I wouldn't do that if I were you—not unless you want Amber to die of a brain aneurysm before you can take another step."

Drew stopped and glared at Greg, then looked at her, his gaze softening, and she saw the frustration mingled with regret in his eyes. She wanted to tell him that it was OK, that she'd be all right, but she couldn't speak. Greg slipped an arm around her waist, and despite his control over her body, she shuddered at his touch. If he noticed or cared, he didn't remark on it.

Sherri's exertions had become less energetic, and she was struggling to breathe.

"We have to do something!" Trevor said. "I don't think she can last much longer!"

"Well, this has been fun," Greg said, "but Amber and I should be going. And since I want to end the evening on a high note . . ." He gestured, and everyone else in the hall began screaming. Some clapped their hands to their heads, while others ran around or attacked those standing closest to them.

Greg surveyed the chaos he'd created with satisfaction. He then turned back to Drew and Trevor, and although he didn't raise his voice, somehow he had no trouble being heard over the terrified screams that filled the hall.

"You might find a way to break Sherri's trance before her heart gives out, but good luck saving everyone else." His lips drew away from his teeth in an expression that bore only the faintest resemblance to a smile. "Come along, Amber."

He started walking toward the door, his arm still curled around her waist, and she went with him, her body moving as if she were a puppet and he the puppeteer. The screams of the reunion attendees followed them as they left the hall, and she wanted to glance back at Drew one more time, but her body refused to cooperate.

She felt something warm and wet sliding down her cheeks and realized she was crying.

FIFTEEN

Drew and Trevor stood in the midst of madness. Their former classmates, as well as the DJ, were lost in whatever nightmarish scenarios were playing out within their minds, transforming the hotel ballroom into a bedlam. People stood shrieking at the tops of their lungs, while others punched, kicked, and bit anyone who came too near. Still others pounded their heads against the floor, walls, or tables, as if attempting to drive out the horrible images that had invaded their heads. Some just sat or lay on the floor, weeping, and Drew found their despair heartbreaking.

Members of the hotel staff arrived, undoubtedly drawn by the racket, but instead of entering, they stood in the doorway, gaping in shock. He understood their reaction. None of them was trained to deal with a crisis of this magnitude, and they had no idea how to react or what was expected of them. Soon one of them would think to call 911, and police and EMTs would arrive—but not in time to help. He didn't know how long it would take for the terror generated by the hal-

lucinations to cause cardiac arrest—he assumed
that the time would vary somewhat from one
individual to another—but he doubted that he
and Trevor had more than a couple of minutes
before people started dropping dead around
them. They couldn't afford to wait for the EMTs
to get there.

"What can we do?" Trevor had to shout to be
heard over the noise of the crowd.

While Drew specialized in working with
patients who'd suffered severe trauma, he had
no experience in helping people who were in the
process of being traumatized, let alone people
who were in the grip of some sort of psychically generated illusions. Hell, he could barely
bring himself to believe such a thing was possible. But if he was going to have any chance of
saving these people's lives, he had to put aside
his doubts.

And as difficult as it was, he also had to put
aside his concern for Amber. It had taken every
ounce of willpower he had not to interfere as
Greg left with her, and he'd only been able to do
it because he'd feared that Greg would make good
on his threat to use his abilities to hurt her. He told
himself that she was safe, that if Greg had wanted
to harm her, he'd have done so already, and he'd
have done it in front of Drew and Trevor. But just
because Greg hadn't harmed her physically didn't
mean he didn't intend to hurt her in other ways,

and with his abilities, he could put her through the tortures of the damned simply by manipulating her mind. And if, as it had appeared, Greg was also able to control her body, there were other things he could do to her or force her to do against her will. Bad things . . .

Stop it! he told himself. This was what Greg wanted, to keep him confused and distracted while people died around him. And he refused to let that happen.

"We need to shock them somehow," he shouted to Trevor. "Jolt them out of their hallucinatory state."

"What, you mean, like, slap them or something? No way we could smack all of them in time. We could turn the music back on and crank it all the way up."

He shook his head. "We need a sudden, strong jolt, and it needs to be something that will affect everyone at once." A thought came to him. "Didn't you say you quit smoking recently?"

"A couple weeks ago, why?"

If Trevor was like most people trying to quit . . . "You still carry your lighter?"

Trevor frowned. "Yeah, but I don't use it."

He felt a flicker of hope. "Get it out!" Without waiting for Trevor to respond, he rushed to the cash bar and grabbed the first bottle of booze he could get his hands on, Bacardi, as it turned out. As he headed back to Trevor, a man came at him—

someone he didn't recognize from high school, and he wondered if it was someone's spouse—eyes wide with terror, teeth bared, hands outstretched as if he intended to fasten them around his neck. Before he could reach him, Trevor rushed forward, slammed into his side, and sent him sprawling. The man fell, then sprang to his feet, but instead of renewing his attack, his expression went slack, and the front of his pants darkened as his bladder emptied.

Drew forced himself to look away, and he ran to the nearest table and splashed Bacardi onto the tablecloth. "Light it up!" he told Trevor.

"Are you nuts? That—" Trevor broke off, grinning. "That's brilliant!"

He flicked on his lighter and touched the flame to a sodden patch of cloth. It caught fire at once, and the flames spread. He didn't stand and watch; he ran to another table, splashed alcohol onto it, then moved on to the next. Trevor followed, igniting tablecloths as they went.

He feared that some of the people might end up stumbling into one of the fires in their delusionary state, but with any luck . . .

The heat and smoke from the table fires activated the room's sprinkler system. Streams of freezing cold water jetted down from the ceiling, dousing the flames and, more important, soaking everyone in the room, Trevor and him included.

As if a psychic switch had been thrown somewhere, the screaming cut off, and everyone stopped moving. They stood, sat, or lay motionless for several moments while water rained down on them, and then they began to look around in confusion. Drew wasn't certain, but at a quick glance, it appeared that everyone was still alive. He saw Sherri Wackler over in one corner, looking as dazed as everyone else but otherwise unharmed.

Trevor laughed and clapped him on the back. "Hot damn! We did it!"

He smiled. "Looks that way." He turned to Trevor and pointed at the lighter still gripped in his friend's hand. "Good thing old habits die hard."

Trevor laughed again. "Guess so."

But the triumph of the moment faded, and he took hold of Trevor's arm and started pulling him toward the door. "C'mon, we need to get out of here before the police arrive."

"We're going to go get Amber, aren't we?" Trevor said.

He nodded. "And I think I know where Greg's taken her."

Still shivering and soaked from the sprinklers, they got into Trevor's Prius and were backing out of its parking space as the emergency crews arrived. The police and EMTs parked in front of the hotel's main entrance, while Drew and Trevor pulled out onto the street unnoticed.

"At least this time, the EMTs won't find any dead bodies waiting for them," Drew said.

"I'm just glad we got out of there before the cops showed up," Trevor said. "They'd want to question us for sure, and who knows how long it would be before they released us? The sooner we get to Amber, the better." He turned the heater on full blast.

"Head for the Lowry House," Drew said. "That's where Greg will take her."

Trevor stepped on the gas, and they zoomed down the suburban streets at highway speeds.

"You do remember the house burned down a decade and a half ago, right?"

"The physical building doesn't matter so much as the symbolism of it," Drew insisted. "Greg fed us hallucinations of the Lowry House—or at least its location—at different times in its history. For whatever reason, that place is important to him, and that's where he wants us to go."

Ash Creek wasn't all that large, but the rec center was on the other side of town from the hotel, and even as fast as Trevor was driving, Drew knew it would take several minutes for them to get there. He knew that Amber would have no way of knowing it, but he mentally urged her to hang on, they were coming as fast as they could.

"Are you sure that's where he'll take her?" Trevor asked. Despite his words, he turned left on the next street and started heading in the direction of the rec center. "And even if that is where he's gone, if he has the ability to manipulate people's minds, he could make it so that we couldn't see him even if we were looking straight at him. Hell, he could be sitting with Amber in the backseat, and we might never know it."

"I thought of that," Drew said, resisting the urge to turn around and check the back. "But if Greg wanted to hide from us, why would he have manipulated her into convincing us to come to the reunion in the first place, and why would he toy with us the way he has? Sending hallucinations, killing two men in front of us, attempting to kill an entire roomful of people and challenging us to save them. He chose to reveal himself to us and let us see the kind of power he wields. It's all part of an elaborate game he's playing. It's why he took Amber. Well, one of the reasons," he amended. "He wants us to chase him, as if he's a child playing a game of keep-away."

"But why?" Trevor asked. "What could he want with us?"

He shrugged. "Payback, maybe. We may have let him hang out with us in high school, but we never accepted him as a friend, at least not a close one."

"And he had a thing for Amber," Trevor added, "which means he's jealous of the two of you."

"There is no two of us," Drew said. "We're

just . . ." He trailed off when Trevor gave him a look. "All right. Maybe he *is* jealous. But the most important reason is likely something we don't remember. He was with us that night in the Lowry House, and something happened to him, something that he blames us for." He turned to look at Trevor. "The paranormal is your realm of expertise. Where do you think he got his powers from?"

Trevor thought for a moment before answering. "I suppose it's possible that he's been possessed."

"You mean by a demon?" He couldn't believe he was suggesting such a thing, but then, before this weekend, he hadn't believed in psychic abilities, either, and he'd come to accept that Greg had them. He wondered how many more impossible things he'd come to believe before the night was over.

Assuming he lived that long.

"Maybe not by a demon per se," Trevor said. "If a place can become a repository of negative psychic energy, why not a person?"

"You think Greg was . . . what? Infected by the evil of the Lowry House?"

"Something like that. But the amount of power he wields, I've never heard of anything like it. I've interviewed people who claimed they could read people's minds or move small objects telekinetically, though most of them were never able to do so in my presence, and those who could, well, I was never able to prove beyond a doubt that they were the real deal. But what Greg can do is light-years beyond anything I've ever read about, let alone seen."

They fell into silence for a time after that, and Drew gazed out the window as they drove. It was full night now, and although streetlights were illuminated and porch lights glowed, they did little to dispel the surrounding darkness. He found himself thinking that in a sense, humanity hadn't come all that far since its primitive beginnings, when people huddled close together in their shelters, fires burning to ward off the dangers lurking somewhere in the shadows. Before tonight, he would have said that those lights, while practical safety precautions, served primarily as psychological comforts. But he had a different perspective now, for he had a better idea of what truly dwelled in the darkness, and he knew that whatever else happened this night, he would never again look at the world in the same way.

He was pulled out of his thoughts as Trevor turned another corner. He recognized the neighborhood and knew it would be only a few more minutes until they reached the rec center.

Evidently, Trevor was thinking along the same lines. "At first, I was all for rushing off like the cavalry to save Amber—and don't get me wrong, I don't want to turn back—but now that I've had

time to think, I'm wondering if we're ready to face
Greg on our own. I mean, neither of us is an action
hero. We don't have guns, and we're hardly masters
of hand-to-hand combat. Maybe we should call
the police and tell them Greg kidnapped Amber.
I mean, we have to do everything we can to help
her, right? What if the two of us aren't enough to
get the job done?"

Trevor sounded scared, and Drew didn't blame
him. He was scared, too.

"Greg wants us to come to him, so he's not going
to kill us—at least, not until he's gotten whatever it
is he wants from us. But if anyone else shows up,
there's a good chance he'll kill them on the spot.
So even if we could convince the police that he's
kidnapped Amber and taken her to the rec center,
they wouldn't be able to deal with him, guns or no
guns. All we'd be doing is sending them to their
deaths. And we can't do that."

Trevor sighed. "No, I suppose we can't. Too bad.
I'd feel a whole lot better about this if we had a
SWAT team or a squad of Navy SEALs accompa-
nying us."

Despite the seriousness of the situation, Drew
couldn't help smiling. "I guess the two of us will
have to do, you armed with your knowledge of the
paranormal and your rapier wit, me with my psychological training and penetrating insight."

Trevor moaned. "Oh, man, we are *screwed*!"

The car's interior had gotten quite warm while

they drove, but the heat hadn't done much to dry their clothes. Instead, Drew felt wet and hot, and the sensation was far from comfortable. He reached out and turned down the heat. Trevor glanced at him but didn't say anything.

Trevor continued driving in silence after that, and Drew mentally reviewed what they'd learned earlier about cleansing rituals. That knowledge might be the only real weapon they had to use against Greg, assuming that it still applied.

The rituals they'd read about on various paranormal-centered Web sites or from e-mail queries and live chat sessions with Trevor's somewhat dubious contacts had only addressed cleansing "Bad Places." They'd said nothing about cleansing bad *people*. Still, it was all that they had, and maybe the knowledge could be adapted to their situation. The rituals, while having some features in common, could be divided into three basic types: magical, religious, and what Drew thought of as psychic-spiritual. Magical cleansings depended on arcane rituals and evocations of ancient spiritual entities. Certain physical items were required, too, such as chalk for drawing mystical symbols, candles and incense, musical instruments such as bells, and the like. Religious cleansings were also very ritualized, but they relied on spoken prayers addressed to a specific deity. Psychic-spiritual cleansings were less structured and depended more on countering a negative spiritual force with positive psychic energy in order to nullify it or at the very least drive it away from the location it had attached itself to. Meditation and visualization played primary roles in this type of cleansing.

Before the banquet, the three of them had debated the merits and drawbacks of each approach. They'd decided against the magical approach because there were too many rituals to choose from, and all required materials they couldn't easily get their hands on. They'd decided against a religious approach for similar reasons. While they all had their own spiritual beliefs, none of them was a strong adherent to a particular religious tradition, so which ritual would they choose? And without deep, sincere faith backing it up, how would a religious ritual stand any chance of success? In the end, they'd decided to go with the psychic-spiritual approach for practical reasons. While the rituals were less tied to magical or godlike forces, at its core, the basic approach was the same as the magical or religious variety: marshaling positive psychic-spiritual energy to counter negative energy and nullify it or at least drive it out of a location. The plan was for the three of them to return to the location of the Lowry House, find a way into the rec center, confront whatever force inhabited it, set their combined will against it, and, if possible, cast it out.

At least, that *had* been the plan, until Greg had stepped in and abducted Amber.

Then again, Drew thought, this development could work in their favor. It seemed clear that Greg was somehow linked to the negative energy that infested the Lowry property. Greg was a person. He could be talked to, reasoned with . . . True, he'd struck Drew as a sociopath, and his actions up to this point didn't belie that impression, but what if he had been acting under the influence of the darkness that had taken up residence inside him? If they could reach the person hidden beneath that darkness, maybe he could help them counter the negative energy that had soaked into the Lowry property over the long years like toxic spiritual radiation.

A lot of ifs there, Drew thought. Still, they had no choice but to play the hand they were dealt and hope for the best.

Trevor had been silent for the last few moments, but then he said, "This would be easier if we had our memories back. That way, we might have a better idea of what we're going to be up against."

"I don't know," Drew said. "Maybe it's better we don't remember. If we did, maybe we'd be too damned scared to go inside."

"That's a cheery thought," Trevor muttered. "Do me a favor: don't ever try to get a job writing greeting cards."

He was about to reply when they turned onto the street where the rec center was located. A Lexus was parked on the street in front of the center, and Trevor pulled up behind it.

"That must be Greg's car," Drew said.

"Of course it is. The villain always has a sweet ride, doesn't he?" Trevor put his Prius in park, turned off the engine, and removed the keys from the ignition. "There's a flashlight in the glovebox."

He got it and opened the passenger-side door. Before he climbed out, Trevor said, "Don't close it all the way. We want to make as little noise as possible."

Once outside, Drew stood and looked at the rec center, but there was nothing much to see, just a dark shape sitting on the spot where the Lowry House had once stood. If Greg and Amber were inside, there was no sign. No lights burning in any of the windows, and no neon sign over the entrance proclaiming "Heroes Enter Here."

Trevor headed toward the rear of the car, and he followed. He didn't turn on the flashlight yet, but he figured that was likely an unnecessary precaution. As powerful as Greg was, he had probably already sensed their arrival. Still, no point in making things any easier for him, was there?

Trevor thumbed a button on the car remote, and the trunk popped open. He reached inside and pulled out a tire iron.

"What's that for?" Drew asked. He spoke in a near whisper, and Trevor answered him the same way.

"Whatever else he's become, Greg's still a man, isn't he? That means he's got a skull to bash in, and since I don't have any automatic weapons stashed in the trunk, this is better than going in unarmed."

Trevor didn't close the trunk, not wanting to make any noise, and he pocketed his keys without thumbing the remote to lock the car, presumably for the same reason.

"Ready?" Trevor said.

Drew nodded, and the two of them started across the lawn toward the rec center. As they approached the quiet, dark building, he couldn't help thinking of the old poem that started with the line "'Will you walk into my parlor?' said the Spider to the Fly."

He hoped things would turn out differently for them from how they had for the fly. But as they drew near the rec center's entrance and saw that the front doors were open wide, as if the building had been waiting for them, he felt his hope fade.

Beyond the open doorway was a solid wall of darkness, and there was no way to see what might be lying in wait for them there. Despite his earlier reluctance to turn on the flashlight, Drew saw no help for it now. He flicked the switch, and a feeble beam of light emerged that did little to push back the shadows within the building. In some ways, the ineffectiveness of the light made the darkness that remained seem all the thicker and more impenetrable.

Drew and Trevor exchanged a last look, and then together they entered the building.

SIXTEEN

Since the rec center wasn't open to the public yet, Trevor expected the interior to be unfurnished. Floor tiles not in place, electrical wires exposed, plaster walls unpainted . . . But as Drew played the flashlight's meager beam back and forth, they saw that everything was finished, floor, wall, ceiling all complete, surfaces painted, tiles in place. And the air, while a bit stuffy, held the smells of new construction: freshly cut wood, untarnished metal, and the chemical tang of recently applied paint. They stood in the reception area, a counter to their left, men's and women's restrooms to the right. The space behind the counter was empty, though. No desks or chairs, no computers or office equipment of any kind. From the state of the reception area, Trevor assumed that the rest of the building—gym, track, exercise rooms—would be completed last, as they would only be needed when the place was open and ready for business. After that, all that would be necessary was for the office equipment to be delivered and set up, and the good people of Ash Creek would be able to enjoy the newest indoor playground their town had to offer.

Assuming, of course, that what the two of them were looking at was real. Greg had already demonstrated the ability to enter their minds and make them experience realistic hallucinations. What if he was doing so now? Maybe the two of them weren't really here at all but rather back at the hotel, only believing they'd left and driven to the rec center. For that matter, maybe they hadn't come to the reunion in the first place. Maybe the three of them were still at home, lying unconscious in their beds and only dreaming they'd returned to Ash Creek. And who said that Drew and Amber were really here at all? Maybe Greg had made Trevor only *think* they were, when in truth, he was the only one caught in Greg's psychic trap, and Greg was using the illusion of his two friends to torment him further.

Trevor felt panic beginning to well up inside him. If he *was* alone, what could he do against a being with Greg's power? Without his friends— without Drew's intelligence and Amber's heart— he wouldn't stand a chance against Greg. He was just a man with strong curiosity about the paranormal, and the last time he'd checked, that didn't count as a superpower. What could he do? Pester Greg with questions and annoy him to death?

Stop it! he told himself. Indulging in an existential crisis right now wasn't going to help anyone. Yes, Greg could use his abilities to make them believe whatever he wanted, and that meant they couldn't trust their eyes and ears, at least not completely. But they had work to do, and instead of standing around wondering what was real and what wasn't, they should get down to it. Besides, he had his tire iron, right? He gripped the makeshift weapon tighter, and while he knew that it probably wouldn't do any good against Greg, the solid feel of metal in his hand was reassuring nevertheless.

He looked at Drew, who nodded, and they started walking forward, moving past the reception counter and into the center's main hallway. They did their best to walk quietly, but their footfalls echoed in the still, stale air, sounding as loud as gunshots to his ears. There was no way Greg didn't know they were coming, but what else could they do? Run down the hallway as fast as they could, shouting at the top of their lungs for Greg to come out and face them?

He leaned closer to Drew and whispered, "Here we are, back inside the Lowry House after fifteen years, on our way to confront an evil force, and I still don't remember anything more about that night than I did before we entered. Too bad. If we did, maybe we'd gain some insight into how to deal with Greg."

They came to a place where the hallway

branched off to either side and stopped. Before they could discuss which way to go, a figure emerged from the shadows on their left and stepped toward them. Trevor raised his tire iron and started to swing it at the figure, but Drew reached out and caught him by the wrist before he could strike a blow. Drew then shone the flashlight onto the figure's face, and he was horrified to see that he'd almost smashed his tire iron into the side of Amber's head.

Her expression was blank, her eyes as empty as a doll's. But then she blinked several times, her eyes focused on them, and she frowned.

"Trevor? Drew?" she said. Her tone was soft, her words slurred, as if she'd just woken from sleep. "What are you doing here?"

"Coming to your rescue," Drew said. "At least, that's what we thought."

"A couple of knights in tarnished armor," Trevor added. "That's us."

"Are you all right?" Drew asked. He moved the flashlight beam up and down Amber's body, checking her for injuries, but there was none—at least, none obvious to the naked eye. He touched a pair of fingers to the side of her neck to check her pulse.

She smiled and removed Drew's hand from her neck.

"I'm fine," she said, sounding more awake this time. "Greg didn't hurt me." She paused. "At least,

I don't think he did. He sent me to meet you. He's waiting in the gym for us."

Trevor and Drew exchanged a look before turning their attention back to her.

"Is he planning on challenging us to a game of hoops?" Trevor asked.

"I don't know what he wants," she said. "I just know we're supposed to go into the gym." She frowned. "Actually, that's *all* I know, and I'm not sure how I know it. The last thing I remember is everyone going crazy at the dance, and then I was standing here in the hallway, talking to you two. What happened back at the hotel? Is everyone . . ." She trailed off, probably because she didn't want to add the word *dead* to her question.

"They're OK," Trevor said. "Drew figured out a way to break Greg's hold over them."

She smiled in relief. "Good. So . . . are we going to do what he wants and go into the gym? I mean, it's some kind of trap, right?"

Trevor wasn't sure how to react to her. It would be horrible to be someone's puppet, and if she truly had no memory of Greg controlling her, he was glad. But just because she appeared to be OK didn't mean that Greg had released her from his control. He could still be pulling her strings, using her to draw them into his trap. Even worse, if he was still in the driver's seat of Amber's psyche, he could use her as a weapon against them whenever he wanted. Evidently,

Drew was thinking along the same lines, because even though the two of them had acted like a couple on the dance floor back at the hotel, he made no move to touch her now. Instead of offering reassurance, he was holding back, and Trevor knew that he'd only do that if he wasn't certain they could trust Amber. It might not even be her talking to them but rather Greg speaking through her. How could they know?

When neither Drew nor Trevor responded to Amber's question right away, she scowled. "What's wrong with you two? Why are you—" She broke off as comprehension dawned on her face. "You think Greg might still be controlling me."

"Please don't take it personally," Drew said, "but we—"

That's as far as he got before she leaned forward and pressed her lips against his. He stood there at first, as if he was unsure how to respond, but then she put her arms around his neck, his arms slid up around her waist, and their kiss deepened. After several moments, she stepped back, gazed into Drew's eyes, and smiled.

"Well?" she asked.

He smiled back. "OK, I believe you're you."

When she turned to look at Trevor, he said, "I'm still not convinced. Maybe you should kiss me, too."

Instead, she punched him on the arm—hard.

"*Ouch,*" he said, rubbing the sore spot on his arm. "*Now* I'm convinced."

"Trap or not," Drew said, "we came here to confront Greg, and that's what we're going to do. Let's find the gym."

Amber pointed down the hallway. "It's this way. I think."

The three friends headed in the direction she indicated. Drew shone the flashlight ahead of them, Trevor continued to grip his tire iron—which he felt foolish for carrying into battle against a man who commanded dark psychic forces—and Amber walked between them, holding on to Drew's arm. Regardless of how the night played out, Trevor was glad that his two friends had admitted their feelings for each other. At least they wouldn't go to their graves not knowing how they felt.

Greg's voice whispered in his mind then, and he sounded amused. *What a morbid thought. I approve.*

"Fuck off," Trevor muttered. "I have an automotive tool, and I'm not afraid to use it."

When his friends looked at him, Trevor realized he'd spoken aloud.

"Sorry. Greg just sent me a message on his private psychic hotline."

"He wants to remind us how powerful he is," Drew said. "Let us know that no matter what we do, he's the one in charge."

"Really? And here I thought he was just being an asshole."

Greg's thought-voice returned then, and he sounded even more amused this time. *Go ahead and make all the jokes you want, but you can't hide how you really feel from me. I know how scared you are. But you know something? You're nowhere near as scared as you should be.*

Trevor didn't have any smart-ass comebacks for that, so he kept his mouth shut as they continued walking down the dark hallway of the rec center, toward whatever horror Greg had planned for them.

As they drew closer to the gym, Trevor said, "What's the plan? We waltz into the gym and say, 'Hey, Greg, how's it hanging?' We came here to rescue Amber, and here she is, safe and sound. Maybe we should get her out of here while we can. You said it yourself, Drew. He's playing a game with us, but that doesn't mean he intends to play fair." Trevor fixed Amber with a penetrating look.

She frowned. "What are you trying to say, Trevor?"

Drew had a good idea of the direction in which Trevor's thoughts were running. "Greg didn't need to send you out to escort us," he said. "We would've eventually checked out the gym on our own. I think Trevor's concerned that he had another reason for having you meet us." He glanced at Trevor, who nodded without taking his eyes off Amber.

"Maybe Greg's not controlling you right now," Trevor said, "but that doesn't mean he can't take control of you again whenever he wants. He could wait until our guard is down and then use you to attack us."

Drew understood where his friend's paranoia was coming from. Greg's psychic taunting had frightened him and put him off balance.

"If he can control me, he can control either of you," Amber pointed out.

Trevor looked startled, as if he hadn't thought of that. But then he went on. "Or maybe he implanted some kind of posthypnotic suggestion inside you, one that'll make you turn against us without knowing you're doing it." He turned to Drew. "It's possible, isn't it? Especially with the sort of power he wields."

"I have no idea how his powers work," Drew admitted. "None of us does. But I think it's safe to assume he's capable of manipulating our minds on various levels."

Amber started to protest, but Drew reached out and squeezed her hand to reassure her.

"But I don't think he intends to use you against us. I may not understand how psychic abilities work, but I understand enough about Greg to know that whatever moves he makes, they won't be obvious ones. He wants to impress us with how clever he is, so whatever we anticipate him doing, you can bet he'll do something else."

"Especially if he's reading our minds," Amber added. "If he is, then he knows what we're thinking and can adjust his plans."

"Great," Trevor said. "So, not only are we facing someone who can create realistic illusions in our minds—so realistic they can make people's hearts stop—we're up against someone who knows our every thought. How do we stand a chance in hell of beating someone like that?"

Amber smiled. "By not thinking too much, I guess."

Drew reached out and laid a hand on Trevor's shoulder. "And by sticking together," he added.

Trevor looked at both of his friends, sighed, and nodded. "All right. Let's go kick Greg's supernatural ass."

Amber continued leading the way through the rec center's corridors to the gym. Despite the fact that she'd never been there before, or at least had no memory of being there, she knew the way. Probably because Greg wanted her to know. Not that they needed his help to find it. There were no signs up yet to tell people where to go, but it wasn't as if a gym was easy to conceal. Down one more corridor, hang a right, and there they were.

When the three of them had been reunited a few minutes earlier, Drew had asked if she was all right, and she'd said yes. While not a lie, it wasn't the entire truth. She hadn't lied when she'd said she had no memory of Greg taking control of her body and abducting her, but now that she knew what he'd done, she was struggling not to freak out. She had no way to know what, if anything, he had done with her—or, worse, *to* her—while she'd been under his control, but the knowledge that he could have done anything he wanted and she'd have been powerless to stop him horrified her. She felt violated in ways she could never have imagined, in both body *and* mind, and it took all of her strength to keep her emotions at bay so she could do what she had to. Greg had to be stopped before he hurt anyone else, and that's what she'd focus on for now. And then, assuming that she survived, she could deal with what he'd done to her later.

As they approached the gym doors, she glanced at the tire iron that Trevor held in his hand.

"I don't suppose you've got an extra one of those that I can borrow," she said.

"Sorry," he said. "This is it. You're welcome to it, though."

She considered taking the makeshift weapon, if for no other reason than for the reassurance the weight of it in her hand would bring. But even after what Greg had done to her, she didn't think she'd be able to use it when the time came.

She shook her head. "Thanks, but on second thought, I'm good."

The gym doors were light yellow wood with small rectangular windows set into them and chrome metal bars instead of handles or knobs. Drew put his hand on one of the bars, but he didn't push right away. Instead, he turned to look at Trevor and her.

"Remember that Greg can make us see and hear whatever he wants, and while his illusions may not have any physical substance, we know they can kill if someone believes they can."

"And it might be even worse than that," Trevor said. "We don't know the extent of his powers. Don't forget, both Sean's and Jerry's bodies had some very nonillusory physical residue on them."

Amber felt a chill upon hearing Trevor's words, but she forced a wry smile and feinted another punch to his arm. "Don't be such a pessimist," she said.

Trevor made a show of rubbing his arm as if her punch had connected, but he smiled.

Drew took a deep breath and let it out. "Ready?" he asked.

Amber and Trevor nodded. Drew pushed the gym door open, and the three of them stepped inside, Amber reaching for Drew's hand as they entered.

At first, the beam from Drew's flashlight cut through the darkness, illuminating a polished wooden floor. But then the light cut out, and she felt a sudden wave of dizziness overtake her. Her legs weakened, and she thought she might collapse to the floor. She tightened her grip on Drew's hand for support—or at least, she tried to. She'd been holding his hand when the flashlight cut out, and she hadn't let go, but she couldn't feel him now.

Panic welled within her, and she cried out Drew's name. Once, twice, three times, but he didn't answer. Panic threatened to overwhelm her, but she told herself that despite appearances, she wasn't alone. Drew and Trevor were still there, and even though she couldn't feel it, she was still holding on to Drew's hand. Greg had used his powers to make it seem as if she was isolated in some dark limbo, and for all she knew, Drew and Trevor were experiencing the same thing. But they were still together, still in the gym.

Greg's voice whispered in her mind. *Still in the gym? Don't bet on it.*

The darkness eased up a bit, the stuffy air in the gym grew cooler, and Amber felt a gentle breeze kiss her skin. Small pinpricks of blue-white light appeared above her, and while she first thought that they were on the ceiling of the gym, she sensed that they were much farther away than that, and that's when she realized that she was looking up at the stars in a night sky.

The flashlight beam came back on, and she saw Drew and Trevor once again, both of them standing close to her. Except that it *wasn't* them, not exactly. They were younger and thinner, and although she could scarcely believe it, she realized that they were teenagers again. Drew wore a blue windbreaker and jeans and carried a backpack and a flashlight, a different one from the one he'd had a moment ago. It wasn't quite as powerful, and its beam did little to push back the darkness. Trevor's hair was shaggier, and he wore a black suede jacket he thought made him look cool. *How could I have forgotten that stupid jacket?* she thought. Trevor had worn it all the time, even when it was warm out, taking it off only during the hottest part of the summer.

She looked down at herself and saw that she wore an oversize red Ohio State sweatshirt instead of a coat. *It's my dad's,* she remembered. She'd borrowed it so often from him while she'd been in high school that he gave up pretending it was his and let her keep it. She reached up to touch her hair and found that it was long. She'd worn it that way when she was a teenager, nearly down to her waist. She'd started wearing it short in her early twenties because she'd grown tired of taking care of it. She hadn't realized how much she'd missed having long hair until now.

This was how they'd looked in the picture on Drew's laptop, the one he'd shown her and Trevor yesterday. Their clothing and her hair had meant nothing special to her then, hadn't sparked any memories. But she remembered these details now, so strongly it was as if she'd never forgotten them.

The three of them stood on the front lawn of the Lowry House. The house, miraculously restored, loomed before them like a hulking black mass, blotting out a portion of the night sky. Off to the side sat a smaller dark shape, which she knew was an old, lopsided barn on the verge of collapse.

"This is the night, isn't it?" Amber asked. Her voice sounded different to her, younger and lighter somehow, more filled with energy.

She didn't have to say which night she meant. Drew and Trevor knew.

"I believe so," Drew said. His voice, while also more youthful, still retained the mature confidence of adulthood. "But we're not really here. It's another hallucination."

"I don't know," Trevor said. His teen voice was higher-pitched than Drew's, and she remembered that it had taken a while for his voice to deepen, something some of the other kids in school had teased him about. "This feels different somehow."

"That's because we *are* here," she said. "Kind of, anyway. This isn't just a hallucination. We're inside our memories of that night." Amber wasn't sure how she knew this, but she sensed it was true.

Neither Drew nor Trevor questioned her knowledge, perhaps because they sensed the same thing.

Or maybe, she realized, because they trusted her feelings.

"But we're also still adults, still standing in the gym," Trevor said. "It's like we're two places at once, isn't it?"

"Does that mean you're still holding the tire iron?" she asked.

Trevor frowned. In his left hand, he held a camera, but his right, the hand in which he'd been holding the tire iron, was empty. He held up his right hand, looked at it, and wiggled his fingers.

"Doesn't feel like it," he said. He lowered his hand to his side. "I suppose there's no way to know for sure. Greg could've made me drop it without my knowing."

"We need to proceed carefully, as if what we're experiencing is real, even if it's not," Drew said. "Reality, unreality, they're just different sides of the same coin for us right now."

"Thanks for the cryptic advice," Trevor said in that too-high voice of his that made her want to giggle. "Maybe you should think about giving up psychology and get a job writing sayings for fortune cookies."

Drew gave Trevor a look that said he wasn't as funny as he thought he was.

Trevor went on. "So, what are we supposed to do? Reenact what we did back then?"

"That would seem to be the logical course,"

Drew said. "Do either of you remember what we did first?"

"No," Amber said. "But if I had to guess, I bet we decided to walk around the outside of the property before going in to get a feel for the place."

"Right," Trevor said, sounding excited. "And I would've wanted to watch the windows to see if we'd witness any figures moving inside and maybe get some pictures."

Drew nodded. "And I'd have kept the flashlight turned off so no one would see us snooping around and call the police." As he said this, he turned off the flashlight, and the three friends began making their way across the property. They circled around the west side of the house, staying about fifty feet or so from it, the dilapidated barn off to their left.

It was so strange seeing the Lowry House reborn like this, although Amber couldn't make out many details of the structure, as dark as it was. What was even stranger was that with every step they took, she experienced an eerie sense of déjà vu. Not memories, precisely, but a strong sense that she'd been there before, done these things before, and she suspected it was the same for Drew and Trevor.

The dark, the stars above, the cool breeze, the soft whisper of grass beneath their feet as they walked all seemed so familiar. While she knew that they inhabited a mental landscape created by their former friend, who was in the grip of dark forces they didn't understand, a friend who'd killed two people and had attempted to kill dozens more, in a strange way, she couldn't help feeling excited to be there.

As they walked, they kept an eye on the house, but it remained dark and still. Despite his earlier words, Trevor didn't take any pictures. She supposed there was no real reason for him to do so. After all, they weren't investigating the actual Lowry House; there were no ghosts hiding inside the building. She supposed that the house itself and its grounds were ghosts of a sort but not the kind you took pictures of, not the kind that provided evidence of life after death. Besides, the camera itself wasn't real, so what would be the point in using it?

Trying to make logical sense of their situation was making her head hurt, and she understood the wisdom of Drew's advice to take everything as both real and not real. Best not to think about it too much and get on with what they had to do.

She reached for Drew's hand and clasped it, and he turned and gave her a smile that, considering how dark it was, she sensed more than saw. If they were going to die tonight, at least she'd admitted her feelings for him, and he'd returned them. And while that gave her even more reason to live, she wouldn't die not knowing if he cared for her as more than a friend, and that was something.

They'd still seen nothing as they circled around

to the rear of the Lowry House. No hint of movement from within the building, no glimmer of light shining in any of the windows, as it had been on that night so many years ago.

"I understand there's an art to the building of suspense," Trevor said, "but this is really starting to drag on. I wish Greg would do something and get it over with."

Greg's voice seemed to echo from the air around them: *Careful what you wish for.*

SEVENTEEN

A fresh wave of vertigo gripped Amber, this one so strong that she feared she'd fall to the ground for sure. But it passed, and when it did, she saw that their surroundings had changed. The house and barn were gone, and more trees covered the grounds. The three friends stood in a clearing in the midst of a dozen dome structures made of bark, mud, and thatch. The air, which had been so silent a moment ago, was now filled with the sounds of struggle, the harsh crack of gunfire, people shouting, screaming, sobbing, and in some cases laughing. There were no other people visible, but the noises made it sound as if they were surrounded by bloody mayhem. It was awful to hear the clamor of people suffering and dying and not be able to see them, not be able to help them.

Drew turned to her and spoke loudly enough to be heard over the din. "This is the setting of the dream you had, isn't it? The massacre of Native Americans by British hunters."

She nodded. "I didn't see outside, though. I was inside one of the homes."

A crazy thought passed through her mind then. If she were to go from home to home and peek inside, would she discover herself within one, her mind inhabiting Little Eyes' body? And would Greg be in there, too, masquerading as one of the hunters? Should they search for him here and try to confront him? She started to ask Drew, but then Trevor spoke.

"This isn't just the setting of Amber's dream," he said. "We saw this the night we came to the Lowry House." He frowned. "At least, I *think* we did. I don't have an actual memory, but this feels familiar, you know?"

Amber knew exactly what Trevor meant, for she felt the same way. She looked at Drew, and from the expression on his face, she knew that it was the same for him, too.

The sounds grew louder then, and images began to form, just shadowy figures at first, but they soon took on distinct features. White men garbed in simple fur-lined jackets, trousers, and boots wielded flintlock rifles, knives, and hatchets. Bodies lay scattered on the ground, mostly Native American men, although there were a few women and even children. Most of the bodies had blood on them, sometimes copious amounts, and more than a few had been savaged to the point where it was difficult to tell that they were human, let alone what gender. Only their clothes, blood-soaked and rent by sharp blades, remained to provide any clue to their identities. And the bloodshed was far from over. Hunters aimed their rifles at anyone who wasn't white and put a round in them, fought hand-to-hand with the village's men who sought to protect their wives, mothers, and daughters, while others entered unguarded homes in search of easier prey.

The sights, sounds, and smells of wholesale slaughter sickened Amber to her core, and while she'd only imagined being a member of the tribe, had never been a Native American girl called Little Eyes, she nonetheless felt a deep kinship with these people and their plight, and she felt a mounting white-hot anger at witnessing the unspeakable crimes being committed against them.

"We have to do something!" she said. "We have to stop them somehow!"

"There's nothing we *can* do," Drew said. "This isn't happening now. It's a . . . a replay of events from the past. These people died a couple hundred years before we were born."

Intellectually, she knew that Drew's analysis was true, but emotionally, it was unbearable to stand there watching and do nothing to help.

As if by some unspoken agreement among the combatants, the fighting stopped, and an unsettling silence fell over the clearing. The hunters, most of whom had blood on their clothes, hands, and sometimes their faces, turned to look at

Amber, Drew, and Trevor. The hunters glared at the three friends and gripped their weapons but made no move toward them.

"It's like they're waiting for us to do something," Amber said.

"Whatever we do, we'd better do it fast," Drew said. "This may not be real, but we know Greg's hallucinations can kill. It doesn't matter if the ax that gets buried in your skull is real or illusory— either way, you're just as dead."

The hunters exchanged no words, didn't even look at one another, but they all started forward. They came slowly, not running, walking at a measured pace, and somehow that was worse. It was as if they felt there was no need to run because there was nothing their prey could do to escape them. They grinned with bloodlust as they approached, eyes glowing with dark hunger, weapons held tight, blade edges dripping with blood, flintlocks reloaded and ready to fire.

And then things got worse.

As they walked, the hunters raised their heads and drew in deep breaths through their noses, as if they were animals scenting the wind. With every step the hunters took, they changed. Their faces, already unshaven, sprouted dark fur, and their mouths and noses joined and lengthened to form snouts. Their teeth became fangs, and long pink tongues lolled out the sides of their mouths. Their hands became fur-covered claws with long black talons, and their eyes turned feral yellow and fixed on the three friends with a savage hunger. As they continued forward, their bodies hunched over, as if their spines had re-formed and they were no longer capable of standing upright, and their legs bent at strange angles. A chorus of low growling came from the hunters as they approached, and the sound caused a ripple of atavistic fear to run down Amber's spine.

The hunters—no, the pack, for that's what they'd become—growled and snarled as they came, white froth flecking their muzzles, eyes dancing with wild delight in anticipation of the slaughter to come.

And then Amber felt a strange calm come over her. "I'm not running," she said. "One way or another, I've been running for the last fifteen years, and I'm sick of it."

The hunters seemed to grin upon hearing these words, as if pleased that she was going to spare them the effort of having to chase her down. She knew she should have been frightened by the sight of them approaching, knew that Drew was right. Illusions or not, they could still kill. But she'd been afraid for so long, and she supposed she just didn't have any fear left.

"This isn't a real place," she said. "It's all in our minds. The hunters aren't real, and neither are the people they killed. The only real things are Greg and us. And if that's true, then if Greg can make things happen here, so can we." She spoke more loudly then as she addressed the hunters. "This was *their* land. You came here to take it from them by force, but you had no right to it. Their blood was always in this land figuratively, but thanks to you, it's literally there now. And it calls out for justice."

She crouched down and jammed her fingers into the ground. Grass and soil gave way before her hands as if they were no more substantial than water, and her hands sank up to her wrists.

The hunters hesitated when they saw what she'd done, expressions of confusion on their bestial faces. But when nothing happened right away, they grinned and started forward once more.

They didn't get very far, though.

Tendrils emerged from the ground around their feet, as thick and sinuous as serpents, but instead of green, they were a deep, dark crimson. The tendrils coiled around the hunters' legs as they stretched up their bodies, wrapped around their waists, chests, necks . . . The hunters let out animalistic roars of frustration at being bound by the blood tendrils. Those who reacted swiftly enough to keep their arms from being pinned to their sides fought back, slashing at the tendrils' rubbery surfaces with their claws, while others bent their heads down and tried to bite their way free. The crimson substance turned to gore beneath their hands and in their mouths, but the tendrils repaired the damage, new blood filling their gaps until they were whole and strong once more.

Amber felt a cold satisfaction as she witnessed the hunters' futile struggles. "You know the old saying about how blood is thicker than water? Well, it's stronger than steel, too."

Tendril tips stabbed toward the hunters' mouths and slithered inside. The hunters' eyes bulged in panic and pain as the tendrils forced their way down their throats, plunging deep into their bodies. And once they were deep enough, the tendrils went to work. It didn't take long.

The hunters thrashed and jerked for several moments but eventually fell still, and the tendrils retracted. As they released their grip on the hunters, their corpses slumped to the ground, and the tendrils returned to the earth from which they'd been born.

She pulled her hands free from the ground and stood, wiping bits of soil from her fingers as she did.

Trevor and Drew looked at her.

"*Damn,* girl," Trevor breathed. "That was hardcore!"

She gave him a weak smile. Now that it was over, she felt shaky and more than a little queasy at the thought of what she'd done. "I didn't plan that out," she admitted. "It just kind of happened."

"Your subconscious mind tapped into the virtual

world Greg created," Drew said. "And it found a way to counter the threat he'd sent against us." He reached out and gave her shoulders a loving squeeze. "Thanks to you, we now know we can fight him on his own terms."

The Native American village and the forest that surrounded it began to fade then, and the dark shape of the Lowry House reappeared.

"Looks like we're back to square one," Trevor said.

Drew shook his head. "No, we dealt with one challenge. If Greg is playing a game, then we just scored our first point. That means it's time for the next move."

"Greg's using our past as a model for his game," Amber said. She glanced at the old barn on the side of the property. "If the hunters chased us fifteen years ago, we would've run. And if that's the case, the closest place to hide is there." She pointed to the barn.

"I don't remember going to the barn," Trevor said. "Do either of you?"

"No," Drew said. He turned to Amber.

"Me, neither. But it makes sense, doesn't it?" she said.

"All right, let's go see what Greg's got planned for us next."

Drew took her hand. Despite the circumstances, she smiled, and the two of them headed for the barn, Trevor walking alongside them.

For the first time since Greg had revealed his powers to them, she felt as if they might have a chance not only of surviving but of actually beating him. Of course, the game was far from over yet.

They continued walking toward the barn and whatever waited for them within.

They'd experienced a lot of weird stuff this weekend, but Trevor thought that the walk to the barn was in some ways the strangest of all, and not just because the three of them looked and sounded fifteen years younger. This was, in a sense, the third time he'd been there. Once during the previous hallucination that Greg had caused him to experience when he'd been at the Historical Society with Amber and once before that, when the three of them had been there as teenagers. And now here he was again, heading for the location where the bootlegger Stockslager had buried his victims.

He wasn't at all certain that they were doing the right thing by following the path Greg had laid out for them. Sure, they'd made it through the first scenario he'd set up, and Drew and Amber were emboldened by that victory, but Trevor wasn't quite as encouraged. Greg might not be a god, but he'd do until the real thing came along, and Trevor had a hard time believing that the three of them had escaped the Indian massacre so easily. He suspected they'd been able to do so only because Greg had wanted it that way, that he was playing a deeper, more subtle game than they were aware of. How could they hope to fight Greg if they didn't understand the rules he was playing by? How could they hope to survive, let alone win?

He was still having trouble accepting that Greg was the dark guiding hand behind the supernatural occurrences they'd experienced this weekend. He hadn't seemed like the evil-genius type back in high school. Ever since Greg had revealed himself back at the dance, Trevor had been sifting through his memories of him, fragmented and incomplete as they were. He remembered him as a hanger-on who'd professed an interest in the paranormal but had really just wanted to be a member of their little group. He'd rarely contributed anything, never offered any ideas, hadn't even kicked in any money when they ordered pizza. And he'd often gotten in the way during investigations.

He'd seemed nice enough on the surface, especially to Amber. But Trevor had detected a mean streak in him, one that manifested in small ways—a snide comment here, a curled lip there, a look as if you'd just said the stupidest thing a human being could express. Amber hadn't seemed aware of it, which didn't surprise Trevor, since she had a tendency to see the best in people. But what had surprised him was that Drew had never seemed to notice. Even as a teenager, Drew had been more empathetic and perceptive than most people, but, like Amber, he tended to be optimistic and give people the benefit of the doubt. Trevor was more pragmatic and clear-eyed, if not cynical. But even so, he had a difficult time seeing how a kid like Greg had turned into a stone-cold killer. But he hadn't done it on his own, had he? The Lowry House had had everything to do with it, which begged a question: If fifteen years ago, Greg had been corrupted by the evil that inhabited this place, why hadn't they? And that led to an even more disturbing thought: Just because they'd escaped corruption last time didn't mean they'd do so this time.

They reached the barn door, and Trevor saw that the wood was far more weathered than it had been in the vision he'd experienced at the Historical Society. The night air was warmer, too. It was still April, not January as in the vision, and there was no snow on the ground. This must have been the way it had been fifteen years ago, the night they'd investigated the Lowry House.

"The door was unlocked," Amber said. "At least, I think it was. But I still don't remember what we found inside."

"I have a pretty good idea," Trevor said. "Let's get to it."

He stepped forward, gripped the barn door handle, and slid the door open.

The barn was dark inside, and the air that wafted out smelled thick and musty, as if the barn hadn't been opened in decades. There was a faint sour-sweet underscent that made him think of old decay, like leaves rotting on a forest floor, and his stomach did a somersault because he knew where the smell came from.

Drew shone his flashlight beam into the gloom to illuminate the way for them, and then the three friends stepped into Stockslager's barn.

Drew panned the flashlight beam around the barn's interior, revealing it to be empty. The homemade still was gone, and the bare earth of the barn floor had been smoothed over, leaving no signs of the fire pit or the still or the graves that had once been there.

"The police must've cleaned out the place," Drew said. "And removed the bodies to bury them elsewhere."

The door slammed shut behind them. Trevor tried to open it but without success. The door, while not locked, refused to budge.

The barn lights were still intact, and they came on now, filling the place with sour yellow illumination.

"Something's coming," Amber said. "I feel it. Something *bad*."

The ground in the middle of the barn began to bulge upward as if something was pushing from underneath. It pulsed once, twice, and then, on the third time, soil burst upward and an obese form dragged itself into the light. It was Stockslager. The front of his clothes was soaked with blood, a result of the multiple gunshot wounds he'd suffered when the police ended his life, Trevor guessed. His head lolled on his fat neck, and his eyes . . . his eyes were gone, replaced with flickering orange-yellow light, as if a fire burned inside his skull.

Once he'd fully emerged from the earth, Stockslager stood and regarded them for a moment. At least, that's what Trevor thought he was doing. It was hard to tell with his eyes glowing like that. Waves of heat emanated from the man's body, and the interior of the barn became hot. Trevor sensed what had happened. Stockslager had emerged from the exact spot where his fire pit had been, and he'd somehow internalized the flames that had once burned there. Beads of sweat formed on Trevor's forehead and began trickling down his face, and he felt sweat roll down the length of his spine. The heat continued to increase and reached the point where it felt painful on his exposed skin, as if he was being stung by tiny insects. Stockslager's dead flesh fared far worse. It began to redden and sizzle, as if being cooked from the inside out, and the smell of burning skin and meat filled the air. Trevor felt his gorge rise, and although he told himself that this was all part of the illusion and that he wasn't really smelling anything, it didn't help.

Stockslager opened his mouth wider, and the heat coming off him increased even more. Trevor had a bad feeling about what was going to happen next, and he shoved Drew and Amber to the side as a gout of sharp-smelling clear liquid shot forth from Stockslager's mouth. The liquid missed them and splattered the sealed-shut barn door. He feared that Stockslager wasn't finished, and he pushed Drew and Amber even farther away. Stockslager made a harsh coughing sound then, and a stream of flame blasted outward from his mouth, blackening his dead lips, and struck the barn door. The alcohol ignited, and a mass of bright orange flame *whooshed* into life and began devouring the wood.

Stockslager had internalized more than just the fire pit, Trevor realized. As bizarre as it sounded, he had the still inside him, too.

"Thanks," Amber told Trevor, and gave his arm a quick squeeze. The heat had continued to intensify, and sweat poured off her. She wiped a hand across her brow to mop it away, but she only succeeded in smearing the moisture around.

Drew looked equally uncomfortable, but he didn't bother trying to wipe his sweat away. He just let it drip off him and fall to the ground. "Whatever we do, we'd better do it fast, before we succumb to either the heat or smoke inhalation."

The latter was a real problem, Trevor thought,

as smoke was rising from the fire Stockslager had started, a fire that was spreading. How long would it take for the smoke to build up in the barn, as closed as it was? More to the point, if the fire continued to spread, how long before they couldn't escape it and were burned to death?

Stockslager came toward them, raising his hands and reaching for them with sausage-thick fingers as he approached. His dead face remained expressionless, but Trevor sensed a malign delight emanating from the man as he headed toward them.

"This is an illusion, right?" he said. "Maybe we can wish it away, use our minds to dispel it."

Drew shook his head, keeping his eyes on Stockslager as he came toward them. "If it were that easy to counter Greg's illusions, they'd never have progressed to this point. They'd have disappeared the moment we saw them, if for no other reason than our subconscious minds would've rejected them."

Stockslager was coming uncomfortably close by this point, and the three friends ran past him to the other side of the barn. He shot another stream of moonshine, followed by another burst of fire. Both missed, but now a second section of the barn was aflame. Stockslager could only move so fast on his dead legs, and although he turned and continued toward the friends, he did so slowly, giving them time to talk.

"But we *can* counter the illusions," Trevor insisted. "Amber did it with the hunters."

"She did it using the scenario against itself," Drew said. "That's what we have to do here."

Something about what Drew had said spurred a thought in him about how Amber had used the last illusion against itself. When he had been there before, during his visit to the Historical Society, it had been during the time period when Stockslager had been alive, and it had been winter outside. This current scenario was the spring of fifteen years ago, but both times were illusions, so why couldn't they *both* be real? Or at least as real as they needed to be?

He specialized in paranormal and supernatural lore, and he knew that elemental forces often played a large role in various mythologies, belief systems, and magic rituals. Not only that, but the concepts of opposing and complementary forces were also vital. Right now, Stockslager was, at least symbolically, a creature of fire. And the opposite of fire was water. They had no water on them, but water could take on different forms, and one of those forms was present in abundance on the night when the police had come for Stockslager. But to access it, Trevor needed to make an opening in the barn, an opening between this time period and the earlier one. But how could he do that? Drew, at least the teenager he appeared to be, carried a backpack, but he knew there were no tools in there, nothing that could bash a hole in the side of a barn. Drew hadn't packed such tools fifteen years ago, so there wouldn't be any in there now. If only he still had hold of the tire iron he'd carried with him into the rec center. If he had, he could use it to—

Wait a minute. He didn't remember dropping the tire iron. He *did* remember dropping the camera he'd been holding when they'd been transformed into their teenage selves—he'd let go of it when the werewolf hunters had attacked—but not the tire iron. It had seemed to vanish when they'd become teenagers again. But just because he could no longer see the tire iron or feel it didn't mean it wasn't still gripped tight in his hand. He might look like a teenager, but in reality, he was a man in his early thirties. And there was a good chance that the man still had hold of a tire iron and didn't know it.

Unless, of course, he'd dropped the tire iron when he thought he was dropping the illusory camera . . .

Stockslager shot a third stream of 'shine at them, and Trevor was so lost in thought that the alcohol would have hit him full on if Drew hadn't caught hold of his arm and yanked him out of the way. As before, Stockslager followed up with a blast of flame, and a third fire blossomed into life.

"I've got an idea," he told Drew and Amber. "Keep an eye on him, OK?" Without waiting for their acknowledgment, he turned to face the wooden wall. He looked down at his right hand. It appeared empty, but he told himself that it wasn't, that he held a solid length of metal in it. Then he closed his eyes, and, concentrating as hard as he could, he raised his hand and swung it at the wall—

—and was rewarded with the solid *thunk* of metal striking wood.

He kept his eyes closed and continued concentrating as he swung a second, third, and fourth time. He felt the wall give way with the last blow, and a gust of cold winter air hit him in the face, the sudden change in temperature coming as a shock.

He opened his eyes, and although he still didn't see a tire iron in his hand, he did see the splinter-edged hole he'd made in the wall, and he smiled with satisfaction. He then turned around to face Stockslager, who'd advanced much closer while Trevor had been making the hole.

"Stay clear," Trevor warned his friends, and then, remembering how Amber had plunged her hands into the earth to summon the blood tendrils that had defeated the hunters, he slammed his palms against the wood to the left of the hole he'd created and thought about the blanket of snow that lay beneath the moonlight outside the barn on the night the police had come for Stockslager.

Frigid wind gusted through the hole Trevor had made, a hole that was more than a passage through space but also one through time. The wind brought snow with it, only a few flakes at first, but it became a torrent of white that streaked toward Stockslager. The snow struck his hot, reddened skin and turned to hissing steam. But more and more snow came billowing in, flying so forcefully that it broke more wood and widened the hole in the wall, making room for even more snow to enter.

Stockslager made no sound as the snow continued to pummel him, but he stepped backward on his unsteady dead legs, fat arms flailing in a vain effort to ward off the attack. The snow melted at first, forming a large puddle beneath Stockslager's feet, but the sheer amount of it overwhelmed the fire raging inside him, and his body began to cool. Snow began to collect on him after that, covering him, and still more blew in from outside, packing onto him until he looked like a giant snowman. A giant immobile snowman, for he'd stopped moving.

The snow did more than cover him. It swirled around the interior of the barn, cooling it to winter temperatures and piling onto the fires he had ignited, smothering them.

Trevor turned to his friends and grinned. "Now, *that's* how you bust a ghost!"

The snow-wind died away but not before opening a large enough hole in the barn wall for them to climb through. They went out one at a time, and when they were outside again, they were once more on the Lowry House property of fifteen years ago. It was still a cool April night, and they were still teenagers.

Well done, Greg said. *Two down, one to go.*

All three friends heard his voice and looked at the Lowry House looming before them in the dark. Without exchanging a word, they started walking toward it.

EIGHTEEN

As the three friends stepped onto the porch of the Lowry House, Drew processed what they'd learned from the last scenario they'd experienced. The longer this extended psychodrama continued, the more it told him about Greg's mind-set. He might be infected by some kind of evil supernatural force that gave him his powers, but he was still a man, and Drew was certain that if they were going to have any chance of stopping him—and maybe even freeing him from the darkness that possessed him—it lay in understanding his psychological makeup. He told himself to remain calm and consider Greg as just another patient who needed his help, to think in terms of diagnosis and treatment. But it wasn't easy to do, considering that they'd barely survived two nightmare scenarios and were about to walk into a third. If they hoped to survive this next test, he needed to remain sharp and stay in the present, be ready for anything. But to defeat Greg, he needed to be able to stay detached so that he could function as a psychologist. How could he do both?

Maybe he was thinking too much. Both Amber and Trevor had managed to exert control over Greg's scenarios and nullify them, and they'd both done so by listening to their instincts. Maybe he should take a cue from his friends and let up on the intellectualizing a little.

Then again, perhaps they'd made it through the last two scenarios because Greg had wanted them to. If he *was* a sociopath, that meant that he was a master manipulator. Maybe he hoped to lull them into a false sense of security and then hit them with the most deadly scenario, one that they couldn't defeat. Or maybe he wanted Drew to be thinking along these lines to foster a sense of paranoia so he'd begin making mistakes.

Thinking too much, he decided. *Definitely.*

They walked up to the front door of the Lowry House, and he shone his flashlight on the doorknob. "It wasn't locked the night we came here as teenagers," he said. He tried the knob, and it turned beneath his hand as if freshly oiled. He pushed the door, and it swung open without the obligatory screeching hinges that one might expect of any self-respecting haunted house.

He led the way with his flashlight, and Amber and Trevor followed, Amber keeping close behind, her hand on his shoulder. The air inside the house smelled stale and moldy, and it felt several degrees cooler than outside.

The short foyer was empty of furniture or carpet, and there were no pictures on the walls. The plaster was cracked in several places and splotched with dark patches of mold.

"When we were teenagers, did we leave the door open or close it behind us?" Trevor asked. He spoke in a hushed voice, as if they were in church.

"We probably closed it," Amber said. "Just in case any police drove by and noticed that it was open."

Trevor turned to close the door, but Drew stopped him. "We don't have to worry about police now," he said. "And who knows? We might need to make a quick getaway."

"But if we don't close it—and better yet, lock it and shove a couch or something up against it— something nasty might sneak in when we're not looking and creep up on us from behind," Trevor said.

"Whatever surprises Greg has in store for us, a locked door isn't going to stop them," Drew pointed out. "Especially since the door, like everything else around us, is only an illusion created by him."

"Which means leaving it open doesn't matter, either," Trevor countered. "He can just think it closed whenever he wants."

Before Drew could respond, Amber cut in. "I'm not sure all of this is just an elaborate figment of Greg's imagination. Remember, I said that he's making it, at least partially, from our memories. We're also standing on the physical location where the Lowry House once stood. However powerful he is, he still needs material to work with, like a sculptor needs clay. What if he is not only using our memories but also drawing on the spiritual forces on the land here?"

"It makes sense," Drew said. "It would explain why we've been able to intuit some of the details of our original investigation of the Lowry House as we go and why we've been able to influence the scenarios. They are, at least partially, ours, too. And if this location possesses strong residual psychic energy, maybe we're tapping into it as well."

"In that case," Trevor said, "maybe I can wish up an Uzi that fires silver bullets." He squeezed his eyes shut in concentration and held out his empty hand, but no weapon appeared. He opened his eyes and sighed. "It was worth a shot."

"Let's go," Drew said. "It's rude to keep our host waiting."

They walked into the living room and found it as empty as the foyer. No furniture, no carpet, no wall decorations. Drew felt a coldness in the pit of his stomach as he remembered the hallucination he'd experienced while talking with Greg in the hotel lobby.

"This is where I saw Mr. Lowry sitting on his couch, gripping his nine-millimeter. He had a hunting knife sitting by his side, and he said he was trying to decide which one to use. I vote we head straight upstairs. That's where Lowry killed his family and himself. Whatever's waiting for us in this scenario is probably up there."

Amber and Trevor nodded their agreement, and they left the living room in search of the stairs. They were easy enough to find, at the end of a hallway that led to several smaller rooms on the ground floor.

The air seemed to grow colder as they reached the second floor, and Amber began shivering. Drew put his arm around her shoulders and pulled her close.

"I'm cold, too," Trevor said. "Who's going to warm me up?" He spoke in a near-whisper, and his breath misted on the cold air.

"I think I remember that," Amber said, ignoring him. "The cold, I mean. It got a lot colder as we came closer to the bedroom where Mr. Lowry killed his children."

Drew shone his flashlight beam on the door to their right. "This is the room," he said.

They looked at the door in silence for a moment. There was a light coating of frost on the door's surface and the knob, and waves of cold radiated from the wood.

"So, do we go in or not?" Trevor asked. "If we want to continue following in our teenage footsteps, we should go inside. It's what we would've done then."

Before they could debate the issue further, the frost-coated knob turned, and the door swung open on its own.

"Guess Greg thought we needed a hint," Trevor said.

Drew shone the flashlight into the room and stepped inside, Amber and Trevor following close behind.

This room, unlike the others they'd seen in the Lowry House, wasn't empty. It was a child's room—two children, actually—with a pair of beds and shelves containing books, toys, and stuffed animals and more stuff scattered on the floor. The walls were painted a cheerful lavender, and curtains displaying cartoon animals covered the window. There were four people in the room, but only one of them was alive. A child lay in each bed, a boy and a girl, both of them little more than toddlers. Their throats had been cut, the wounds so deep that their heads were almost severed from their bodies. Blood soaked the bedclothes, coated their headboards, was splashed on the wall. The children's eyes were wide and staring, and their mouths were open, as if they'd died pleading for their lives. A blond woman in her thirties wearing a sheer blue nightgown lay on the floor, stretched at the feet of both beds. She lay on her side, revealing that her throat had been cut as savagely as her children's, and blood soaked her nightgown and the carpet around her and matted her hair.

The only living denizen of the house stood near the window, blood-slick knife held at his side, tears streaming down his care-lined face as he gazed on his grisly handiwork.

"This time, I used the knife," he said in a toneless voice.

It was John Lowry, looking much the same as he had in the hallucination Drew had experienced in the hotel lobby. Except that now he held his hunting knife instead of his gun, and his clothes were covered in his family's blood.

He didn't tear his gaze from his family as he spoke once more. "I didn't want to do it. Really, I didn't. But I had to, so I decided to do it as fast as I could, to minimize their suffering, you know? The kids first, so they wouldn't have to hear their mother die, in case I couldn't keep her quiet when I killed her. But Jimmy woke up as I was doing his sister and screamed, and that brought Helen." He nodded toward his wife's body. "So I had to do her while Jimmy watched. A hell of a thing, a boy having to watch his mother die. I'd have done anything to stop it, but the voices wouldn't let me." He let out a mournful sigh. "Only one thing left to do now."

With a trembling hand, Lowry raised the knife to his own throat and pressed the edge of the blade to his flesh.

"Wait!" Drew said. "You don't have to do that!"

Lowry stood there, trembling, tears continuing to slide down his cheeks and drip onto his shirt, mingling with the blood of his family. But he didn't draw the knife blade across his throat. And then he stopped shaking, and a sly smile spread across his face. He lowered the knife.

"You know something?" he said. "The voices have changed their minds. They've given me a new task to do before I can rejoin my family. I'm supposed to kill you three."

He raised his knife and started forward.

"Time for us to beat feet," Trevor said.

Drew doubted that it would be that simple, given the variations that they'd experienced in the last two scenarios, but they could hardly stand there and let Lowry open up their throats, so the three friends turned and ran out of the room, history once again repeating itself.

The air in the hallway seemed even colder than it had a few moments ago, and their breath gusted clouds of steam as they hurried toward the stairs. But before they reached them, long metal blades, like knives only far larger, shot forth from the stairs, walls, and ceiling at haphazard angles, as if the friends were trapped inside a gigantic version of one of those boxes that stage magicians thrust swords into. The crisscrossing blades formed an impenetrable barrier, so rather than plunge ahead and be sliced into ribbons, they stopped running and turned back to face Lowry.

He'd followed them into the hallway, taking his time and grinning as if he enjoyed it, his demeanor far different from that of the sorrowful father he'd been only a few moments ago. As he came, knives jutted forth from his body, bloodlessly cutting through skin and slicing through clothing, until he resembled a nightmarish human porcupine with sharp steel blades in place of quills.

"Do you like my new look?" he asked. "I think it ups the entertainment value, don't you?"

Although they heard Lowry's voice, Drew knew that the words he spoke were Greg's.

Amber gripped his arm tightly. "It's your turn," she said. "Trevor and I handled the other scenarios, so this one has to be yours."

He saw a certain twisted logic to what she suggested. It fit with the way Greg had been playing this game so far.

He knew they had mere moments until Lowry reached then, and either he'd impale them on his body or force them into the blade barrier on the stairs. Either way, they'd be just as dead. Time to think fast.

Both Amber and Trevor had beaten the last two scenarios because they'd understood something profound about the scenarios themselves, and they'd used that knowledge as a weapon. But he was a healer. He'd dedicated his life to understanding people, to empathizing with their pain so he could discover how best to help them. He wasn't a fighter. No, he realized. He *was* a fighter, a warrior, but one of the mind instead of the body. And considering that this scenario was a psychic landscape with no physical reality, that meant that he was standing on his preferred battlefield.

"They forgave you, you know," he said. "Your family, I mean."

Lowry stopped and stared at him. The grin fell away from his face, but he said nothing.

Drew didn't know if Lowry was really there or if he was talking to Greg in disguise. But the last two scenarios had appeared to have at least some independent reality of their own, so he decided to proceed as if things were as they seemed. If there was even a sliver of Lowry's spirit present, he'd do his best to attempt to reach it.

"They knew you loved them," he said. "And they must've heard the voices, too. At the very least, they'd have sensed the darkness in the house. Yes, they were terrified when you attacked them, and they died in horrible pain. But once that pain ended and they were freed from their mortal flesh, I'm sure they could see what had been done to you, how, despite your best efforts, you'd become corrupted by the evil that infested your home. Once they understood that, they knew that what you'd done wasn't your fault, and they forgave you."

Lowry continued looking at him, and while it was difficult to read the man's expression, given the fact that his face was covered with protruding knife blades, he seemed to be experiencing an internal struggle. Drew didn't know if he'd managed to reach Lowry, but the man wasn't rushing forward to impale them, and he decided to take that as a good sign.

But then Lowry's expression hardened, and although it now seemed more than a bit redundant, he raised the knife he held and started toward them again.

For a terrible instant, Drew feared that he'd failed, and while the prospect of his own death was bad enough, the thought that he'd doomed Trevor and Amber—especially Amber—filled him with sorrow.

But then rustling sounds came from the children's bedroom, causing Lowry to halt once more. He lowered his blade and turned back to face the open doorway, curiosity mingled with more than a little fear in his gaze.

They came lurching out into the hallway, mother and children, drenched with blood and moving with awkward, spastic motions, as if they were having trouble getting their dead bodies to function.

The mother—Helen, Lowry had called her—opened her mouth and spoke a single word in a thick, liquid voice. "Forgive . . ."

The children echoed her, speaking in the same wet tones. "Forgive . . . Forgive . . ."

They reached out for Lowry as they came, and he raised his knife. For a second, Drew thought he might attack his family and attempt to finish the job he'd started, but then he lowered his hand and let the knife slip from his fingers. It fell to the floor with a solid thump, and as it did, the blades protruding from his body retracted, until they were gone.

A strangled sob escaped his lips then. "I'm sorry," he said. "So very sorry."

He walked forward to embrace his family, and with fresh tears pouring down his face, he stepped into their arms and hugged them back as fiercely as they hugged him.

And then Lowry screamed as his wife and children began tearing away chunks of his flesh with their hands and teeth. He collapsed to the floor, still screaming, and his family fell on him with savage enthusiasm.

He didn't scream much longer after that.

When Lowry was silent, his wife looked up at Drew, Amber, and Trevor, her husband's blood dribbling down her chin.

"Forgive," she said. "Not forget."

Then she rejoined her children in their feast, and an instant later, their forms, Lowry's included, became insubstantial and drifted away like so much mist. The blood they'd spilled vanished with them, and when Drew turned to examine the stairs, he found the blade barrier gone, too.

Feeling more than a bit queasy, he turned to his friends and managed a feeble smile. "Three down," he said. "What now?"

"The basement," Trevor said, looking more than a little green around the gills himself. "Where else?" He let out a weary sigh. "I never thought I'd say this, but I think I've had enough paranormal experiences tonight to last me the rest of my life. How about we head back to the hotel, get a good night's rest, and come back and confront Greg tomorrow after a nice breakfast?" He raised his voice, and his tone took on a hysterical edge. "How's that sound to you, Greg? You have to be bushed yourself, what with creating all these scenarios for us."

At first, nothing happened. Then Greg's voice echoed around them. He sounded amused. *Thanks for your concern, Trevor, old buddy, but I'm still holding up fine. But I suppose there's no reason to put this off any longer.*

The hallway began to become indistinct and hazy, as if losing its grip on reality, or vice versa. Everything around them became dark then, and although Drew's flashlight continued to shine and illuminated the immediate area, they could see nothing.

No need to rely on your flashlight alone, Greg said. *Not when I brought my own light.*

A soft glow came into existence about ten feet from where they stood, and Drew realized that he was looking at a kerosene lantern, the kind people used when camping. It rested on a concrete floor, and sitting cross-legged next to it was an overweight teenage boy with acne-dotted skin and oily hair, wearing an old Army jacket, jeans, and running shoes. He was grinning, but his gaze held no mirth.

"It's Greg," Amber said. "The way he used to be."

And then, in a sudden rush, the last pieces of Drew's missing memories returned, and he knew everything.

NINETEEN

"**Aren't you going** to thank me?" Greg asked. Although he resembled a teenage boy, the mocking tone in his voice and the matching smile were those of an adult.

"*Thank* you?" Trevor stepped forward, hands balled into fists as if he wanted to hit him. "You just had us fight our way through your version of a low-rent carnival spookhouse, and you expect us to *thank* you?"

Amber wondered if Trevor still held the tire iron in one of his hands. Just because she couldn't see it didn't mean it wasn't there. He had used it to bash a hole in the side of Stockslager's barn, and the tire iron hadn't been visible then. She wondered if he even remembered the tire iron by this point, and if so, if he was tempted to use it on Greg. She wondered if she wanted him to. Before tonight, she couldn't have imagined wishing harm on another person. Not seriously, anyway. But after everything Greg had put them through, not to mention the two people he'd killed and the dozens more he'd tried to kill, if she'd had a tire iron, she'd have smashed his head in right then without a moment's hesitation.

Greg focused his gaze on her, and his smile softened. "No, you wouldn't. At your core, you're too gentle a soul. It's one of the qualities I admire most in you."

Drew and Trevor looked at her.

"He's reading my thoughts." She was surprised to hear how calm she sounded. Here they were, confronting a man who possessed the power to kill with his mind, and she was acting as if it was no big deal. Maybe she was numb from everything they'd gone through to get to this point.

Greg rose to his feet, but he made no move toward them. "Or maybe you realize that I mean none of you any harm."

Drew's brow knitted in a skeptical frown. "Are you saying that despite the way it seemed, none of us was in any danger as we made our way through the scenarios you created?"

"Well . . . maybe I should say that I *hoped* no harm would come to any of you. Believe it or not, I was rooting for you the whole way. The challenges—and the dangers they presented— were very real. In a metaphysical sense, at least. They were re-creations of what you experienced when you came here as teenagers. And the three of you performed magnificently! You didn't shrink before any of the obstacles I set before you, and you found a way to counter each one. And now, like all triumphant heroes, you get to receive your just reward."

"What the hell are you talking about?" Trevor demanded.

"Our memories," Drew said. "They've been restored. That's what he was referring to when he suggested we should thank him." He turned to Greg. "Isn't that right?"

He nodded. "That's what this whole weekend was about, after all. Well, a big part of it, anyway."

Amber couldn't believe what she'd heard, but when she thought back to the night when they'd first explored the Lowry House, she found no blank spaces in her memory. It was all there, every moment, every thought, every emotion she'd experienced back then. The sheer amount of information that inundated her was so overwhelming that she thought she might become lost in all of it, but then it began to settle, like the silt at the bottom of a stream after someone has tossed in a very large rock.

"It's true," Trevor said, his voice filled with awe and excitement. "I remember that after we saw Lowry, we came down to the basement." He glanced around. "It looked just like this. Empty like the rest of the house." He turned back to Greg. "Empty except for you, that is."

"You were sitting cross-legged on the floor," Drew said, "just as you were a moment ago. And the lantern was sitting on the floor next to you."

"We tried to talk to you, find out what you were

doing here, but you didn't respond," Amber said. "You sat and stared straight ahead. We tried to shake you to rouse you, and when that didn't work, we shook you harder."

"And when *that* didn't work, I smacked you across the face," Trevor said. "Like they do in the movies. I have to admit I enjoyed that, but it didn't work, either."

"We discussed what to do," Drew said. "None of us had cell phones back then, or we'd have called nine-one-one, despite not wanting to get in trouble with our parents for sneaking into the Lowry House."

"We thought about one of us running home to get our parents while the others stayed with you," Trevor said. "But I convinced Drew and Amber that we needed to get you out of the house. After everything we'd experienced, I was sure that the spiritual forces in the house had affected you somehow, maybe even taken you over. I hoped you might return to normal if we could put some physical distance between you and the house."

"Drew and Trevor each took one of your arms and tried to haul you to your feet," Amber said. "But the moment they touched you, you began to laugh."

"It was one of those creepy this-guy-has-lost-his-mind laughs," Trevor said. "The sort of thing I imagine Drew hears a lot in his practice."

"Bad as it was, the laugh was far from the worst

part," Drew said. "The flame in your lantern began to burn more intensely, becoming so bright that we couldn't look at it. Trevor and I let go of you so we could shield our eyes, and we backed away because the heat became so intense."

"They were on one side of you, and I was on the other," Amber said. "I was covering my eyes, too, so I didn't see it, but I heard the lantern shatter. I peeked through my fingers and saw flames begin to spread outward from the lantern, moving almost as if they were alive. I was cut off from Drew and Trevor, and I shouted Drew's name."

"The flames rose higher, forming a barrier between us," Drew said. "I didn't hesitate. I pulled off my backpack and dropped it to the ground. Then I put up my arms in front of my face to protect my eyes, squeezed them shut, and leaped through the flames. I found Amber, took off my jacket, put it over her head to protect her, and together we jumped through the flames."

"I tried to reach you, Greg," Trevor said, "but the flames blazed higher and brighter, and you just kept on laughing."

"There wasn't anything in the basement for the flames to consume," Drew said, "but they started producing smoke anyway. We started coughing, and since we were unable to get to you, we started for the stairs. I forgot all about my backpack and left it behind, which is why we lost the equipment we'd brought."

"The flames followed as we ran, as if they were chasing us," Amber said, "and the stairs caught fire even as we reached them. The flames continued after us as we ran through the house and out the front door. When we got outside, our clothes were on fire in several places, so we threw ourselves to the grass and rolled back and forth to extinguish them."

"We were coughing and shivering in the night air," Trevor said. "We knelt on the grass, huddled together, and watched the flames rise into the night sky as the Lowry House burned. We heard your laughter above the roar of the fire for a time, but then it faded away, and when it was gone . . ."

"So were our memories," Drew said. "We became catatonic and didn't return to conscious awareness until the next day in the hospital."

Greg smiled. "Bravo." His form blurred and grew thinner, and when he came into focus again, he was his adult self once more, although Amber noted that the kerosene lantern continued to glow on the floor next to his feet. She looked down at her hands and saw that they'd again become the hands of a woman in her thirties. She looked at Drew and Trevor, and they, too, had returned to their true selves. Drew held a different flashlight from before, and Trevor's tire iron was now visible in his hand. They still appeared to be standing in the basement of the Lowry House, though. Whatever was happening, it wasn't over yet.

"I'm glad it worked," Greg said. "To be honest, I wasn't certain you'd get *all* of your memories back or, if you did, that the process wouldn't end up traumatizing you even further." He smiled. "Hell, for all I knew, you might've ended up with large sections of your brains burned out. But it looks like everything turned out fine."

Drew scowled. "What are you implying? That your illusions were some kind of *therapy* to help restore our memories?"

"Essentially," Greg said. "If you toss some psychic surgery into the mix." The three friends looked at him, and he laughed. "Surprised, aren't you? You thought I was out for revenge against the three kids who'd wronged me back in high school."

"Uh, well . . . yeah," Trevor admitted.

"Maybe it'll all make more sense if I tell you my side of the story," Greg said. "In the weeks before you decided to investigate the Lowry House, I'd become aware that you tried to ditch me whenever you went on an investigation. I pretended that I didn't have a clue, but in truth, I became angry and resentful, and I decided to get back at the three of you. So, when I realized you were planning on coming here, I sneaked in earlier and waited for you. My plan was to hide in the attic and walk around, make some noise, and get you all excited, thinking that you'd encountered solid evidence of a haunting. And then, when you came up into the attic, I'd jump out yelling and scare the hell out of you. But not long after I entered the house, I found myself drawn to the basement. It was almost as if a voice was calling me, a voice that I couldn't quite hear but which I could *feel*.

"So I came down here." He gestured at their virtual surroundings. "It looked like this. Just an empty basement. No furniture, no boxes of forgotten junk. Just some dust and cobwebs." He smiled. "Kind of a disappointment, really. I mean, you'd expect a haunted house to have a basement with *some* atmosphere. This was where Stockslager killed his victims, after all. He buried them in the barn afterward. But what the basement lacked in appearance I found it made up for in power, for as I sat on the floor, I sensed that this was the center of the Lowry House—its dark heart—and once I settled in, it began talking to me in earnest. And it told me many strange and wondrous things . . ."

He trailed off, his gaze becoming distant and unfocused as his mind drifted back to that time. Amber wondered if he heard the Lowry House speaking to him now across the decade and a half since it had been destroyed. If so, she wondered what it was saying to him.

Finally, Greg's eyes came back into focus, and he looked at each of them in turn, as if he'd forgotten all about them and was surprised to see them standing there. But he picked up his story, as if he hadn't lost a beat.

"I learned a lot that night. I learned that places

like this begin as natural phenomena that serve as focal points for negative energy. They draw it from the surrounding area, gather and concentrate it. And once they get strong enough, bad things begin to happen there. Plants grow stunted and twisted, and animals too dumb not to stay away find themselves becoming aggressive, if they didn't weaken and die. It's worse if people come into one of these Bad Places. We already carry so much darkness inside us—fears, jealousies, hurts, and hatreds . . . It's all fertile ground for a Bad Place, allowing it to manipulate a person's mind and spirit, bringing their darkness to the forefront, making them do things they'd never consider doing otherwise. Terrible, awful things. Things that cause pain and suffering, which in turn feeds a Bad Place even further, helps it grow even stronger.

"That's what happened here. Over the centuries, this land, which was originally a focal point for negative energy, grew so strong that it achieved a sort of sentience. It became self-aware, intelligent. Not like us, though. Different. And it was tired of being bound to a single location. It wanted to be free, wanted to roam the world. But to do that, it needed a body." Greg smiled. "It needed me. But why settle for one body when it could have four?"

Amber felt a sick chill as the full implications of his words sank in.

"So, we waited for the three of you to arrive. Through me, the Darkness in the Lowry House understood what you'd come to see, so it gave it to you. Ghostly scenarios drawn from the land's dark past, designed to scare you, thrill you, and ultimately lure you down here to me. You were supposed to join me in becoming vessels for the house's energy, and together we would walk in the world and spread its Darkness throughout the land." His voice had taken on a dreamy quality as he said these last words, but it returned to normal as he added, "But something went wrong, and the three of you escaped.

"After you fled, the Darkness reached into your minds and sealed away the memories of what you'd experienced here in order to protect itself. It was somewhat clumsy and brutal, I'm afraid, and you lost more of your memories than intended. Large chunks of your high-school years became blocked off, though they should've returned with the rest of your memories by now."

"What happened to you after we got out?" Trevor asked. "Neither the police nor the fire-fighters found any indication you'd been here. You escaped the fire, but how?"

Drew shook his head. "He didn't escape. He managed to get out but not unscathed." He looked at Greg. "Isn't that right?"

Greg looked at him a long moment before smiling. "Always the smart one."

He did nothing obvious, but his face and hands changed. His hair vanished, and his flesh was now puckered and wrinkled, like wax that had partially melted and cooled before setting once more.

"You've been using your abilities to disguise your true appearance," Drew said. "But we got a glimpse of the real you yesterday at the hotel bar, just for an instant. What happened? Did your control slip, or did you decide to give us a little peek at the real you for fun?"

Greg's burn-scarred lips stretched into a tight smile. "The latter, I confess." His voice had changed, too, becoming rough and guttural. "You're right, of course. I got out before the house burned down but not before taking some damage. The Darkness settled for using me as its sole avatar, and I carried it with me as I left. Its power allowed me to withstand the pain and sped my healing process, though as a creature composed of spiritual energy, its ability to affect the physical world is limited, as you can see."

He gestured at his ruin of a face. "I was able to hide my transformation from my parents, and I returned to school. When the three of you got out of the hospital, I said nothing to you about what had happened. The Darkness wanted me to keep its existence a secret. It didn't want me to have any contact with you, in case seeing me might somehow trigger your memories. And that was the end of our friendship. I regretted that, but after a while, I became convinced it was for the best, and so we went our separate ways."

"We know you moved to a different school soon after that," Drew said. "What happened to you then?"

"I didn't move," Greg said. "After my parents died, I decided to strike out on my own and explore the newfound abilities the Darkness had granted me. Chief among them was the power to sense other Bad Places, large and small, ancient and newborn. I began seeking out those places, and once there, well, the Darkness within me was alive, wasn't it? And that meant it needed to feed. We absorbed all the negative energy we could find, and we continued to grow stronger. And that's what I've done for the last fifteen years: travel the country and feed my Darkness." He smiled and spread his arms. "And now here we all are."

"But *why* are we here?" Trevor asked. "And don't tell me it was all so you could restore our memories. I'm not about to buy you as Greg Daniels, Supernatural Doer of Good Deeds. It must be the house or, rather, the Darkness that once inhabited it and now lives in you. It lost us once, and now it wants us back."

Drew shook his head. "I don't think so. If it wanted us so badly, why wait fifteen years? We had no memory of its existence and no way to protect ourselves against it. It could've taken us whenever it wanted."

"No," Amber said. "It couldn't. Greg said something went wrong when it tried to possess us. Do you remember when that happened? I do. It was when Greg's lantern began to glow bright. I heard the voice he told us about whispering to me inside my head, telling me how much it wanted me, how much it needed me . . ."

"I heard the same thing," Trevor said. "And the next thing that happened was the flame burst out of the lantern and began growing. You called for Drew, and he got you, and the three of us . . ." He trailed off. "That's it! That's how we resisted the Darkness. As we fled, the Darkness reached out for us, but we were together, our minds and spirits joined. Remember the cleansing rituals we researched? They all came down to the same thing in the end: positive energy marshaled to counteract negative energy. Our combined psychic energy formed a protection against the Darkness's influence." He turned to face Greg. "That's what happened, isn't it?"

Greg looked at Trevor without answering.

"I suspect tampering with memories is a lot less invasive than full-out possession," Drew said, "which is why the Darkness could still block our memories even though it was unable to take us over. We were already traumatized by the events of that night, and we were physically and emotionally exhausted, not to mention suffering from burns and smoke inhalation. It wouldn't have taken more than a psychic nudge for the Darkness to give us selective amnesia."

"So, we flew the coop, and the Darkness decided to forget about us and make do with Greg," Trevor said. "But that still doesn't explain why we're here now."

"You're right about the Darkness settling for me," Greg said. "And we've done very well on our own for the last fifteen years. You're not here because the Darkness wants you but, rather, because *I* do."

The three friends stared at him.

"I knew you had the hots for Amber," Trevor said, "but all *three* of us?"

Greg laughed. "Not what I meant. For the first few years after my transformation, I was content to be by myself, traveling in search of focal points of negative energy to absorb. You wouldn't believe all the different ways such energy can manifest. I've seen some bizarre things, even by my standards. But somewhere along the way, I began to miss having anyone to share my experiences with, and I found myself thinking back to high school and those investigations of yours. There I was, living proof that the paranormal was real, visiting one Bad Place after another, and I thought how much the kids you'd been would've loved to know even a fraction of what I'd discovered since my rebirth. Then, one day, it occurred to me. Why not get the three of you together, see if I couldn't restore your memories, and then, once I'd shown you the truth of what I'd become and what I could do, I'd ask you."

Drew frowned. "Ask us what?"

But Amber had already guessed. "To allow part of his Darkness to enter us and make us like him. And then we could accompany him on his search for more Bad Places to drain of negative energy." She looked at Greg. "It's simple. You're lonely."

"It's true, and I admit, the change comes at a price." He gestured to his face. "At least, in my case it did. But consider the great gift I'm offering you. When you were kids, you wanted to find evidence that there was something more to existence than what appears to be reality. Once you've changed, you won't just be investigating the hidden world, you'll be part of it! The knowledge you'll gain, the things you'll see . . ." Excitement rose in his voice. "I'm not exaggerating when I tell you human language doesn't possess the capacity to communicate what your lives will be like once you accept the Darkness. What you've experienced this weekend is nothing more than the merest appetizer for what awaits you."

"And all we'd have to do to accept your so-called gift is to allow ourselves to be possessed by a force that can only be termed evil," Drew said. "Assuming we were insane enough to allow such a thing to happen, how much of *us*—our thoughts, our feelings, our very selves—would be left?"

Greg shook his head. "Evil is a human concept, Drew. Energy can't be good or bad. It just *is*. True, I've used terms like *Bad Place* and *Darkness* but only for convenience's sake. As I said, human language lacks the capacity—"

Amber interrupted. "Cut the crap. When we knew you, you were a socially awkward outsider, but you weren't a killer. You've said a lot of things tonight, but you've neglected to mention the two men you killed this weekend: Sean Houser and Jerry Cottrill."

"And I doubt they were the first," Drew said. "Knowing what we know now, it's more than a little suspicious that your parents died in a car wreck not long after your change, as you call it. What happened? Did they somehow discover the truth of what their son had become? Or did they simply stand in your way?"

Up to this point, Greg had been coming across as someone who had genuine affection for them. But now his gaze hardened, and his voice grew cold. "Neither. I just grew tired of them. And as for Sean and Jerry . . ." He shrugged. "I had to do something to amuse myself while you three jumped through the hoops I set up for you. What can I say? Boys just want to have fun."

"You're not human anymore, are you?" Drew said. "Maybe you still were when you first changed, at least partially, but the years continued to change you. The more negative energy you found and absorbed, the less human you became. The whole process was something like fossilization. You're like a skeleton whose bones were replaced with minerals over millions of years, until there's no bone left, only rock. You look like Greg, you walk and talk like him, but the man you were died long ago. You're not even a ghost. You're nothing but a bad copy that doesn't even *know* it's a copy."

"How many other people have you killed over the years?" Trevor demanded. "Do you even remember?"

Greg's grin answered for him. Then the grin fell away, and he let out a weary sigh. "I'm disappointed, but I can't say I'm surprised. I didn't think you'd take me up on my offer. Not willingly, anyway." He glanced down at the kerosene lantern, and the light within began to glow more strongly, just as it had fifteen years ago.

Amber understood what was happening. "The lantern is the focal point for the house's negative energy, isn't it? We keep calling it the Darkness, but it first manifested as fire when we were teenagers."

"It couldn't take us over back then," Trevor said. "What makes you think it will be successful this time?"

The glow inside the lantern burned even brighter, until it became too painful to look at, and the basement, which up to this point had been cool and damp, began to heat up.

"The Darkness is far stronger than it was then," Greg said. "And fifteen years ago, it had only a short time to probe your psychic defenses and search for weaknesses. This time, it's had an entire weekend.

Plus, now it has *me,* and I know the three of you. I can help it find your weak spots."

"We're older now," Drew said, "and we're stronger, too."

"You're right on one count, at least," Greg said. "You're older. But during the intervening years, your psyches have acquired as much bad as good. More hurts, disappointments, regrets, self-doubts, and every one of them is a chink in your spiritual armor for the Darkness to exploit."

"That's how it got to you, isn't it?" Drew said. "You came here as a teenager filled with resentment, determined to get back at us for leaving you out of our plans. The Darkness used those negative feelings to create an inroad to your psyche, and while you sat here waiting for us, it poisoned you and took you over."

"Yes," he admitted. "So, in a sense, I'm *your* fault. All three of you. If you'd been better friends to me, I wouldn't have been so full of resentment, and the Darkness would never have found a foothold in my soul."

While he spoke, the "Darkness" grew even brighter, filling the basement with so much light that even with her eyes squeezed shut, Amber could still see its glow through her eyelids. She couldn't see Drew or Trevor, but she assumed that they also had their eyes closed. She wondered if Greg did or if, as a servant of the Darkness, he had no need to avert his gaze from its full glory.

"You're full of shit!" Trevor snapped. "We managed to resist the Darkness, and you could've, too, if you'd really wanted to. But you wanted to be strong, wanted to have power like no one else had ever known."

Greg said nothing, but an instant later, the lantern's light winked out. Amber opened her eyes a crack and saw him illuminated in the beam of Drew's flashlight. His burned lips formed a half-smile. "Don't think it's over," he said. "The Darkness is loose now, like a genie that's escaped its lamp, and it's ready for you."

Amber wasn't certain what he was talking about, but then she noticed the basement walls rippling, as if they were made of some soft spongy substance. The ceiling did the same thing, as did the concrete floor beneath their feet. She started to lose her balance, so she reached out toward Drew and Trevor. The three of them grabbed hold of one another and huddled close to keep from being knocked off their feet.

"The Darkness was, for all its age, inexperienced the last time you encountered it," Greg said. "It reached out for you like a toddler stretching out its hands to try to grasp hold of a toy it wanted, and you were able to run away from it. But it's learned a lot since then."

Pseudopods emerged from every surface in the basement. Thick tentacles formed of wood, plaster, and concrete extended toward them, wrapped around their legs, caught hold of their arms, encircled their chests, coiled around their necks. The tentacles pulled them away from one another until they were no longer touching. Amber tried to reach out toward Drew and reestablish physical contact, but she was bound tight in the tentacles' hold and could barely breathe, let alone move. She thought she heard a soft whispering just beneath the threshold of hearing. A voice speaking words that she couldn't make out but could sense the meaning of. It promised her strength, promised her power, promised to show her sights beyond anything she'd ever imagined. All she had to do in order to accept its gifts was submit and let it in.

She fought to resist the voice, but its promises were so tempting. She'd lived the life of an invalid for so many years, gotten by only with the help of copious amounts of meds. The Darkness promised her that if she let it in, she'd never feel weak or scared again. Tempting . . . *so* tempting . . .

The tentacles had reached around Greg, leaving him untouched. "I'm not going to lie to you. The change is going to be unpleasant, but it'll go more easily if you don't resist. But either way, in the end, you'll belong to the Darkness just as I do. I'm so excited! I can't wait to share the things I've learned with you." He turned to Drew. "And don't worry. I'll be happy to share Amber, too." His smile became a leer. "After all, we're going to be one big, happy family."

The tentacles had left their mouths uncovered, and Drew shouted, "Don't do this! You might feel like you don't have a choice, but you do!"

Greg sighed. "Really? I thought you said I wasn't human anymore, that I was just a fossil. If that's true, how can I have a choice? Make up your mind."

"I was wrong," Drew said. "You still have some humanity left inside you. Maybe just a spark or a distant echo, but it's there."

The whispering grew louder, threatening to crowd out Amber's thoughts. She felt herself growing weaker, becoming almost drowsy, but she forced herself to ignore the voice's urgings and focus on Greg. "He's right. If you weren't still human, at least a little, you'd never have gotten lonely, never have sought us out and brought us back here to join you."

"And if you're still human, you *do* have a choice," Trevor insisted, "whether you want to believe it or not. That means Sean and Jerry died not because some big, bad bogeyman made you do it but because they pissed you off back in high school, and fifteen years later, you decided to get back at them. End of story."

The voice inside Amber's head had grown so loud by this point that she had trouble hearing Trevor speak.

Greg still smiled, but he looked uncertain now.

"Do you really like what you've become?" she

asked, barely able to hear her own voice. "Is that what you want for us? For me? If you truly care about us, you won't let this happen!"

The last of Greg's smile fell away. "I . . . I don't know."

"We could've been better friends to you," Drew said. "*Should've* been. But we were just kids. We all were. You can't condemn us because of that."

The tentacles of wood and concrete that had hold of Amber tightened, as if the Darkness was becoming worried. The voice inside her head became even louder, and now it seemed as if it was screaming at her to listen to it and nothing else.

She spoke again, although she could no longer hear her own voice and wasn't certain that any words emerged from her mouth. "Separating us so we can't touch doesn't matter, Greg. Drew, Trevor, and I were united the first time the Darkness tried to claim us, and our minds and spirits are just as united now. Even more so because of what you've put us through this weekend. Thanks to you, we're stronger than we've ever been."

And it was true. She could feel it, feel Drew and Trevor with her, their minds and spirits one. And together they directed their combined positive energy at the voice shrieking inside them. That was all a cleansing ritual was, after all. Positive energy versus negative, one pushing against the other, fighting to nullify it and cast it out. She felt their energy pushing against the Darkness, and at first, it seemed as if there was no hope, for the Darkness was so old, so powerful, and it wasn't just the negative energy that had built up on the site of the Lowry House. It was the combined energy of the dozens, maybe hundreds, of Bad Places that Greg had visited and drained over the years. How could the three of them, no matter how unified their spirits, stand against such power? They were, in the end, only human.

Her vision went blurry around the edges, and she felt her identity slipping away, her thoughts being replaced by those of the voice.

In one last, desperate attempt to resist the Darkness, she reached out to Drew and Trevor in the only way she could now, calling out to them with her mind and her heart.

She found Trevor first, heard his response inside her mind, far softer than the Darkness's voice but still there, still able to be heard. *Amber? Is that you?*

She felt a wave of relief. *Yes! Can you feel Drew? We need to connect to him, too, so the three of us can stand against the Darkness together.*

I'll try, Trevor thought.

She felt him add the strength of his willpower to hers, and together they stretched out their minds toward Drew. He didn't respond at first, and she feared that they weren't going to be able to reach him, perhaps because deep down, he still didn't believe in psychic communication. She redoubled her efforts, concentrating on how she felt about him, and she reached out to him with her love.

She called his name as loudly as she could. *Drew? Drew!*

Amber? I . . . feel you. What's happening? How are you—

No questions, she thought, with more than a little amusement. Even now, in the midst of all of this, he was still being analytical. *Just trust me.*

She felt a wave of his love wash over her. *Absolutely.*

Trevor broke in then. *So, now that we're hooked up in a three-way psychic conference call, what do we do?*

We perform the cleansing ritual, she said. *We pool our energy against the Darkness and kick it to the curb.*

She closed her eyes, sensed that Drew and Trevor did the same, and pictured the Darkness as a black wall of solid shadow standing before them. She imagined the three of them stepping forward and placing their hands against the wall's ebon surface and was surprised to feel a sensation of freezing cold against her palms, as if she were literally touching the wall. She ignored the sensation and imagined the three of them pushing against the wall, leaning forward and really putting their backs into it. The wall didn't budge at first, so the three friends pushed harder, giving it everything they had. And the wall retreated, not far but enough to prove that they *could* move it, and the knowledge that it was possible boosted their confidence and fueled their determination, giving them renewed strength.

But no matter how hard they pushed after that, the wall moved no farther, and soon it began advancing again, inch by inch, forcing them backward, and no matter how hard they fought, they were unable to slow its inexorable advance.

It's not enough! Trevor said. *We're not enough! We might've been able to counter the Darkness when we were teenagers, but it's grown so much stronger over the years. Our combined energy isn't a match for it!*

Then we need more, Drew said.

At first, Amber didn't know what he meant, but then she remembered that the three of them weren't alone here.

She reached out to Greg's mind. As psychically powerful as he'd become, connecting to him was as simple as taking a breath. *Greg, I'm talking to the part of you that's still human. We need you. Help us—please!*

The thought-voice that answered her sounded nothing like the cocky, self-assured adult Greg. Instead, it belonged to a confused teenage boy. *Amber? Drew? Trevor? What are you guys doing here? Where is here, anyway? I feel funny . . . like I've been asleep for a long time, and I just woke up.*

There's no time to explain, Trevor said. *A dark*

force is trying to take us over, and we need you to help us fight it.

I'm not sure what you mean, but I feel something here with us. Something bad. Really bad. And so very strong. I don't think I can help you. I'm . . . I'm scared to try.

This might not make much sense, Drew said. *But connected the way we are now, I hope you'll be able to sense the truth of my words. That bad thing you sense got hold of you fifteen years ago, and it changed you. Turned you into a monster and made you do terrible things. And now it wants to do the same to us.*

In her mind's eye, Amber still saw the three of them pushing against the great dark wall, but now teenage Greg appeared. He stood close by, looking at the wall with a mixture of confusion and fear, but he didn't step forward to help them.

What can I do? he asked.

What the hell does it look like? Trevor said. *Get over here and help us push!*

Greg still looked scared, but he came forward and joined them, taking up a position on Amber's right. He took in a hissing breath when his flesh came in contact with the wall's cold black surface, but he didn't remove his hands.

The four of them pushed, fully reunited for the first time. The wall's advance slowed, then stopped, but no matter how hard they tried, they couldn't push it back.

We're still not enough, Drew said. *The best we can manage is a stalemate.*

So what does that mean? Amber asked. *That we're going to be stuck here for the rest of our lives, pushing against this damned wall?*

Maybe longer, Trevor said. *Our physical bodies will die of thirst in a few days, but our spirits could be trapped here, battling the Darkness forever.*

They continued putting all of their psychic strength into pushing back the wall, but it was no use. It couldn't advance any farther, but they couldn't force it to retreat. Trevor's dire assessment of the situation began to seem more likely, and Amber wondered what it would be like to remain trapped like this, fighting to hold back the Darkness for the rest of eternity.

I won't allow that to happen, Greg said. *Not to the three of you. And especially not to you, Amber. I don't remember everything that happened to me, but I remember enough. I know I chose to let the Darkness take me, and on some level, I was aware of what I was doing all those years. I can't make up for the awful things I've done, but I can keep from hurting the three of you. Good-bye, Amber. Take care of her, Drew. And Trevor? See you on the other side someday.*

Amber watched as Greg pulled his hands away from the wall. He looked at her and gave her a last smile before once more facing the wall and stepping toward it. The dark surface parted like water to accept his body, sealing up behind him as he passed through.

She felt a sudden twist of vertigo, and then she was standing within a pool of light in the middle of a gym floor. Drew still had hold of the flashlight he'd brought into the rec center, and Trevor still held his tire iron. Greg—adult again, scarred and bald—lay on the floor in front of them, unmoving.

"No," she whispered.

Drew rushed forward to check Greg's pulse. He started performing CPR, but after several minutes, he checked Greg's pulse again and shook his head. "He's gone."

"Unless this is another illusion," Trevor said.

"It doesn't feel like one," Amber said.

After a moment, Trevor nodded. "You're right. It doesn't."

Drew rejoined them and put an arm around her shoulders.

She encircled his waist with her arms and pressed her body close to his for comfort. "What happened?" she asked. "Is the Darkness gone?"

"I think so," he said. "I'm not sure how, but it appears Greg sacrificed himself to save us. It looks like he died the same way Sean and Jerry did. His heart gave out."

"Did the Darkness kill him?" she asked.

"No," Trevor said. "Remember how he told me he'd see me on the other side someday? He wanted to draw the Darkness away from us, and there was only one place he could take it where it couldn't get to us. He used his psychic abilities to will his physical body to die, and since the Darkness was bound to his spirit, when he crossed over to the afterlife, he pulled the Darkness along with him. He not only saved us, but he also made sure the evil he'd collected over the years could never hurt anyone again."

The three friends gazed at Greg's body in silence for a time after that.

It was Amber who finally spoke. "He turned out to be a good friend in the end, didn't he?"

Drew and Trevor agreed.

TWENTY

"Nice day for a funeral," Trevor said.

Amber and Drew looked at him.

"Well, it is! It's warm and sunny, and the sky's clear. Beats cold and rainy, doesn't it?"

Amber smiled. "I guess so."

It was Wednesday morning, four days after Greg had sacrificed himself to save them from the Darkness. Ash Creek Memorial Cemetery was pleasant enough as graveyards went. The grass was trimmed, the grounds free of leaves and fallen branches, the headstones unmarred by bird droppings or mold. The three friends stood next to Greg's freshly dug grave, which lay not far from a good-sized oak tree. They'd been the only ones in attendance at his funeral. He'd had no family, and no one from the reunion had attended. Most of their former classmates didn't live in town and had already headed home, and after everything that had happened that weekend, those who did live in the area hadn't felt like attending a funeral.

Considering how the Ash Creek police had reacted to their being present at the scene of a third death in one weekend, Drew, Amber, and Trevor were lucky to be able to come to the funeral themselves. The police chief would have loved to lock them up, and if he'd had even a shred of evidence to tie them to Greg's death, he would have done so.

They wore the same clothes they'd had on at the banquet, since they'd been staying at the hotel for the last few days. The three friends looked more festive than somber, mostly because of Amber's green dress, but their clothing seemed to complement the nice weather.

"Thanks for paying for Greg's funeral expenses, guys," she said. "I wish I could've chipped in, but disability checks only stretch so far."

"We may have footed the bill," Trevor said, "but you did the important part. You picked out everything. The grave site, the coffin, the headstone . . . You did a great job, too."

Drew nodded and squeezed Amber's hand.

It would take several weeks for the headstone to be delivered. Right now, the space was empty. The stone itself was going to be a light gray, the letters black but not too stark. They would spell out "Gregory H. Daniels: Friend."

"I wish I could've come up with something better to put on his headstone, though," she said.

"I think what you chose is perfect," Drew said.

"Me, too," Trevor agreed.

They stood there a little while longer. Finally,

Amber wiped away a tear and whispered, "Good-bye, Greg."

Trevor drove the Prius while Amber and Drew sat in the backseat. He'd joked that he was their chauffeur and made a show of opening their doors for them. Now they were on the road, driving away from the cemetery.

"Now what?" Trevor asked.

"Now lunch," she said. "I'm not all that hungry, but we should probably eat something."

"How about Flying Pizza?" Drew suggested, and both Amber and Trevor thought that sounded good, so he headed for the restaurant.

"That wasn't what I meant when I asked now what," he said. "I meant where do we go from here? More to the point, are you two going to get married or what?"

Amber and Drew laughed.

"Don't rush us!" she said. "We only held hands for the first time a few days ago. I'm feeling a lot better now, and I haven't needed any of my meds at all. But I want to take some time and find a real job and a better place to live. Get a real life for myself, you know?"

Trevor looked at them in the rearview mirror. "Does that mean you two aren't, uh, an item any-more?"

"No," Drew said. "We are most definitely an item. But we're going to take things slow for a while and let our relationship develop naturally. I'll go back to work at the hospital—"

"—and I'm thinking about moving to Chicago," Amber said. "After that, we'll see, you know?"

"Sounds good," Trevor said. "But don't move *too* slow. It took you more than fifteen years to get to this point, after all."

"How about you?" Drew asked. "What are you going to do?"

"Keep writing," he said. "Though I think I'm done covering haunted tourist attractions. After what we experienced this weekend, I think I'm going to try to focus on more substantial subjects. Greg showed me that there's even more to the paranormal than I thought there was. I'd like to learn what's *really* out there." He paused. "Of course, it would be more fun to have some friends along to keep me company. We make a good team. Not only did we stop the Darkness, but we gave Greg a chance to redeem himself. There may be other people like him out there who can use our help. What do you say?"

Amber and Drew looked at each other, then smiled.

"You have our numbers," she said. "Call when you need us."

And Drew nodded.

Trevor grinned. "I'm glad you said that! Yesterday I got an e-mail from an ex-girlfriend of mine. She lives in Exeter, Indiana. You ever heard of it?

It's famous for being the most haunted town in America. Anyway, she told me that there's been some really weird stuff going on there lately."

He kept on talking as they drove, and Amber and Drew listened.

ACKNOWLEDGMENTS

Thanks to Simon & Schuster for their support and assistance. And to Tim, for your ability to take our stories and help us turn them into masterpieces.

Also a special thanks to my wife, Kristen, for helping me keep my drive alive and standing beside me, never in front or behind me.

And to all of my children, to have your love and support has been all I have ever wanted. You have made me what I am today. You are forever my world.

—Jason

Thanks to my wife and my boys for always sticking by me. To the whole crew at Pilgrim Films for believing in us and in the paranormal field. To Jody Hotchkiss and Jen Heddle for their tireless work. And, of course, to Tim Waggoner, without whom this book would not exist, quite literally!

—Grant

Special thanks to Christine Avery, John Helfers, Russell Davis, Jennifer Heddle, and Wendy Keebler. This book is far better for their feedback and guidance, and I'm very grateful to them all.

Extra-special special thanks, of course, to my collaborators, Jason and Grant. Thanks for sharing with me the shocking truth behind your investigations. I promise never to tell a soul!

—Tim